MW00960510

ONCE UPON A PRINCE SERIES

KRISTIN J. DAWSON

THE
POISONED
PRINCE

ONCE UPON A PRINCE

A SNOW WHITE RETELLING

Copyright © 2023 by Kristin J. Dawson

All rights reserved.

No portion of this book may be reproduced in any form without written permission from the publisher or author, except as permitted by U.S. copyright law, or trolls may find you and take you to the nearest dragon's nest.

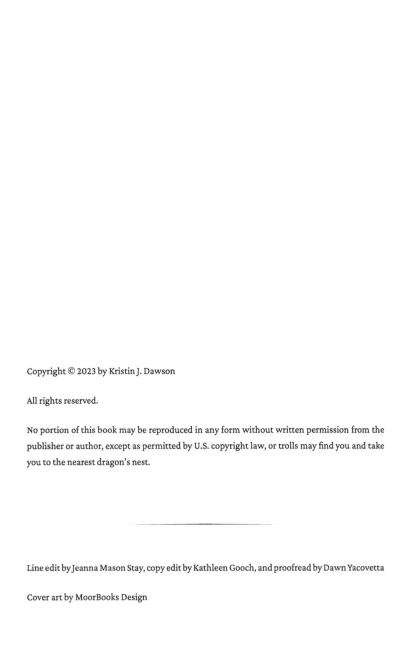

Line edit by Jeanna Mason Stay, copy edit by Kathleen Gooch, and proofread by Dawn Yacovetta

Cover art by MoorBooks Design

To Kara

(and to everyone who marries their best friend)

CONTENTS

CHARACTER LIST

Snow White: A servant of the king's castle
Maximilian Hunt: Apprentice to the royal huntsman

King Friedrich Albrecht: Ruler of the kingdom of Solinsel
Queen Agnes Ulrich Albrecht: Wife of Friedrich
Reinhold: Bonded fae to King Friedrich
Heinrich Hunt: Royal Huntsman of Solinsel
Princess Elisabeth Albrecht: Younger sister of Friedrich
Hildaruna "Runa": Dwarven friend of Maximilian
Fritzgrim "Grim": Dwarven friend of Maximilian

The Abundant Ones: Three Goddesses (Child, Maiden, Crone)

Note: The calendar cycles when the Goddess comet appears, once every 20 years.

PROLOGUE

I'd merely meant to be an apathetic witness to the birth. After all, the pregnant woman was just another low-born. Then while our carriage rumbled through the city, snow began to fall. Odd, but not because daffodils had already bloomed and wilted. Not because the valley rarely saw snow. But because the hair on my arms stood on end.

Something stirred inside me. Did the sky itself warn of tumult? As the snow became a heavy slush, I focused my magic on keeping the rented carriage's wheels from slipping against the cobblestone roads, though my thoughts swirled more than the storm.

Inside the cottage on the outskirts of the city, I dropped our glamours. My Bonded human, my mentee since his birth, rushed to his mistress's side, his favorite of several years; the woman was a great beauty of the countryside, my Bonded's weakness and his comfort. I had only ever cared that she was like the others: discrete.

Sweat glistened on her pale skin, and her wheat-colored hair shone like silk in the candlelight. She cried out as the babe was born, the sound muffled *by the weather. When the child was lifted, I should have felt a sense of relief at seeing her thick, raven curls, just like the six children who had come before her. Hair like their father's. Unlike him, this babe's skin was as white as the snow that fell outside the window.*

"The child's vitality holds steady, my Lord," I said, sensing the babe's health.

"She's inherited your strength, Rosalind." My human kissed his love's forehead as the servant wrapped up the babe, who wailed along with the storm.

The howling wind beat on the glass panes, threatening to shatter them. My heart pounded with the vibrations, though I was more than powerful enough to protect us, even if the roof caved in. What weighed on me, I couldn't fathom. Would this child, the seventh born, bring her own squall to the kingdom? I trembled at the possibilities, but I wouldn't turn away. I needed to act. To guide her. To give her what only a fae could offer.

I took the child in my arms and sent away the servant. The child's mother stiffened, her hand gripping her lover's arm. But he simply looked at me with open curiosity.

"I would like to gift the child," I said.

The woman gasped, obviously honored by what I offered.

My Bonded cocked his head, his brow furrowed. Then he stood and clapped me on the shoulder. "It would be a great honor, my friend."

I held the babe close, considering the many gifts she would've received if she was a recognized high-born. But this girl was unheralded. A guarded secret. However, the stoutest souls are born in the shadow of a storm.

"I gift this child with discerning emotion," I said. "With practice, she will sense even the quietest feeling."

"Not beauty?" her mother asked. "Not physical strength?"

"It is a wonderful gifting, Reinhold," my human said, stopping his mistress before she insulted me further.

However, he need not have worried; such a speck of a human could not offend me. I could not care less about her, other than she was the mother of this baby, touched by destiny. Even if the babe's destiny was to receive nothing beyond my fae gifting, it was greatness nonetheless. Amid my thoughts, I dimly heard a discussion of the babe's name. My Bonded didn't have long until he'd be missed, so we needed to return home. Still, I wanted to know the name. Who knew how long he would continue with this peasant woman, and I desired to keep track of the child. This little human bundle was of interest to me. I felt something I hadn't in decades — curiosity.

"Let us call her 'Snow,'" the woman said. "Snow White."

CHAPTER 1: SNOW

YEAR 8 OF THE MAIDEN COMET, LATE SPRING

S now White scurried through the palace kitchens like a scullion, assisting with the king's evening meal. She drizzled the buttered breadcrumb sauce over the boiled asparagus, a favorite delicacy. Everything about the royal dish, from the texture to the colorful presentation, was fit for a fae.

Despite the importance of her task, as Snow worked, the weight of the allowance in her pocket itched to be secreted away. But she couldn't leave—not yet.

Finally, servants marched up to the royal wing, carrying trays laden with fine food. With her responsibilities done for the day, Snow wanted to dash into the forest. But the brief lull in the kitchens provided the best time to teach.

Before servants returned to help clean up, Snow placed a slip of parchment on the table between a dirty bowl and herb scraps.

"You're a darlin', Snow," said Dottie. The cook used her height to oversee her sizeable staff, and her humor made the endless work more enjoyable. "You have the patience of an Attuned watching unruly children."

"Well, Dottie, no one accused you of being a child."

Dottie barked a laugh. "An unruly adult, then. Fair enough."

"I'm happy to help," Snow said sincerely. "Soon, you'll be able to send and receive proper missives on your own."

Dottie smiled as she wiped her hands on her apron. Her brow scrunched as she worked through the parchment scraps that Snow had collected, with more words thoughtfully added to expand Dottie's vocabulary. Ever since Snow had been offered a position in the royal wing, her honorable, new duties had her running all over the castle. So, she relished any time back bantering with her old friends. Too soon, the kitchen servants returned, ready to wash dishes.

"Now, be off with you," Dottie said to Snow as she signaled to a scullion to clean the counter.

"Well then, I'm off to rumple clean laundry and harass the king's dogs," Snow teased.

"Have a jolly time, lovie," the cook replied with a wink, "I'll keep thy secret mischief safe as a vixen minding her kits."

"Thank you!" Snow grabbed her cloak and ran into the courtyard.

The cool, early spring afternoon was a stark contrast to the fiery kitchens. Snow gathered the cloak tighter around herself, glancing up at Clarus Castle. The structure perched on the side of a mountain and was split into two perpendicular wings, with a balcony stretching across the second story of the east wing. Between the castle and the outer wall, a lone tree stood in defiance of the rocky mountaintop, a feat of magic combined with the sheer determination of the gardener, keeping it not just alive but thriving. Snow passed the gardener as he inspected the spring buds on his prized charge, the precious apple tree.

"Will ye be back before dark?" he called out to her. The aging gardener tended to fret about the safety of the younger servants when they left the protection of the castle walls. Some found his questioning annoying, but Snow didn't mind.

Snow turned, assuaging his worry. "The cook will listen for me tonight as the pots are polished. I won't be locked out."

The gardener put two fingers to the tip of his brow, near his cap, signaling his approval. Snow waved and jogged out of the courtyard through the enormous, open gate. From the mountainside vantage point, the sun lowered, nearly kissing the tops of the distant, unending forest. Below, farmland lay like a skirt fanned out around the base of the mountain. Beyond the treeless buffer in the west, the city of Caston sprawled between Clarus and the nearest port. To the east and south lay the King's Forest. Further still, at the bend in the distant mountain, the keenest eye could spy where the forest turned into a thicker, darker mass.

Snow jogged down the mountain road, zig-zagging toward the valley. By the time Snow entered the forest, the light changed, taking on a warm, golden hue, signaling the coming sunset. She didn't have long. Glancing over her shoulder, making sure she was alone, she darted through the trees. Listening as she went, she wove an irregular pattern until she reached her hiding spot. Then, she quickly dug up all her savings, wrapped in burlap. She was overly cautious, but she wouldn't let a careless mistake keep her from her dreams. As lovely as Clarus was, she longed to return to her childhood home. Only there would she find the answers she needed.

"Do you need a lookout?" a voice said right over her shoulder.

Snow let out a yip and jumped to her feet, her coins dropping into the dirt before her mind registered the speaker. Just two steps away, Max stood with his arms crossed and a smirk on his face. Dappled light danced upon his tousled sandy blonde hair and accentuated his broad shoulders. Dressed in his worn hunting attire, the earthy tones of his clothing blended seamlessly with his surroundings, and the hint of stubble on his chiseled jaw was evidence of a recent hunting expedition.

"Max!" Snow shouted, stepping forward and giving him a good shove. "You gave me a fright, you troll!"

"Aww," Max said, his piercing gaze holding a mix of mirth and warmth. "Such flattery. Besides, you'd be lucky if I were a troll and not a fae. They may be pretty, but they're twice as dangerous."

"Pft! You underestimate the fae."

Max chuckled and helped pick up the coins she'd dropped, not bothering to wipe the grin off his face.

"I swear, Maximilian Hunt, if you ever do that again, I'll shave your head one night."

He laughed, handing over her bronze.

"And an eyebrow," Snow added. "But only one."

Snow wrapped up the coins in the sack, shoving her treasure back into its hideaway. She should have known Max would show up. And not because his family's cottage was nearby. But because Max was her confidant and closest friend. He'd taken her under his wing ever since she'd arrived at Clarus when she was eleven years old. Max's father had fetched her over five years ago, after the attack, and she'd never been back home.

Though one day, that would change. She needed answers and the distant town of Isolzing held them.

"You could stop sneaking around and just hide your treasures at the cottage," Max said as he helped her disguise her hiding spot.

Snow was tempted to allow herself to feel Max's emotion, to know if there was something more behind his casual teasing. But instead, she stood up and brushed off her hands, as well as his kind suggestion, ready to change the subject. Besides, she'd already been too much of a burden on his family.

"You're such a spider—how long have you been spinning your web?" she asked, changing the subject.

"You give me too much credit." Max put his arm around her neck, almost like he was wrestling a brother, and tromped back through the forest at her side. Snow enjoyed the comfort and friendship, drinking it up as he continued. "I knew the royal staff got paid today. And you get this way every spring. Jumpy."

She knew what he meant, and she didn't deny it. "I can't help it. This time of year brings back so many memories," she said. "So much of childhood is repetitive between chores and schooling. But once a year, around my birthday, Mama chose a day and made it all about me. Special."

"Tell me a story," Max said, with genuine interest. Snow had already shared her birthday tales a hundred times, but she was always glad when he asked.

"Every spring, after the tulips faded, Mama bought the most expensive lamb on the market," Snow began. Like most commoners, only the great Abundant Ones, the three goddesses, knew the exact day of her birth. "Not the biggest piece; the perfectly marbled loin. And wine far beyond our means. Then, she'd go to the finest dressmaker." Snow skipped the part where Mama got measured in the back room, away from the windows. She wasn't good enough to be seen by shopping nobles, but merchants took Mama's coin without reservation. But not wanting to dampen the mood, this time, she only retold the happy parts. "Mama made a delicious stew and invited the neighbors. We all laughed, danced, and ate. Oh, Abundants, did we *eat*. Then, later, she would take her new dress from the year before and sew matching dresses for me and my doll."

Snow reached up and gripped Max's forearm, which still hugged near her neck, and she let the glow of the past wash over her. She sensed a quick rush of tender emotion from Max, but she blocked it out, as she'd learned to do. As a child, the emotions of others had overwhelmed her, but she'd been taught how to keep them out. It was for the best.

Besides, Snow had goals. One day, she'd have enough money to investigate the night her life had changed. The night she'd been scooped up and moved across their island kingdom of Solinsel. Sharp memories from that night were broken fragments, like a jar shattered against the rocks. Her best chance of finding clues lay in Isolzing, where she'd grown up. Despite the six years that had passed, Snow hadn't given up hope that someone knew the truth. She needed closure; otherwise, that night would never stop haunting her. Snow's sensitivity to others' moods was a distraction she'd never been able to afford, especially not now if she planned to traverse the kingdom.

As they neared the edge of the forest, Max slowed, pulling his arm away, and rested a hand on her shoulder. "I have an idea to get you to the edge of the king's forest. But it involves you asking the king for a favor. You've served the king for two years. He trusts you."

Earning enough trust to work for the royals was a rarity, a coveted honor unlikely to be repeated. When Snow left Clarus, she would forfeit her position. Getting an offer to work in the royal wing was a shock—not even Dottie expected the steward to offer Snow the position. Hundreds of merchants, servants, guards, and officials hurried through the castle each day. How had the steward even noticed her?

"When the king's health returns, I'll arrange the perfect hunt with my father," Max continued. "The king will benefit from fresh air, and you'll ask to join his retinue. And we'll travel deep into the king's forest. To the edge, in fact."

"To the Wildwood," Snow breathed the word, almost a curse on her tongue. The king's forest abutted the magical woods filled with deadly plants and strange, wild creatures. Few ventured inside and survived. Snow had read many books about the dangers and wouldn't risk entering. Instead, she'd take the King's Road that circumvented the whole treacherous forest on her way to Isolzing. Even the main road could be dangerous; occasional attacks happened, regardless of station, status, or even the time of day.

"I could take you myself—"

"I'd never ask you to do such a thing. It wouldn't be fair."

To you. Snow kept the last thought to herself, quickly adding an excuse. "The Wildwood is far too dangerous."

Snow's parentage limited her prospects. Abandoned by her father, Snow's mother had told her the same thing every fatherless girl was told—that she was the child of a great man who loved her—lies, of course. Unlike Snow, Max came from a respectable family. One day, he'd earn his father's title and be the Master of the Hunt, the Royal Huntsman of Solinsel. She wouldn't mar his reputation by asking him to travel alone with her. Nor did she have the funds for an escort. Not yet.

"We'll stay on the roads," Max said.

"Aww, the chivalry! Offering to brave the roads *near* the creepy, magic forest," Snow said as she skipped away, teasing over her shoulder. "There's a chance I may not need to shave your eyebrow after all."

"Not the eyebrow!" He mockingly protected his face with his hands.

Snow laughed and jogged across the buffer to the main road. Max was the one person she never tired of, and she would miss him when she left Clarus. Once she got the answers she needed, she'd return. She could not fathom leaving Clarus forever, especially not Max. She'd lose her position in the royal wing, of course, but any amount of status was far less precious than her closest friend. She wouldn't risk losing Max forever. Not for anything.

A thought bubbled up in Snow's mind, one she'd never dared voice—she was beginning to suspect that the king himself had requested her. The idea was ludicrous. Yet, King Friedrich Albrecht often spoke to her, and not just commands for linens or food. They spoke on many subjects. In fact, he'd even asked her *opinion* on occasion. Only the queen knew of their discussions, as she was present for a few of them. With a snap of her fingers, Queen Agnes could have Snow removed for impertinence.

Snow never spoke to Max about her casual conversations with royalty. Max would mention them to his father, who happened to be the king's closest friend. She bit the inside of her cheek, imagining a conversation between them. Snow sensed that Heinrich wouldn't approve of the king treating Snow with such familiarity. Though some servants had jealously reacted to Snow's appointment, she had expected Max's parents to celebrate the news. But they'd given Snow strained smiles and she'd caught the wary look between them.

So, Snow kept her interactions with the king to herself; the last thing she wanted was to be a source of contention between the hunter who'd rescued her from destitution and the most powerful human in the kingdom. That couldn't be good for her or for Max's future.

CHAPTER 2: MAX

YEAR 8 OF THE MAIDEN COMET, LATE SPRING

"The queen asked to see me," Max said to the maidservant, showing her the note with the queen's now-broken seal.

"She's with the king. I'll take you there," she said, leading him down the corridor. "We're getting together tonight in Caston. The weather's been nice. You should join us. Even the apprentice to the royal huntsman should take a break every once in a while."

"Oh, um," he stalled. This was the third person to mention it, but with his father gone, Max had his hands full. Firewood to chop, thatch to gather, and a dozen other tasks needed attention.

"It'll be loads of fun." She slowed to a crawl, waiting for a response. Not getting one, she continued, "My brother is bringing his lute. I love to dance, don't you?"

Was the king's door getting *further* away? Max wanted to escape the conversation; the sooner, the better. He hated crowds and only rarely tolerated social gatherings if Snow attended. She had a knack for putting him at ease. But orphans with no connections were often invisible within the hierarchy of the servants, which irritated Max to no end.

"I'd need permission from the huntsman," Max said, hoping to put an end to it.

The maidservant's smile signaled that she didn't think his father would be an obstacle. Max picked up his pace. Had she noticed his father's absence?

With his father gone, Max had been fielding questions from everyone from the steward to the nobles. He had made excuses, everything from 'he has a fever' to 'you just missed him.' His father had said he didn't know exactly when he'd return, but three weeks was too long. Max's initial irritation was turning to worry, but revealing Heinrich's absence would cause a stir of gossip.

Max had never been so glad to see the guards as the ones at the door. Thankfully, the maidservant continued down the hall while Max flashed the missive to the sentinels who granted him access. Inside the king's chambers, the cloying scents of garlic and burning incense layered over a deeper, sickly-sweet smell that threatened to close Max's throat. He breathed through his mouth and reminded himself that King Friedrich had the best healers in the kingdom tending to his every need.

The king rested under a mound of blankets, his head propped up on pillows, his eyes closed. His pale skin looked less waxy than last time and the circles under his eyes had lightened. Max's mood brightened—the rumors of the king's demise were nonsense. On one side of the bed stood a tall column with a flat top where Reinhold could stand and converse with the king in his natural, small faerie form. On the other side, the queen perched on the edge of a cushioned chair. She closed the lid to a box on her lap and set her quill on the cluttered table that sat between herself and the king, and then she bade Max closer.

"The king is feeling better," the queen said quietly, her lilting accent still thick even after a decade in Solinsel. "He would like you to take him on a hunt."

Max paused, wondering if Reinhold knew about the ride. The fae didn't hover while the king rested, and Max rarely crossed paths with him, thank the Abundants. Surely this excursion was a bad idea. But it wasn't Max's place to argue. The king and queen might listen to the fae or to the royal huntsman, but not Max.

King Friedrich and Heinrich Hunt, Max's father, grew up together at Clarus. While in the forest, the two men were equals. No, they were more than simply on equal footing; they were best of friends who trusted and relied on each other. Max was no replacement for the royal huntsman, especially with the *king* as the guest. And certainly not with the king's delicate condition.

The king hadn't sent for Heinrich in many moon cycles, and was likely unaware of his absence. Revealing both his father's absence and his breach of royal protocol was the last thing Max wanted. But, how could he hide his father's disappearance any longer?

Perhaps he shouldn't. The king cared about Heinrich, and what if his father needed help? This was Max's chance to ask.

"My apologies, Queen Agnes," Max began. "I'm afraid that my father has been—"

"Whatever the problem, I'm sure you can overcome it," Agnes said, cutting him off. She quickly looked at her husband, and seeing his eyes closed, her shoulders relaxed.

While she inspected the king, Max couldn't help but notice vials of medicine, a half-eaten bowl of soup, and a goblet of wine on the side table. The box in her lap had three holes in the top, strategically allowing the ink to dry away from wandering eyes. Perhaps it was correspondence with one of her respected noble siblings across the sea. The queen was nothing if not private.

"I'll prepare the horses," Max said, stepping back with a bow.

"On your way, go by the kitchens and have them send spring water." She moved the wine goblet further away to the king's dresser, which held ornate glass decanters and a cask. "No more of the wine. It makes him drowsy. Have the cook fetch one of my apples. He rather likes them, and it will give him strength for the ride."

"Of course," Max said, taking another step back.

"And Maximilian?" she asked, slowly emphasizing each word. "I don't know when the king will be ready to leave. Will *you* be prepared?"

He stiffened, realizing she definitely knew his father wouldn't be the escort. But clearly, she didn't want to discuss Heinrich's absence in front of the king. Why?

"I'll be ready," Max said, bowing, before leaving the room.

The horses would be ready soon and could wait all day if needed. Because, of course, everyone served at the leisure of the king. So why would Queen Agnes specify? Her words meant something more, though Max had no idea what. He wished his father was back to deal with the vague innuendoes fraught with political dangers.

Max stormed through the castle, discomforted by the conversation. He understood why she wanted the king to be seen riding; showcasing his stamina would quell rumors that he wasn't fit to rule. But how would they keep him upright long enough to walk from his rooms to the courtyard, let alone ride down the mountain and *through* the forest?

And, when Max's father returned, would the queen punish Heinrich for the long absence? Max would need to perform well to help protect his father's reputation. Even so, there could be consequences.

In the courtyard, Max quickly greeted the gardener, who was pressing his hands against the rocks that circled the base of the tree. A tree was a ridiculous luxury on the rocky, cold mountain, yet it thrived. The last of the apple blooms clung to the branches, bees buzzing.

The tree was a wedding gift from the king to his new bride, a noblewoman from a wealthy, fertile kingdom across the sea. Though it was a political alliance, Friedrich had wanted to ease Agnes's transition by bringing a sapling from her family's orchard. Max remembered the massive hole prepared for the roots. Only dwarves with their axes could dig deep enough. Max remembered them, too.

The day the tree arrived, the air seemed to crackle with anticipation. Max's mother had said it was probably all the magically treated soil, not to mention the rocks—the same ones the gardener was currently checking—which magically heated the soil to the perfect temperature, even turning a lighter shade of grey when the soil was too dry.

If the king died, Queen Agnes would rule unless someone else had been selected. Or until distant cousins or high-ranking nobles battled for the throne. Max shook his hands out. Political concerns were above his station. Whatever the king's plans, they were done behind closed doors. But surely Friedrich had a contingency. Didn't he?

Ignoring the pit in his stomach, Max entered the open corridor that split the two wings of the castle. In the shadows of the lofty tunnel, he found himself tapping the pin on his coat, an amulet passed down from generation to generation in his mother's family. He dropped his hand away, hoping no one had noticed. Any fae-created protection would be valuable to someone grasping to secure the throne.

A breeze cut through the stone corridor and Max turned to buffer against the chill. The darkened walls around him framed the courtyard beyond. Delicate pink petals swirled and fluttered to the ground in a mesmerizing last dance. Or a last gasp. Perhaps both.

CHAPTER 3: SNOW

YEAR 8 OF THE MAIDEN COMET, LATE SPRING

I n the kitchens, Snow ladled the chicken broth into a ceramic bowl rimmed with gold. She arranged the bowl on the tray, adding two slices of bread while enjoying the general bustling of the servants.

"Hope springs eternal," Dottie said to Snow, inspecting the tray. "The king has his appetite back?"

"I'll find out soon enough," Snow said.

A week earlier, Max had taken the king on a hunt, and he had barely lasted an hour in the forest. Snow suspected the king and queen rode to just beyond the trees and rested out of view of spectators. But even that had cost him dearly; the king had been bedridden ever since.

Max appeared at the doorway, carrying two pheasants. Several kitchen servants giggled at his arrival, hurrying to take the birds off his hands. Dottie muttered about geese flocking around their crust of bread, and Snow quirked a grin.

"Should I bring food for Reinhold as well?" Snow asked.

"Aye, that picky fae creature," the cook tsked. "I thank the Abundants above for the protection and guidance the fae provide for the lordly sorts, but those creatures have insatiable appetites. Like starving vultures, but by me truth, they'd be eating all the day long!"

"And night," Snow added. They'd all seen Reinhold flit through the kitchens, helping himself to his favorite foods, but fae didn't speak to lowly servants. Ever.

Snow didn't know how to explain it, but she always had a sense of those around her. As a child, she'd tried to keep her distance from others, but her mother was quite social. When Snow was too young to know any better, she revealed a villager's duplicity. The peasant woman quickly retaliated by telling everyone that *Snow* was the liar. For moons, Snow's heart was crushed as the villagers' gossip grew into horrible rumors. The villagers stopped letting their children play with her, but what truly hurt was how they'd shunned her mother. Even in the middle of summer, Isolzing had become as cold as the snow-capped mountain.

Yet, deep down, Snow felt gratitude for being ostracized. Even before the incident, the constant, secret jagged thoughts of the villagers cut deeper than any freeze. And then Snow had felt guilty over her gratitude. Between the cruel villagers, Rosalind's sadness, and her own erratic emotions, Snow curled up in a ball, unable to study or even eat. Her mother eventually hired a witch—a dangerous proposition—in a desperate attempt to help Snow block the overwhelming emotions. It had worked, and the rumors faded.

But Snow remembered.

Even with the witch's magic spell, when Snow wasn't vigilant and she was focused on an individual, feelings crept through. The cook generally felt calm, and Max felt protective. But the king's fae emanated 'cold calculation,' as if Snow were a science experiment and he held a scalpel.

"Reinhold once flit through the kitchens in the predawn, practically salivating while I kneaded dough." Snow remembered that morning clearly because Reinhold had talked to her. Soon after, Snow had been elevated to serve the king. She shrugged off the discomforting memory.

"Were you alone? You must've been nothing but nerves," Dottie said, though her attention stayed on the kitchen preparations.

"I fixed him a plate of cheese and bread, and he left."

"You got off lucky. I'm surprised he didn't want a side of lamb," Max said, moving closer. "The whole side. Braised in mulberry wine and rosemary."

"With a helping of buttered potatoes." Snow reached for a plate to prepare for Reinhold, but Dottie lightly smacked her hand away.

"I'm near finished getting the nobles' morning meal." Dottie slid the king's tray into Snow's arms. "Tell that hungry vulture he can stoop to dining with the human upper crust."

Princess Elisabeth, the king's younger sister, along with visiting nobles, dined in the Sunrise Parlor. Servants piled platters with sliced meats, including smoked ham, cured sausages, and spiced beef. A basket of fresh-baked rolls, and a variety of spreads, including butter, honey, and jam, were already being whisked away. The nuts and cheeses would follow soon behind, along with the juice and wine.

"Another fantastic feast. Not even a fae can complain," Snow complimented as she scurried to join the servants headed to the royal wing.

Max started to follow after her, but Dottie chastised him to clean up. Instead, he dashed after Snow and dropped three white-petaled anemones on the tray. Max gave them to her every planting season to mark her birthday.

"Thank you." Snow grinned, remembering when he once said the dainty flowers looked like snow against her dark hair.

"My father returned yesterday," Max whispered, determination and frustration rolling off him. Snow didn't feel his every passing emotion, only the more intense ones, so something was amiss. She'd suspected as much, but now she knew for certain.

Before he could say more, Dottie shouted a reminder for him to get to the washroom. Snow wanted to talk to him further, but it was just as well. A crowded castle was no place for private conversation, and wherever Max went, servants thronged, wanting his attention. Between Max's father's friendship with the king and his mother's noble family, everyone valued his friendship. But Snow hadn't known who he was when they'd met. She only knew him as the boy who had treated her kindly after her mother was killed.

Snow clutched the tray, careful not to spill, and continued to the royal wing. Though Friedrich was the king, Snow pitied him. All the gold in the seven kingdoms couldn't cure his frail body. Snow almost pitied his stoic fae, Reinhold, too. Almost. Snow didn't know much about the magical bond between royals and fae, other than it strengthened them both. Fae lived long lives and cared for nothing beyond their cherished meals; though they were said to deeply mourn the loss of their human companions. If the king died, his people wouldn't be the only ones to sorrow—Reinhold's broken Bond would pain him, too.

When Snow entered the king's rooms, she slipped the flowers into her pocket while Queen Agnes set down a plate of fruit on the side table. The queen carefully placed her hands into her lap, the rings on her fingers glittering in the light streaming from the open window. It wasn't unusual for the nobles to quiet when servants entered, but the queen always seemed to prick at Snow's presence. The king, on the other hand, brightened.

"Snow," the king said, sitting up straighter. "It's good to see you."

As Snow neared, the queen jerked to her feet and excused herself. When she left, the silent tension lifted by a degree. Setting the tray down on top of the blankets across the king's lap, Snow checked for any dirty dishes to clear away. But, she saw only a near-empty goblet of spring water and the plate the queen had set down next to her husband. A plate of thinly sliced apples.

"Wasn't that sweet of Agnes?" The king said, seeing Snow's attention on the fruit. "She brought me an apple from last season. I feel terrible as I don't have the stomach for them. You should have one."

Snow's eyes widened. "I couldn't, my Lord."

He chuckled, "Who would know?"

The queen. She'd know. Agnes had each apple waxed, wrapped, stored, and numbered. Not a single apple went unaccounted for. They were the queen's gifts to dole out to whom she wished, and they never went to anyone other than herself, the king, visiting royals, and as the occasional prize for the most devoted nobles.

"Never mind the apples, Snow," the king said, waving to the queen's vacated chair. "Sit, sit, please."

Snow sat on the edge of the seat, nervous that another servant or a guard would see her resting and report her to the steward. The king asked Snow questions about the people she interacted with, which he'd done before. Just like Dottie and others, he assumed she was simply observant. Snow gave him silly insights and stories, figuring it did no harm to make the ill king smile.

The king quieted, his usual laughter replaced by a somberness. "What do you think about my queen?"

Snow's stomach dropped. This line of questioning was different. And potentially dangerous, which set Snow on edge. She barely knew the queen, and what she had sensed from Agnes was a swirl of uncomfortable emotions.

"The queen is clever." Snow scanned the room for ideas, hoping the king didn't notice her hand tremble. "She enjoys puzzles."

"Her silly puzzle boxes." He grinned when he spotted the wooden cube the queen left on the side table. "And what else?"

"She's beautiful and, um,"—Snow strained to think of positive attributes—"aloof."

As cold as the fae. Snow quieted the treacherous thought. The king swiftly punished anyone who impugned his wife's character.

"I hear rumors. The people say my queen is vain. What do you think?"

Snow clutched her hands together in her lap and determined to give the queen the benefit of the doubt. Besides, even if Agnes were vain, she was far from the only one. The servants gossiped about the long hours the nobles spent primping. "I think she just appreciates her mirror." Though most nobles sought size rather than quality, the queen had the largest sheet of glass Snow had ever seen. "The craftsmanship is very fine."

The king chuckled, and the tightness in Snow's chest unwound. "I remember the day Agnes arrived at the castle with that mirror," he said. "It was a gift from her parents when she was a child, and she couldn't bear to leave it behind. It was beyond impractical, but I demanded we get it into her rooms. Builders created a system of pulleys and widened her window because it was too large to make the corners in the hallways. Can you imagine such a feat? You were about six years old at the time."

The king paused, his attention on the untouched tray on his lap. Snow thought he might be drifting off to sleep when he suddenly spoke, his voice soft. "What do you think about me?"

"I think if you want to go hunting any time soon, you should eat your broth." Snow kept her tone light, though she wondered at the sudden seriousness. A king didn't care about a servant's opinion. Still, his sincerity and vulnerability poked at her conscience, so she added, "You're a good king. Your people love you."

"I'm sorry about what happened to your mother," the king said, ignoring his food. "I can't stop thinking about Rosalind's last hours. How terrified she must've been. How brave you were."

Snow clutched her aprons in her fist, surprised he knew her mother's name, let alone thought about her.

"A long time ago," he continued, "I cared for Rosalind deeply."

Snow stilled. How could he have known her mother? Snow recalled that her mother had spoken of living in Caston. Had her mother worked in Clarus? Perhaps she was a trusted servant, which could explain why Snow had been elevated to such a high position.

The king paused, his expression earnest. "Snow, I came to see you as often as I could. Reinhold glamoured me, so no one knew about our relationship. You were adorable; the way you flexed your hand deepened the dimples in your knuckle. As you grew a little older, you were always rescuing insects by putting them into a mug and skipping outside, your black curls bouncing down your back." He sighed, his eyes unfocused, lost in memories. "Your mother knew I would marry soon, and she itched for her own new adventure. So she moved to Isolzing when you were five years old, and I've had a hole in my heart ever since."

"What?" Snow heard herself saying in disbelief. It was as if part of her soul had lifted out of her body, and she distantly watched the exchange.

"I sent funds every spring on your birthday," the king said. "Your tutors kept Reinhold and Heinrich apprised of your accomplishments. Your last tutor was the one who fled back to the castle after the . . .

attack. You'd already been taken to the local Attuned, so he left you in safe hands and reported the incident to my fae adviser."

Snow sat dumbfounded, realizing the king had financially supported her and her mother all those years. Why? Perhaps Snow's mother had fallen for a wealthy noble, a friend of the king. But why would the king send funds? Why would the tutor report to Reinhold?

Could you be my father?

The mere thought surged through Snow like a tumultuous wave, stirring a maelstrom of emotions within. Disbelief consumed her, making her question the validity of her suspicion. Could she have been so oblivious?

Her past suddenly appeared distorted as if seen through a cracked glass. Yet, the pieces of her identity, once scattered, now began to align.

Not wanting to assume anything through her confusion and unable to ask the most important question directly, she asked another. "You remembered my birthday?"

"Of course I remember that storm. Who doesn't? Only the fae-protected orchards and fields survived that cold spring."

Snow shook her head, unable to make sense of the conversation. Her mother said the best magic was found in everyday serendipity; she was a romantic who followed her whimsy. Yet under her carefree exterior, she'd clearly known how to keep a secret. Why was he admitting to the truth her mother had hidden on the king's behalf?

"Why are you telling me this?" Snow asked.

The king turned his hand over and lifted his palm. Snow's heart tightened at the gesture. She put her hand into his, trying and failing to grasp a different, logical explanation. His hand was cool and clammy but not unkind. With the other hand, he held a gold ring with the royal Albrecht seal. When he slipped it on her finger, it tightened, fitting perfectly, just before it vanished and then reappeared.

The king put his family seal on my finger. The ring alone confirmed what he'd been unable or unwilling to say aloud. Pieces of a puzzle she never imagined solving snapped into place. Snow was the daughter of King Friedrich Albrecht.

The very foundation of her existence felt shaken, tenuous, as if she were standing on a rock slide. An ache settled in her chest, and her inner defense disappeared as her sense of betrayal, frustration, and embarrassment for her blindness crushed her vigilant wall in one fell swoop.

The king's worry, wistfulness, and hope struck her, flooding her senses. She stared into the king's eyes, the emotion within confirming everything. How had Snow never suspected?

"Consider the ring an early seventeenth birthday present," the king said. "It won't be visible to humans, except to you, until you turn nineteen."

"I don't know what to say. Thank you." Snow's mind swirled with questions. She pulled back from the king, tucking her hands into her lap. Amidst the turmoil, a flicker of hope emerged. A new chapter in her life unfurled before her with blank pages ready to be filled with possibilities. She stood on a precipice, poised to rewrite her story, her future.

"Can I ask you about my mother?"

He nodded. "I'll tell you what I can."

"Do you know anything about the attack that killed her? I only remember flashes. Heinrich said a wolf attacked. But it didn't sound like any wolf I've heard in the forest. And why was it in the village?"

"You know as much as I do. Your tutor was stunned that you survived, and I sent my royal huntsman to Isolzing to fetch you. When he arrived in your village, the rumors were grisly; Heinrich's instinct was to get you away from that place. He didn't ask for details. As soon as you were of age, Reinhold arranged for you to work in the kitchens."

"Because you wanted me to have security?" Snow lifted a brow, grateful for the opportunity for financial means.

"To teach you about the one human resource that fae care about—food. They are powerful allies or deadly enemies. I wanted you equipped to deal with them. And, selfishly, I wanted to know you a bit. Later, I promoted you because I had to find out for myself if you could be more than a royal servant. I needed someone who could become a symbol of security, someone the people could rally behind. The kingdom needs an heir."

Snow gasped, her attention flying to her ring. The king pulled on the silk rope near his bed, which signaled for a servant as he continued. "You're insightful, as I'd expected. But also responsible and kind. I couldn't be more pleased with the woman you're becoming. And I hope one day, you will"—the king paused, struggling for words as tears filled his eyes,—"forgive me. I haven't been quite myself, Snow. I am so filled with emotion . . . finally able to tell you who you are. I hope you will give me a chance. I don't deserve it. I know I don't. But . . ."

His statement hung in the air, and Snow was too surprised to respond before Princess Elisabeth and an older woman entered the room. Right behind them flew the king's fae in his small, natural form, about one hand in height. Snow stared at each of them, the room quickly becoming claustrophobic with emotions. She walled herself off, mentally numbing herself, as she shot to her feet and curtsied.

The king cleared his throat. "Snow, you already know Reinhold. But let me introduce you to the high judge, Helene, well known for her wisdom and knowledge. And my sister, Princess Elisabeth, my dear friend and confidant who proved her loyalty in the deepest way many years ago."

Elisabeth smiled as she rearranged her brother's pillows. The princess's gaze fell on the apples, and a spike of emotion pushed through Snow's defenses—a mixture of concern, grief, and frustration. And something deeper. Jealousy? Whatever it was, it was sharp, like frostbite. Snow reinforced her inner barrier, closing an iron-like wall around her heart, bringing her blissful peace.

Elisabeth moved to the far dresser, poured a glass of wine, and then handed it to her brother. She tenderly patted the king on the shoulder and stood next to Reinhold on his column.

"My dear sister," the king said after taking a sip. "You have the finest eye for beauty. Please commission a painting of Snow, and send it to Prince Leopold."

"Of course, my Lord," she said.

Judge Helene held out a document to the king, and he signed it as he spoke to his sister. "Thank you for acting as a witness, Elisabeth. I appreciate your steady support."

The judge gave a sharp nod. "It is done. Snow White will be known as Snow Albrecht on her nineteenth birthday, the heir to the throne. I trust preparations for her training are underway."

Snow tried to breathe but couldn't seem to get enough air into her lungs. The blank pages flipped forward too quickly, glimpses of challenges flashing in warning.

"Her training started long ago," Reinhold said, looking down his nose at the judge, though she stood taller than him. "The girl will be ready. Don't worry."

The tutors I'd had in the village? Snow wrung her hands, finally understanding why she'd had an education far beyond the average peasant.

"Let Snow have her anonymity for now," the king instructed. "Her training will continue in earnest, and no one out of this room is to know of the arrangement. Especially not the queen. It could cause . . .

unneeded hurt. I intend to be around many years, but if the worst were to happen, my queen will reign as regent until Snow is of age. However, my sweet Agnes need not know before absolutely necessary."

Shouldn't I have been told before it was 'absolutely necessary'? Will the nobles accept me? Am I a worthy choice? Snow's many questions fought for attention.

Her entire life slid, hurling her in a new direction. It was one thing to find her father. It was quite another to be named the heir to the throne. She lost hold of her inner defense, and it dipped long enough to sense fear. The king *feared*, but the protective warmth signaled he was afraid *for* Snow.

"My Lord," Elisabeth said. "You'll have plenty of time to inform Agnes. Long live the king."

"Long live King Friedrich," they all echoed.

He smiled. "You're right, of course. I'll live to a ripe old age. Besides, Snow could practically run the castle."

"That makes her a fit steward. Not a queen," Judge Helene said.

The discussion of tutelage receded in Snow's mind as she attempted to twist the ring around her swollen finger. Why was the king hiding her away? Why was he afraid?

"Training to be worthy of the crown takes more than making fae-pleasing meals and gathering herbs," Elisabeth said. "She seems capable, but she'll need much more in order to rule Solinsel."

"You're right, my dear sister, as always," the king said good-naturedly.

Would anyone ask Snow what *she* wanted? Becoming the secret heir to the kingdom was more than she could comprehend. The room tilted, and Snow leaned against the bedpost, realizing too late that her fingers had choked the flowers from Max—crushing them to a pulp in her fist.

CHAPTER 4: MAX

YEAR 8 OF THE MAIDEN COMET, AUTUMN

"How can you expect us to keep covering for you?" Max shouted at his father inside their family cottage. "When you returned in the spring, I thought you'd be smart enough to stick around. But then you missed three summer hunts and then the first one in autumn!"

"We will make it work," Max's mother, Addy, said.

"No. No, we won't," Max said. "These upcoming hunts are the biggest of the year."

"I can stay for the next hunt, but I must leave directly after," Heinrich insisted.

"Why! Why *must* you leave?" Max had never pushed for answers before, but he was beyond caring about his father's privacy when it impacted them all.

Addy took her husband's hand and squeezed it, giving him a pitying look before excusing herself.

"You forget your place, son. I am a servant of the crown. I might not always understand my tasks, but I do them out of loyalty to the kingdom. You will obey me as I do the throne. And you will continue to hide my absence, or we will all suffer." Heinrich glanced at the door his wife had just exited. "Take care of your mother while I'm gone."

Strained silence hung for what felt like an eternity. Addy's winter melancholia would deepen with the grey skies. Would Max's father bother to return for the worst of it?

"How dare you put all of this on me." Max stormed out of the cottage, fury swelling in his belly.

Mounting his horse, Max galloped down the path from his family cottage, barreling deeper into the king's forest. The autumn leaves fell, signaling deer hunting season. But the king hadn't ridden for moons, not since his exhaustion during his spring ride. What few knew was that a healer from Caston had been waiting to attend the king at the Hunts' cottage. Not even Max's mother had expected him. The healer met privately with the king and queen while Max and Addy waited outside, alert for any potential intruders.

Fortunately, the queen hadn't punished the Hunts after that excursion; she hadn't even mentioned Heinrich's absence. But her sour expression as she left the cottage all those moons ago was still fresh in Max's mind. He told himself she was just concerned about her husband, but he worried her irritation with Heinrich was quietly simmering. Not that he could blame her.

With only an argument for breakfast, Max's stomach growled. But he rode harder, needing distance from his father, which was ironic because their arguments circled around the huntsman's absences. His mother always defended Heinrich, despite knowing she'd need him through her winter melancholia afflictions.

Not wanting to upset her further, Max decided to stay away and scout. Besides, he needed to prepare for the upcoming sporting hunts for visiting nobles. His father wasn't making himself useful, and Max was tired of making up excuses for the *esteemed* royal huntsman.

Gripping the reins, Max pushed harder into the forest, heading toward a stone bridge over the river. If only his father would just explain what was going on rather than brush him off. It didn't help that, whenever Heinrich was in town, he spent more time in the castle than on the grounds. And when he was home, he was irritable.

The springtime river had turned into a stream. As he neared the bridge, he noticed someone sitting on the edge, her legs dangling above the water and a basket at her side.

Snow looked up at him and waved cheerfully. Her raven black hair lay in waves down her back, contrasting against her pale skin and buttery yellow dress. She usually wore linen servant's clothing, stitching and patching any holes until she outgrew each one. He'd never seen this one, but he liked the way the ruffles accentuated her bare shoulders. She never bought new clothing. Did she have an admirer? Jealousy spiked inside him, nearly making his vision blur.

"Are you going to offer me a ride like a respectable knight or act like the rogue we both know you are?" Snow teased.

"Just like old times," he said, his mood instantly lightening as his horse clopped closer. "Though, I worry about my reputation if I'm seen unaccompanied in the forest with a young maiden," he teased. "Respectability and all."

Her smile faded, and he quickly amended his statement. "Everyone knows we're just friends, Snow. And Dottie has never complained."

When Snow had worked in the kitchens, she'd often ridden with him into the far reaches of the forest; Dottie was grateful for the variety of herbs. Kitchen positions were highly coveted, and cooks were the highest-paid staff in any castle as they were the key to pleasing the fae. But, ever since Snow had been promoted to serve the king directly, he'd rarely seen her in the forest. He could only guess why she was here today, but she was a balm to his troubled soul.

"And who would see us anyway?" He held out his hand, extending the offer just like he'd done a hundred times before.

Snow brushed herself off and grabbed her basket before reaching up her free hand. This time, his hand sparked at the meeting. He hoisted her up, wondering if she felt it too. She wrapped her arms around him, and he was conscious of her warmth at his back. As he walked the horse forward, he should've looked for signs of animals, but all he could think about was the place where Snow gripped his waist and how much he wanted her to lean closer.

"What are you doing in the forest today?" Max asked, chastising himself for not asking sooner. What was her destination?

Snow shifted behind him, her grip tightening for a heartbeat. "Um, mushrooms."

"Does the king want mushroom soup for dinner?" Max asked, changing direction.

Snow didn't reply, but he figured it wasn't his business. He tried focusing on anything other than *her*—the colorful leaves, tracks in the mud, or the sound of birds.

Max pushed deeper into the forest, beyond where Snow could walk in a day, and stopped in an area usually rich with mushrooms this time of year. He and Snow split up, both hunting their prey but staying within earshot of each other. Max was grateful for a reprieve, wondering what was happening between them. He found himself drawn to her more each day. But she'd never indicated she cared about anything beyond getting back to Isolzing and learning about her past. Whatever he felt, it was just in his head. The feelings would pass. They had to—Snow was his best friend.

Max took his bow and quiver, but his primary goal was scouting the area for the nobles, not hunting. An hour later, Max had found signs of hare, deer, and the cook's favorite—wild boar. He was elated to tell his father about the sightings until he remembered their argument. His father hardly seemed to care about hunting anymore.

An errant thought crossed his mind. Could his father have been hunting in the dangerous Wildwood? Not only would his long absences be explained but the haunted look in his eyes as well. Some books said magical creatures were so horrifying that they stalked your dreams forever, never quite leaving in the daylight. Max shook off the idea, reminding himself that his father would never be so foolish.

Taking a deep breath, Max jogged back to his horse and rifled through the saddle pack. Relieved, he found an apple and a roll.

Thank you, Mother. He smiled, knowing she had predicted Max's temper and had tucked away something to eat. He made a note to apologize to her later.

Max tracked down Snow, finding her with her basket nearly full.

"Maximilian Hunt," she said, seeing the red fruit in his hand. "Tell me that isn't from the courtyard."

Max couldn't help but laugh, "Uhhh, no. I'd rather keep my neck connected to my body, thank you very much."

She put down her basket and stretched. "That's good to hear because I'd have to turn you in. And I probably wouldn't even get an apple for a reward."

Max snorted, the troubles that plagued him all morning easing away. He set the apple on a stump, walked twenty paces away, and then notched his arrow. He released the arrow, the bow vibrating near his cheek. Even from that distance, the iron tip punctured through the heart of the fruit. Snow clapped, and he bowed, enjoying the lightness of the moment. He hadn't appreciated their afternoons together for all those years and now he yearned for them. He jogged and grabbed the arrow, the apple skewered on the end, and took a bite.

"Max, one day you won't be wearing your pin, and you'll cut your face while you're eating like a three-year-old child," Snow teased. "Sometimes, you need to think ahead."

He rolled his eyes and leveraged the shaft, splitting the apple. "Sometimes, you need to trust your instincts."

Snow flashed him a half-grin as she moved through the dappled light, seeming to glow at each touch of the sun. Without thinking, Max found himself at her side. Awkwardly, he offered the larger piece of the fruit. Snow took the smaller section, but as her hand grazed his palm, she hesitated.

In years past, he wouldn't have noticed. But today, he did. She gripped the apple and quickly put a mushroom for him in its place before stepping back, wrapping her arms around herself.

"Is everything all right, Snow?" Max asked, the air thickening around them.

Snow fidgeted with the basket. "Will you take me to my coins on the way back? I have one to deposit."

"Of course," Max said. "Whatever you need."

In hindsight, he couldn't believe he had been so blind to Snow's radiance, so utterly ignorant of the gem that lay before him. Then again, he'd learned to keep strong feelings buried deep—at times, Snow seemed to know people's emotions even better than people knew themselves.

It was pure foolishness, but he'd hoped to take Snow to her child-hood home one day. Since it was her greatest wish to go to Isolz-ing, he wanted to see the village, too. He wanted to know where she came from—to understand her. They'd need separate rooms, and Snow would want a chaperone, but he didn't trust anyone else with her safe-ty. He'd never paused to ask himself why, beyond simply enjoying time with his best friend. But was it for reasons he hadn't allowed himself to admit?

Snow took a bite of the fruit, and Max was sorely tempted to move closer. His gaze fell on her shoulder then her neck, then her lips, their color even deeper than the red of the apple. But, no, they were friends. And Snow had to untangle her past in Isolzing. But once she found peace with herself, perhaps their relationship might change.

A branch snapped, and without thinking, Max pulled Snow behind a tree. Leaves rustled about fifty paces away. Snow was gripping his tunic, and his hand was at her waist. He put a finger to his lips, begging for silence, knowing only a large animal could cause so much noise. Footsteps clomped closer. Human. Who would dare trespass on the king's lands?

Not anyone with good intentions.

Max grabbed an arrow with one hand and pressed his other hand harder against Snow's waist, signaling her to slide around the tree. As they moved in tandem, she held his gaze, her blue eyes questioning. He blinked away and peeked around the trunk. A young man, about eighteen years, picked through the bushes, growing closer. He was tall and thin, his face gaunt with patchy growth on his chin. The stranger carried a pheasant, and it looked like the man could use the meal. But as the apprenticed huntsman, Max was obligated to report him.

Even if the trespasser were merely curious, he'd be fined. But he'd brazenly stolen royal resources, and technically, poachers were sentenced to hang. King Friedrich's father had begun generously allowing poachers to languish in the dungeon for a time, instead. According to his father, the recent kings' lenience had only been made possible because of harsh past rulers. Solinsel wouldn't return to the previous harsh law, would it?

The trespasser's clothing rustled as he neared the tree where Max and Snow hid. If the young man noticed them, Max would turn him in. Otherwise, word would spread that a royal apprentice flouted the law, which would end Max's appointment and shame his family. Or worse, the judge could throw Max in the dungeon for disregarding the law. To complicate matters, with the king ill, the high judge followed the law with exactness. The queen might not know to request leniency. She might not care. Why would she? Her family lived in a distant kingdom. The only person she cared about in Solinsel was the king.

Max held his breath as the young man passed by. If the stranger turned around, he'd spot them; from that particular angle, the sparse bushes wouldn't hide both Max and Snow. The young man's footsteps slowed. Max peeked around the trunk at the trespasser's back. The young man looked down at something—Snow's basket of mushrooms.

The stranger stilled. Then, his head jerked to where Max's horse was still tied up and grazing. Max released Snow's waist and quietly lifted and nocked his arrow, ready to take the poacher to the guards.

Before Max realized what Snow was doing, she slid around Max and pressed him against the tree, keeping him completely hidden.

"I've already thought this through," Snow whispered, rising up onto her tiptoes to reach his ear. "Wait here. Trust me."

She shoved her hand inside his coat, near his neck. Surprised by her touch, her familiarity, Max didn't realize what she'd done until she'd unlatched his family pin. Before he could stop her, Snow stepped away from Max, revealing herself to the unknown hunter.

CHAPTER 5: SNOW

YEAR 8 OF THE MAIDEN COMET, AUTUMN

S now tucked the amulet into her belt then put her hands out, showing the hunter she wasn't armed.

"Hello," she said softly, not giving her name.

If this encounter went awry, the court would get involved. And with the king so terribly ill, Judge Helene would find herself in an awkward position. More than awkward—potentially treasonous—because if Snow got entangled in a mess, Helene would be sentencing the future heir. As one of the few who knew Snow's true identity but was sworn to secrecy, would the judge disregard the law? Such action could bring anarchy inside and outside the noble hierarchy. Snow's tutors had overwhelmed her with hours of confusing topics, but she'd figured out the basics: one wrong move could topple a ruler.

"Would you like a mushroom?" Snow asked.

The young man stepped back, his attention darting from Snow to the forest around him. Would he believe she was alone? He had to, for his own sake. Max would not hesitate to subdue the stranger. Snow had let her mental guard slip the moment Max put his finger to his lips. When she had, an overwhelming feeling of protectiveness fell over her, and the fierceness of his emotion surprised her. But when she turned her attention to the stranger, she knew he needed help. His desperation was acute as was his fear. Fear made people dangerous.

"Do you know where you are?" Snow asked.

He fidgeted, his fingers flicking toward the slender rope at his waist, his other hand still holding the pheasant. Snow sensed his utter panic.

"If you go home with your pheasant, villagers will talk." Snow quickly spoke before he bolted. "More will hunt. Others won't be as lucky—they'll be caught. You're fortunate the royal huntsman hasn't arrested you on behalf of the king. The huntsman is scouting at this very moment. Are you sure he hasn't spotted you yet?"

Behind her back, Snow signaled for Max to stay put. Thanks to the amulet she'd borrowed without permission, even if the trespasser had a weapon, he wouldn't be able to hurt her.

"Who are you?" the young man asked.

"I work in Clarus, and I'm gathering mushrooms," Snow said. "You're in the king's forest."

Which you obviously already know.

"The queen demands too much," he blurted an excuse. "She takes more than her fair share of our crops, leaving us naught with scraps."

The king is in charge.

Though the king relied on the queen, apparently false rumors swirled about Agnes enforcing ludicrous policies. Even if the queen could increase taxation, any abrupt changes would be illogical.

Wouldn't they? Snow chewed the inside of her cheek, second-guessing herself. Taking a breath, she realized the simple explanation was that this young man had fallen on hard times and unjustly blamed others, exaggerating the situation.

"The crown exports more across the sea than we can spare," the trespasser continued. "The artisans are also bellyaching about their lot. My wife, she's sick. I can't be harvesting for the farmer and caring for her, too. We're all hungry, even the farmers."

"I'm sorry to hear of your plight." Snow fiddled with the ring on her finger, feeling woefully unprepared. She determined to ask her tutors to pause her lessons on foreign currency and focus on local taxation laws and farmers. "The pheasants of the king's forest are for the castle staff. I don't want you to get into trouble. Will you let me buy the pheasant from you?"

The young man cocked his head as Snow slowly put a hand into her pocket and pulled out her most recent bronze payment. Though it felt odd to be paid like a regular servant while training to become the queen, Reinhold had instructed her to keep up appearances. And despite the king's words and his sister's assurances, Snow couldn't help but prepare for the worst. Wars were fought over thrones; even the lowliest beggar knew that. So, Snow had squirreled away every bronze bit.

The stranger set his jaw, his fist around the pheasant tightening. "I'll sell for the coin. And a message to the queen."

"I'm listening," Snow said, feeling his emotions rise like a storm on the horizon. She tossed him the coin, and he caught it deftly in one hand. If Snow had hoped the money would calm him, she was wrong. She pulled her walls up higher, fearing she'd crumble under his swelling frustration. His anger.

He threw the pheasant at Snow's feet. "Tell Queen Agnes to help her people. The winter season comes quickly, and we'll *all* suffer."

***

In the tallest castle tower, Snow tried not to fidget while the painter worked. Her clothing itched everywhere it touched her skin, which was completely unhelpful.

Candles lit the painter's canvas as the rain fell, and the artist exuberantly slashed strokes on the canvas. The circular space was rather bare with a single velvet chair and a silken curtain framing the window, both quietly transported for Snow's portrait. As stark and chilly as it was, Elisabeth had suggested the derelict space as a ploy to keep servants unaware of Snow's special treatment.

After sitting for hours, Snow had grown weary of the artist's scowl. While Elisabeth gave him feedback while he worked, Snow tried not to think about her father. He'd been unconscious for a moon, and she'd overheard Dottie and the steward worrying about his health. A sad tension had fallen on the staff, an unspoken worry. Certainly, no one dared predict that he might die. With her access to the archives, Snow studied the king's family tree, seeing several noble cousins who could potentially bid for the throne. But no distant relative had the armies or the influence needed to wrestle the power from Queen Agnes. Few knew Agnes would merely be the regent until Snow was of age.

Her father had promised a slow transition. But if he died, Snow would be thrown into the light, revealed as the heir. Any perceived weakness on her part would lead to trouble from either within the kingdom or without. Snow straightened her posture, despite the ache in her back and the uncomfortable clothing. If this painting circulated around the northern kingdoms, they would see strength.

"Perhaps if you add more rose to her cheeks?" Elisabeth said, standing next to the artist.

"Perhaps the young woman should rest before our next session," he said, his voice tight. "The circles under her eyes look like bruises. How am I expected to—"

"We're done here," Elisabeth quickly moved to rescue Snow as she dismissed the artist. "We'll see you tomorrow."

Elisabeth escorted Snow out of the tower and down the winding stairs. Then the princess lowered her voice into a whisper. "Snow, is the steward pushing you too hard? I told him you are busy attending to the royal needs and to keep your tasks light. With your studies, I fear you are doing too much."

Snow winced, remembering what she'd overheard between Elisabeth and her last tutor. He'd said, "Snow is not the kind of student I agreed to teach. The curriculum is far beyond her grasp."

Embarrassed, Snow began studying on her own at night . . . until she couldn't keep her eyes open a moment longer. She could read far better than most commoners, but she'd never read such difficult texts. Each dull, arduous page in the thick dusty tomes was a drudgery. However, her tutor had emphasized the books were "laborious but important."

"I'm fine. Just not sleeping well," Snow lied.

In addition to her evening studies and her other duties, she'd also gotten permission from the steward to polish the statues in the Chamber of Tribunals. The work allowed her to eavesdrop on the court proceedings, and she had memorized the names of the lower judges, along with many rules and processes.

She'd also been privy to hallway gossip. Alarmingly, several merchants and farmers were as frustrated as the stranger in the woods.

With the growing rumors, Max had advised Snow to avoid the queen and not mention the trespasser. Furthermore, Snow had never felt comfortable approaching the queen, feeling Agnes bristling even from afar. Would she even receive advice from a commoner? But Snow had promised to pass on the trespasser's message, so she had keenly waited for another opportunity.

Who else might listen? Finding herself alone with the princess in the royal wing, Snow dared share her encounter in the forest, though she omitted the fact that Max was there, too.

"That's bold." Elisabeth tapped her chin, her focus distant. "The people grow desperate."

"I'm just glad I found him instead of Heinrich," Snow said. "His sense of duty would've compelled him to turn the young man over to the guards. Reputation is everything to him."

The princess brushed off the cuffs of her sleeve. "His father was the same. All the Hunts put loyalty to the crown above all else."

"I want to be a good ruler, deserving of loyalty," Snow said, overwhelmed by the importance of her role. "I appreciate all you're doing to prepare me. Thank you for your patience."

"I know you are trying to become what the kingdom needs." Elisabeth's words were infused with a sense of focus. A seriousness. "Your efforts are impressive, and I'm not the only one who has noticed."

"I wonder if the king made a mistake naming me the heir," Snow confessed her concern about the task ahead.

A pang of bitterness shot through Snow before Elisabeth took a breath and smiled, and the sour notes faded. "Unless there's an uprising, usurping, or conquering, the crown follows the bloodline. Of all my brother's children, you're the best fit."

Snow dared to ask what she'd wanted to know for moons. "How many siblings do I have?"

"Eight half-siblings, nine children in all," Elisabeth said, flashing a tight smile.

"I'm sure others have more skills than I do," Snow said, wondering if they even knew their paternity. "I don't understand why the king selected me." Guilt over her appointment and recognition weighed heavy, and she felt more than a little unworthy, considering how she'd disappointed her tutors.

"I don't think he was looking at your skill but at an aspect of your personality that he found appealing." Elisabeth turned, more curious. "Unfortunately, not all your siblings are still alive. I tried to assist those I know of since Friedrich has taken ill, but they are like feathers in the wind. I would arrange for you to meet them, but they tend to move around. I wish I knew where they were located so I could help them as I've done for you. We're all family, and perhaps, one day, you can help me find them."

"I'd like that."

"When Friedrich wakes up, you can ask him all your questions."

Snow's questions for her father were piling up. He had rarely left his chambers since his spring ride. After his confession that he was her father, they'd had several tender discussions. He'd shared stories about his childhood, meeting Rosalind in Caston, and his crowning ceremony. Snow told him about wildflower head wreaths and the Maiden Comet celebration in Isolzing when she'd eaten enough candy to make herself sick. The king had begun to look at her with unabashed care, and Snow had almost started seeing him as a father and less as *the* king.

After reflecting on her childhood, Snow calculated that the king had sent enough resources to allow for extensive tutoring. Enough to even buy into an apprenticeship. Though she had a joyful childhood and the loss of her mother still cut deeply, Snow had been left a destitute orphan in the Blessed House. Fortunately, the king had sent his huntsman to fetch her. Even if Friedrich decided not to make Snow his heir, she had gained enough experience to secure employment at any number of noble houses worth far more than her bag of bronze coins.

"Do you think he will awaken?" Snow asked, feeling unmoored at the thought of losing him. She longed to have more substantive conversations with her father. There were so many things she hadn't asked him yet.

"Anything is possible," Elisabeth said, though Snow sensed her doubt. "He's very sick, though. It might be best if—"

A servant ran to intercept them in the halls, her face wild with panic. Before the servant even said a word, Snow's belly filled with dread.

"The king," the servant said. "I'm so sorry. He's dead."

Then, before Elisabeth could question her further, the servant burst into tears.

CHAPTER 6: MAX

YEAR 9 OF THE MAIDEN COMET, MID-WINTER

M ax stalked through the servant's entrance into the castle. Stomping his feet, snow fell from his coat and shoes onto the threshing. He still boiled from the latest disagreement with his father. Heinrich had never argued in front of the king's stable hands or other servants, not until yesterday. Surely, the servants would be gossiping about the huntsmen's loud, sharp words for weeks.

He no longer cared. His father had become a tinderbox after the king's death, and his mood hadn't softened in the moons since.

Heinrich had hated being confined inside the castle, but once the king grew ill, he spent more and more time among the stuffy nobles. Now, if anyone wanted to find the huntsman, they'd have to look for him indoors—it was unnatural. Max would've kept his distance, but between the questions from the nobles and the strange request his father had left on parchment for him, Max had to find his father.

After asking one of the few discreet servants, Max was directed to the Chamber of Tribunals in the northwest wing of the castle. The grandiose room was designed for holding court sessions and legal proceedings. The soaring ceilings and intricate architecture were lined with paintings and tapestries depicting the laws of the kingdom, and polished statues of past rulers loomed. Max strode through the back of the crowded room, barely glancing around for his father, guessing he wasn't actually watching court proceedings but instead in one of the side chambers meant for formal noble meetings. As he passed the royal receiving room, the largest side chamber by far, he noticed Agnes sitting on King Friedrich's throne.

No, the *queen's* throne.

Queen Agnes sat ramrod straight, her hands gripping the arms of the chair as a merchant spoke in rapid fashion. She didn't speak, but her brows furrowed as she listened. Max shook his head and continued his search for his father. Finally, Max saw his father emerge from one of the archways around the Tribunal. Heinrich turned and strode into the hall, coming straight toward Max.

"Funny running into you here," Max grumbled.

His father gave him a dark look and jerked his head, gesturing for his son to follow. The huntsman led Max down another corridor and into an alcove next to the high judge's personal office.

"What are you doing here?" his father said, keeping his voice low.

"I came to ask you the same thing, royal *huntsman*," Max spat. "I can't keep covering for you. Ever since the king died, the nobles are edgy."

"Maximilian, I need you to look around," his father whispered. "The kingdom is devolving into turmoil. The queen barely understands our court system. She struggles with the finer points of the language, too. I fear some courtiers are taking advantage."

"She's passing laws and putting plenty of citizens in the dungeon, Heinrich," Max said, tired of his father's excuses for the new ruler despite his allegiance and requirement to do so. "She seems to be figuring things out just fine. I'm more worried about you."

"You're supposed to be on a task for me today, remember?" Heinrich's nostrils flared. "You shouldn't be here."

"Why would you ask me to locate elven mistroot?" Trips to the Wildwood were never taken lightly and were usually discussed well in advance.

Heinrich's eyes widened, but then he lowered his voice, his lips barely moving. "Just obey. No questions."

High Judge Helene approached them, and his father straightened.

"Go home, son." The huntsman lifted his chest as if daring Max to argue.

Max clenched his jaw, barely holding back a retort. Why was his father in the castle when he was needed at home? Why was he sending Max into the Wildwood without reason?

"And one more thing," Heinrich said harshly, loud enough for a passing servant to pick up her pace and scurry out of earshot. "Stay away from Snow White."

"What?" A shock shot through him. Why would his father request such a thing?

"Snow has been promised to another. She'll only break your heart."

"She's betrothed? Since when?" Max couldn't believe what he was hearing.

"Just like her mother did to Snow's father, she'll take your heart and your coin but leave you behind."

Max fisted his hands at his side. "How dare you—"

The high judge cleared her throat, "The queen wishes to speak with you. I'll take you now."

Heinrich turned on his heel and followed Helene toward the queen's receiving room, leaving Max alone, stewing in his fury.

CHAPTER 7: SNOW

YEAR 9 OF THE MAIDEN COMET, LATE WINTER

S now awoke to a sharp smell and a stiff hand holding her down. In the darkness of her room, she couldn't see the intruder, and all her senses screamed. Snow tried to wriggle away as she cried for help, but the sound was smothered by the cloth shoved against her face. Panic filled her, followed by a tingling numbness which quickly swallowed her whole.

Snow's entire body rumbled, and her head pounded. She squinted and curled away from the light coming through the tarp overhead. Each breath brought a frigid awareness that she was outside in the winter elements . . . in the back of a wagon, bumping along some unknown road. She fought to *think*. Then the nightmarish event flashed to the forefront of her mind. She buried her face in her hands, trying to sort through her lint-filled head.

Strangely, her hands weren't tied, nor was she gagged. She swallowed, trying to abate the dryness in the back of her throat. The wagon was covered, tied tight with a rope against the sides, giving two hands of space above her body for movement. She shifted, peeking at the driver through the gap in the wagon cover, but saw only a portion of a man's back.

Oh, Abundant Ones, she'd been *abducted*. But how had that even been possible? Elisabeth had moved her into the royal wing after the king's death, afraid of this very thing. How did this man get past the extra guards?

Judge Helene and Princess Elisabeth had debated with Snow about publicly revealing her claim to the throne after King Friedrich's death. Snow sensed both the women's unease, but then Elisabeth confessed her suspicion that someone poisoned Friedrich. Until the culprit was found, any known heir would be in danger. Helene didn't act surprised, yet she still wanted to reveal the king's contract. In the end, Helene agreed to wait until they could quietly investigate Friedrich's death.

Even so, Snow had requested they tell Agnes . . . and soon. Elisabeth paled, clearly concerned. But, Helene gave a curt nod. Unfortunately, they'd never had a chance to inform Agnes that she was merely in a temporary role.

All that strategizing and Snow had been captured anyway. She couldn't change the past, so she fumbled for a plan to escape. She blinked, trying to focus enough to see if the back of the wagon was boarded and secure. But even if she could roll her sluggish self off the back, the driver would certainly chase her. Could she outrun him?

The man spoke as he drove the wagon, and Snow recognized the voice.

"You're awake," Heinrich said without turning around. "Keep yourself hidden. Spies are everywhere." He was somewhat difficult to understand, and then Snow dimly realized he was not only speaking quietly but he was barely moving his lips. He continued, "Water. In the bag."

Snow lowered her inner walls, desperate to get a sense of the huntsman, but got nothing except a buzzing fog. Trusting the man she thought she knew, she reached for the pack and pulled out the bladder, eagerly drinking.

"Why?" Snow squeaked out a question.

The huntsman took a deep breath, his shoulders heaving. "Patience."

Now that she actually needed to know someone's intentions, her ability seemed small and out of reach. The longer they rode, the more irritated she grew with both Heinrich and herself.

They rode in silence, Snow concentrating on breathing as the overhead branches blurred past the gap in the wagon cover. She didn't recognize the area, the snarl of limbs blocking out most of the cloud-covered light. But then again, she didn't usually look at the forest from this angle. The sky grew darker, and Snow wasn't sure if the evening was closing in, the trees were growing thicker, or if it was a combination of both.

Finally, Heinrich spoke, his tone hushed, but clear. "I'm not even sure where to begin, but let me start with today, and I'll work backward. Will that do?"

"As long as it explains why you drugged and kidnapped me, then proceed."

"I always did like your sense of humor," the huntsman said, glancing back at her before continuing. "So did the king. He had a lot of regrets in his life, but you were never one of them."

Snow pulled the woolen blanket up to her chin, acutely missing Friedrich. Finding her father was a gift she hadn't expected, and Snow missed his presence. Though she knew the king was frail, she always hoped he'd recover. Sadly, she'd never said goodbye.

The queen refused to let anyone near his body except for dwarven glaziers, the finest craftsfolk in the Seven Kingdoms. For her father's processional, Princess Elisabeth watched with Snow through a castle window as the dwarves carried his glass coffin down the moonlit road to the royal tomb in the side of the mountain. Later, the princess argued to keep Snow in the royal wing, shifting her duties to Elisabeth, keeping up the pretense that Snow was dusting and sweeping rather than studying. The princess had taken her in just like the Hunts had after Snow's mother was killed.

While the wagon rumbled on, Heinrich explained that he knew Snow's mother; he had known several paramours of the king.

"Once the king married, he was loyal to Agnes," the huntsman said. "Much later, they began to realize she was barren. Your father needed an alternative heir. Someone with the appropriate qualities who the kingdom would also accept as the ruler."

"The king began looking to his illegitimate children?" Snow fiddled with her ring, wondering if Heinrich knew the heir was in his wagon at that very moment. What else did or didn't the huntsman know?

"Friedrich delegated his children's care to me. I'm a peculiar choice, but we grew up together, and he trusted me. Per his instruction, I sent tutors to the elder children and hired more when the younger children were of age. Your mother was protective of the life she'd built for you both, which I respected. The summer before I fetched you, I'd written to Rosalind about possible apprenticeships."

Snow's chest tightened. Her mother had no idea she wouldn't live to see her daughter's next birthday. The drugged fog of Snow's mind evaporated with the jolting memory of the wolf attack. Her mother's shouts. The creature's chilling growl. Black, shimmering fur before her mother shoved Snow out the window.

The hair on Snow's arm rose, even these many years later. Snow wrestled the thoughts away, unwilling to relive the attack again.

"The tutors reported directly to me. I reported to Reinhold and the king, usually on our hunts when we were alone." Heinrich's tone took on a hard edge. "The king was paranoid, and evidently he had good reason to worry."

"What do you mean?"

"For a long time, I pitied Queen Agnes. She's unfamiliar with many Solinsel traditions," the huntsman said, his back hunching lower. "She had me fooled into thinking her a kind woman. All a clever ruse, apparently. Everything changed yesterday when she came to me with a depraved request. She commanded that I take you into the forest and," he paused, before choking out the last words, "bring back your heart and liver."

The air seemed to leave Snow's lungs. As she moved to sit up, the huntsman hissed a reminder to stay put.

"Breathe in slowly through your nose as you count to ten," the huntsman soothed, coaching her.

Snow trembled but forced herself to take deep breaths. Finally, the initial shock passed. "Go on, Heinrich. I'm ready."

"I believe that this is the queen's second attempt on your life," Heinrich said slowly. "I don't think the attack on your mother in Isolzing was an accident."

As unbelievable as the statement was, Snow felt the truth of his words, as if The Abundant Ones tapped on her heart, calling her attention. An awful understanding. Snow clutched the blanket tighter, aching for her mother.

"When I brought you to Clarus, I didn't tell the king everything I'd learned," the huntsman explained. "I can only hope that he will forgive me when we meet again in Fairen'la."

"You know more about the wolf." The words were flat, but inside, the realization that Heinrich had withheld answers she'd longed for left a bitter taste.

"When I arrived in your village, I found you at the Blessed House. The Attuned had questioned the villagers, and two witnesses claimed the attack was done by no mere wolf. It was a Shadow Beast."

"The beasts are bedtime stories Addy made up," Snow retorted, distrustful.

"You'll be surprised to discover how many of those mythical tales are real," the huntsman continued. "Magic is a tricky thing. So I'm taking you someplace the queen can't find you. Can't see you."

"What do you mean, can't *see* me?" Snow asked.

"Fae magic. Your father didn't record the locations of his children. Very few knew you even existed. Yet somehow, Agnes found you. The tutors were not compromised; I questioned them myself. It didn't make sense, but then I realized that magic explained everything. I don't know how, but witches can conjure visions of the present."

That cannot *be good.*

The huntsman took a deep breath. "Your father became very, very careful before he died. Paranoid. Instead of occasional talks in the forest, he began writing me sealed notes and had them delivered to my home with explicit instructions to burn them afterward—he wanted me to relocate all his children. Whenever I asked about the messages, he pretended not to know of the missives. He was protective, which is why the king waited to reveal himself as your father; he kept your identity secret, believing it would keep you safe. But now, with the king dead, the queen stopped hiding her intentions."

The huntsman fell into a dower state, quieting. Snow was grateful for the silence as she tried to untangle what he'd confessed. Knowing a Shadow Beast attacked only brought more questions. The creatures never left the Wildwood. So, did the queen hire someone to direct it to Snow's childhood home? How was that even possible? Furthermore, Snow couldn't quite reconcile that Agnes wanted her dead. Even before the king named an heir, had Agnes viewed Snow as a threat?

If the queen had known all along that Snow was the daughter of the king, it explained Agnes's prickly emotions. Even so, Snow never would've guessed at the queen's depraved intentions. The mere thought of Agnes's request for Snow's organs made her stomach roil.

The thick canopy overhead blocked out the light, and an eerie screeching sounded in the distance. The wagon slowed, and a bone-chilling dread crept over the wagon. The huntsman stopped the wagon, staying silent as if afraid to announce his presence. Snow began to worry that perhaps all his chatter was a preamble, explaining why he had to kill her—to save his own life and family from the queen's wrath. Snow hated that she understood why; she'd do anything to protect Max, too.

Someone drew closer, their footsteps marching right past the wagon bed.

"What is going on?" Max's voice whispered. "I've been waiting in these woods for an hour. Are you going to explain your latest ridiculous request?"

Snow startled. What was Max doing here? He'd been acting strangely distant over the last few weeks. He'd treated her the same, but something had shifted. She pressed her knuckles to her lips, wondering how she'd been such a fool. Had he been planning this abduction, too?

Max continued, "First elven mistroot? And now this?"

Something thudded on the seat next to Heinrich, rocking the wagon.

Heinrich didn't respond to his son, loosening the canopy instead. "It's okay to come out. No one will see you here."

Snow peeked over the ledge at Max. His red face drained of color as his jaw dropped.

"I can't believe you brought Snow here. Of all the dangerous, absurd, *foolish* things to do! You've lost your mind." He turned to Snow. "Come with me. I'm getting you out of here. Now."

Snow gripped the edge of the wagon. Decaying trees punctuated the dense forest, their skeletal limbs poised like claws ready to strike. The overhead canopy choked the light, allowing too little to reach the mossy carpet underfoot, dotted by peculiar vibrant flowers. Ominous vines hung and swayed, despite the lack of breeze. But what alarmed her most was the sense of being watched. Studied.

"Son," Heinrich said. "We must hide Snow where fae magic cannot find her. Here."

"You're leaving me in the Wildwood?" *I am going to die.*

As if in response, a strange animal barked in the distance, followed by two more. Then a keening whine cut through the air before it was cut short with a sickening yip. Snow shivered and pulled her gaze away from the trees and back to the Hunts. Next to the elder huntsman, Snow saw what Max had set on the wagon bench—a juvenile wild boar, dead and tied.

"The queen wants Snow dead, and this is the safest place in the kingdom," Heinrich explained to them both. "Fae magic cannot penetrate these woods."

"You can't be serious," Max said. "Snow will be dead within a day."

Agreed.

"That's where you come in, son," Heinrich said. "Help Snow. Create a shelter and teach her what to gather. She won't be here long."

The huntsman continued with his instructions, but Snow's insides twisted. This whole situation was madness. Snow had many skills, but flying to the moon would be easier than surviving the insidious magic of the unfamiliar wood.

She jumped down, wanting to walk off her nerves, but Max grabbed her arm, stopping her mid-stride while not missing a beat in the argument with his father. She looked down and realized she'd almost stepped on a spiny nettlepox. The drawing and caption came to her mind; the unassuming thorns easily poked through cloth shoes and stockings. Only days later would the infected person realize their mistake, when an itchy rash spread up from the foot or leg and covered their entire body, making their joints ache. With fluids and rest, one would recover, but few travelers in these woods had that luxury. Instead, stiff and tired, they'd be easy prey for the dangerous creatures.

She was barely inside the forest, and she literally needed to watch every footstep.

"But why would the queen come after Snow?" Max speculated aloud. "The servants say she's jealous of anyone's beauty beyond her own."

"Perhaps," Heinrich said, keeping Snow's parentage a secret.

Who noticed a lowly servant girl? Not a queen. Snow knew the truth—Agnes actually feared losing the throne. But the queen had been too hasty in trusting Heinrich. Agnes wouldn't make another mistake. So, how could Snow turn this to her advantage?

She fiddled with the invisible ring on her finger. Max could help her survive a few days, but the Hunts underestimated the threat Snow posed to the queen. She needed long-term shelter.

"Take me to the Darkstone Mountains," Snow interrupted their argument.

Heinrich paused. "To the dwarves?"

And closer to my childhood home and more answers.

Snow nodded. "Max said you've done business with them in the past."

"Yes, but on behalf of the crown," Heinrich said.

"The dwarves are under no obligation to help us," Max added, "but they might."

"It's a good idea, in theory," Heinrich said. "But there's a process, which is lengthy. I'll be back for you long before they'll respond to a request."

"How long until the queen notices Max's absence?" Snow asked. Her eighteenth birthday was a few moons away, meaning she had to hide for over a year. Only those who wielded dark magic could hope to survive that long in the Wildwood.

"Max is supposedly on a mission to gather willow bark for the healer. It grows near the Wildwood border, which is why I selected today to move you," Heinrich said. "But the assignment should only take a day at the most."

Max huffed, leaning closer to her. "I'm not leaving Snow."

"The bark isn't a high priority, correct?" Snow confirmed. "So, let the queen believe that you both want to ingratiate yourselves with the new ruler. When Heinrich returns to Clarus, he will deliver the boar's heart and liver to the queen"—Snow swallowed—"as if they were mine."

Silence hung between them, the whole situation feeling even more real. More dangerous.

"Meanwhile, as far as the queen knows, Max is foraging for a special plant," Snow turned to Max. "Do you have any suggestions? The offering must be something potent. A gift worthy of a queen."

"Ghost crocus." Max grinned. "They're rumored to purify the skin. The queen and nobles are obsessed over appearance. She won't question it."

Plus, the crocus enhanced mental clarity and focus, which was the real reason the queen might be interested, but Snow kept that thought to herself.

Max continued, "The bulb is found where the king's forest and the Wildwood meet, so even if the queen doesn't believe your ruse with the boar, she won't suspect that I escorted Snow all the way to the mountains."

"But ghost crocus can take weeks to find," Heinrich said, doubtful.

Max's grin widened. "I saw some while scouting last week."

Snow gripped his sleeve, wondering if she could really escape the clutches of the queen and get back to Isolzing, all in one move. Heinrich had given her some answers about her mother's death, but they brought so many more questions. Max put a hand over hers, and the touch caused her defenses to lower enough to sense his hope but also his deeper worry. He knew something wasn't quite adding up. She owed Max the truth his father already knew, didn't she?

"Max, you should know what you're getting into before you agree." Snow stepped back, forcing herself to withdraw from his comforting touch. "I'm the daughter of the late King Freidrich."

CHAPTER 8: MAX

YEAR 9 OF THE MAIDEN COMET, LATE WINTER

The space between Max and Snow seemed to widen into an impassable gulf, though they'd both stayed perfectly still. "Y-you are . . ." he couldn't finish the impossible sentence. "I'm still going with you."

Of course he was. Always. Despite the shocking news. Did it change anything between them? No.

Yes?

He didn't know what it meant, but the edge of the Wildwood wasn't the place to analyze the shifting winds.

"I'm afraid there's more." Heinrich sighed and hopped down from the wagon. "Things that neither of you know. About five years after the king married, he reviewed reports of his children and selected an heir:

Snow's studious elder sister, raised by her grandparents. She was gifted with languages and as charismatic as her father. A born leader. But she tragically died about two years before Snow came to the castle."

"That's terrible," Snow whispered, her brows furrowed.

Max still reeled from the knowledge of Snow's parentage—and she had siblings. The thoughts churned like sap in the heat, sticky and unable to be brushed aside.

"The king and I believed your sister's death was an accident until six moons later when your eldest two siblings went missing. His suspicion grew to paranoia after Snow's attack. But it wasn't until a year and a half ago, before the king died, that he requested that I move his children."

As Heinrich continued his explanations, guilt snaked through Max's stomach. He'd been so angry about his father's absences. But all that time, he had been relocating the king's children, just like he'd done with Snow. He'd brought her to their home, but he couldn't do that with every child. He had to make complicated, time-consuming arrangements.

"That must've been hard, living a secret life," Max said, trying not to think about his impatient, biting words.

"It was. But your mother is my greatest support," he said, moving to the wagon bed. "I owe everything to her. Despite her own struggles, she has been a gift, not asking me to divulge the king's secrets and taking Snow in without question."

How long had Snow known her father's identity? Of course, her parentage was her secret to tell, but Snow knew everything about Max's life. Apparently, she didn't trust him in the same way. The revelation punched him in the stomach, leaving him breathless. But he swallowed, trying to ignore whatever emotions were burbling inside, telling himself he had bigger problems.

Snow politely excused herself, claiming to need to prepare for the journey, giving the Hunts privacy.

"Father," Max began, stuttering through an apology, "I'm so sorry about what I said. And about the fighting."

"No, it's exactly what I needed people to see," the elder huntsman confessed as he gathered his field dressing supplies. "I had to make it real. Everyone needed to see us argue, so I pushed you where I knew it would hurt the most, like with my insults about Snow's mother."

So fewer will suspect my involvement if my father is ever caught.

Max's stomach twisted, imagining what Agnes would do if Heinrich's double life was discovered.

"Not that my opinion matters, but I never took issue with Rosalind," Heinrich continued. "And I would've communicated with you about my absences, but I couldn't let anyone suspect the truth. I knew this day would come, and I knew you'd need to help Snow."

"You pushed me away from Snow, hoping servants would assume our friendship had drifted apart," Max said. It would be less obvious that he'd helped her if they hadn't spoken in weeks. If only his father had told him, especially because he *hadn't* distanced himself. But if fae magic was employed, his father had little choice but to stay quiet.

"Be back within two weeks." Heinrich shook a finger in Max's face. "Any longer, and the queen will begin to question."

"I'll be back. You taught me well," Max assured him.

His father had started his training for the Wildwood not long after Snow had first arrived. His mother's stories of the magical creatures began around that time, too. Max embraced his father, awed by his parent's planning and tenacity but also by their confidence in him.

Heinrich stepped back, his attention flitting from the forest to the wagon where Max had tossed the requested animal.

"I'll dress the boar here and bring back the heart and liver. The required proof," Heinrich's voice quivered.

"How could the queen demand such a cruel task?" Max's stomach soured.

"Madness? Greed? Does it matter?" The huntsman hesitated, a hint of uncertainty in his voice. "She met with me in the dungeons, which was unusual. Something about the queen felt *off*. Unsettled. Between the flames of the torch casting strange, moving shadows across her face and the echo of the chamber swallowing her northern accent, the whole situation seemed . . ." his voice trailed off for a moment. "Surreal. I almost thought I'd dreamed it. I wish I'd been so lucky. The queen wants the heart and liver prepared for consumption."

Max pressed a hand to his stomach, sickened.

"I'll ask Dottie to prepare the meal," Heinrich said, straightening. "I'll deliver the dish myself, ensuring that few servants see it. The queen will have no reason to suspect the lie—unless Snow is discovered."

"How long will Snow need to hide?" Max dared ask.

"If the dwarves take her in, we'll have more flexibility. But I have a plan either way." Not wasting time, Heinrich shoved a satchel into Max's hands for inspection. "Food is going missing from the kitchens. The steward is interrogating the servants, but I suspect the king's fae, Reinhold, is still flitting around the castle. I don't know why he didn't return to his realm, but I suppose he's mourning in his own way, not quite ready to leave. If I can find him, I'll ask for his advice. Otherwise, I'll need to approach Elisabeth. She'll want to depose the queen as much as anyone—her family has steered the kingdom for generations. A single, greedy ruler could spoil it all."

"Why not go to Elisabeth now?"

The huntsman looked over his shoulder to where Snow had disappeared and then lowered his voice. "Elisabeth has already suffered great misfortune. Somehow, despite all the rigors of the fae leaders, she was Bonded to a depraved fae as a baby."

Most royals across the seven kingdoms were Bonded to fae; the partnership was a great honor. Fae were not kind creatures by nature, but a wicked fae could easily trick a human child.

"As Elisabeth grew older," Heinrich continued, "she eventually recognized her fae's terrible manipulations. Unfortunately, she'd already damaged her reputation with not only the servants and nobles but with her family. Despite the consequences, she broke her Bond and asked for forgiveness. I can only imagine how difficult that was for her."

Max's jaw dropped, unaware a fae bonding could be broken other than by death.

"It was before you were born," Heinrich continued, "and her brother punished anyone who mentioned Elisabeth's past. But my generation remembers; I'm not sure she'd be supported even if she does help Snow and stop the queen. Friedrich and Reinhold pitied Elisabeth, but her parents treated her mistakes as permanent stains on her character. I suspect many elder nobles feel the same."

Snow re-emerged, gingerly brushing herself off against an invisible foe. Snow and Max had spent plenty of nights in the forest together, but the Wildwood was different. Even on the edge of the dangerous woods, Max was wary, but deeper inside, survival required vigilance.

Heinrich gave Snow the second satchel and the blanket from the back of the wagon along with a dagger. Then he hurried them along. "Get going. The darkness falls quickly."

"I'm sorry for the danger I've put you in," Snow apologized.

"It's not your fault," Heinrich assured her. "Your father told me to abide by the queen, to be her confidant and friend in a kingdom where she has none. I fear she fooled him until the bitter end, just as she'd fooled me."

"Her moods have fluctuated greatly since the king's death," Snow said. "But I still can't believe she wants me dead. And her request seems . . . not like her."

"How well did any of us really know her?" The huntsman shook his head. "Be careful. Stay hidden."

Max was torn. When Heinrich returned, the queen would scrutinize everything he did and said. With Max conveniently missing, some suspicion would be cast on the royal huntsman. But Snow couldn't return to the castle, and Max couldn't let her wander in the Wildwood. Max's stomach soured with guilt about leaving his father, worry swimming inside him. Not to mention Snow's huge secret.

Choosing between his father and Snow was impossible. Even so, he knew what he needed to do. Helping Snow situate her satchel and making sure her dagger was secure at her waist, he started leading her deeper into the forest. He took one last look back at his father just in time to see him wipe a tear. Max waved then turned and focused on their surroundings.

Snow stepped where he stepped, wisely staying quiet. They traveled in silence, and despite his best efforts, Max's mind wandered to Snow. How could she not have told him that the king was her father? True, she hadn't been recognized by the king, but clearly, they had a relationship. A connection she'd never shared with Max. What else hadn't she told him?

When they stopped to eat, Max whispered survival insights. "Don't believe anything you see, especially if the aspect appears human," he warned. "Who knows if there's a witch residing in the wood? They have the power to control glamours."

"Only because they bargained for it with fallen fairies," Snow said.

Max scrutinized her as she ate, trying to recall when his mother had taught a lesson on how dark fae essentially created witches. Heinrich had told Max during their first trip through the Wildwood, but his mother rarely spoke about the fae, preferring stories about Wildwood plants and animals. Had she mentioned the reclusive humans with fae-amplified powers?

Snow shivered as she ate, despite the cloak. He controlled his impulse to wrap his arms around her. How would he have reacted to her need a week ago? What did she expect of him now? Constantly second-guessing every action wore his nerves.

"I thought it was odd that Addy requested books from her family's library when Clarus was so much closer," Snow mused as she finished her roll. "I think she purposely hid our studies of the magical creatures."

Max felt a rush of gratitude for his mother. Even so, Snow had only heard stories of enchanting wisps and poisoned bramble. She hadn't spent a single night in the Wildwood. Which also meant the queen wouldn't suspect Snow to survive here. And no one knew about Heinrich's dangerous training of his son in the magical woods.

As the day stretched on, the tension between Max and Snow thickened, and not just because of the stench of rot, the distant keening, or the ominous trees surrounding them. Part of him longed to hold her hand, to comfort her as he once would have. Their affection was once casual, comfortable even in silence. But something had changed, at least for him. He reminded himself that Snow had lost her home and family for the second time. She was about to start over with strangers that she could only hope would shelter her. So, he would not brood about his own bruised feelings.

And he would absolutely not dwell on how—between the drawn lines of their friendship—he'd completely fallen in love with Snow.

Four days later, cold, muddy, and emotionally wrung, Max closed the distance to the base of the snow-topped mountain. He was sick with worry about his father, hungry enough to eat a toad, and doing his best not to obsess about Snow. An impossibility as she had stayed a step behind him for days. Yet, he'd never felt more distant from her. A brokenness had formed, or maybe it had always been there and Max had been blind to it. Snow wasn't the light-hearted orphan who shared everything with her best friend. She was the daughter of a king, holding a mountain of a secret.

Logically, hiding her identity made sense. But it pained him that she had never hinted at her truth. Even more so, his unrequited affection for Snow cut him to the core. For their entire relationship, a transparent but thick barrier resided between them. He'd never noticed—until now, when the impediment became glaringly obvious, as if the sunlight had bounced off the glass wall, finally revealing it.

Did he ever know Snow at all? Or had he only seen what he'd wanted to see? He wished he could cut out the gutting feelings inside him, hating the battling emotions within. But they only intensified through the journey.

Despite the spiraling sadness inside, he would do whatever it took to keep her safe. As they quietly crept forward, Max taught Snow to survive as they traveled by pointing out landmarks, warning of dangers, and pausing to eat the few safe plants. If the dwarves didn't take her in, he'd have precious little time to build her a shelter before he'd condemn himself and his father by not returning.

"Avoid speaking about the king's Bonded fae at all," Max whispered his last advice to Snow as they wove through the trees toward the hidden entrance to the dwarven caves. "Dwarves hate fairies, and they use a significant amount of their resources to block fae magic. Their mutual animosity is your advantage."

Snow raised a brow but nodded and followed. He tried to ignore the blue tint to her lips, reminding himself that warmth wasn't much farther. The trees thinned as they climbed the mountainside, avoiding patches of snow between the branches overhead. The rockface steepened, and a sheer, smooth slab sat amongst the rocky outcroppings. The door looked like a natural formation, easily missed. Heinrich had brought him to meet the dwarves years ago. On the second trip, Max had to find his way on his own. His father traveled alongside but was as helpful as a gnat. Max had found the door. Eventually. He'd been tricked by a wisp but was only waylaid an extra day.

Max passed by the sheer section of rock and hiked a few steps parallel. He counted over five hands, finding a section of rock that looked like a face. Well, that's what the dwarves said, but Max thought an ant with a dented thorax was more apt. A difficult marker, but the dwarves were discreet. He tapped a rhythm on the ant, which didn't budge. But in the center of the sheer rock face, a geometrical design appeared, carved by invisible hands.

Max jumped down in front of the carving. "Dwarves of Darkstone Emerald Clan, may I, Maximilian Hunt, and my guest, Snow White, be granted access?"

Silence greeted them, and sweat beaded along Max's forehead. Finally, the doorway shifted, and bits of dust rained down. The door opened, and a dwarf stood there with arms folded, staring at him with a glare. Great. Of course, Karldorin would greet them.

"First, you must answer my riddles three," the elder dwarf said, his lip curled.

"What?" Max had never been tested before. They stared at each other for what seemed like ages, Karldorin scowling.

"I'm joking!" the dwarf said, his expression unchanged. "What do you take me for? A bridge troll?"

Snow shot Max a questioning look then snorted a laugh.

"Welp, she passed. Come on in, my lady; you're letting out all the warm air. Yes, you too, ya dimwit huntsman," he demanded before turning his attention to Snow. "And how did this dolt convince a charming young lady to join him? You'd better meet the family. They're gonna want to get to know the woman who's finally stolen Max's heart. Or are you a magical creature? Elven, perhaps? I mean, you did travel through the Wildwood, did you not?"

Snow stuttered nonsensically, and Max's ears burned. Karldorin finally stepped to the side, allowing them entrance. But before Max could budge, six other dwarves rushed toward them, each one talking over the other. They pulled Snow inside first, pelting her with questions.

Gertrild grabbed Max's arm, holding him back. "Who is she?"

Max shook his head, unsure himself.

CHAPTER 9: SNOW

YEAR 9 OF THE MAIDEN COMET, LATE WINTER

The dwarves pulled Snow into a dazzling cave, nothing like the book illustrations she'd seen. Welcoming light streamed down from the vaulted ceiling, and whimsical, delicate trees stretched tall despite the encasing rock. Rough walls enclosed the massive, circular space, and a set of wooden double doors dominated the opposite wall from the entrance. The space was bigger than the home she grew up in, and the dwarves' loud questions bounced off the walls—deafening after days of near silence.

"Slow down," Max laughed. "Let me introduce you before you pelt Snow with more questions." He gestured to a matronly dwarf wearing an apron, her red hair pulled up into a bun, showcasing several thin, gold earrings up her ears. "This is Gertrild. She's in charge around here, and don't let anyone tell you any different."

"Blast it, young huntsman! My mother is the proper matriarch." She punched Max in the hip before giving a quick curtsy to the eldest female dwarf. "Ingrihild Oremind is the reason our mining is the most successful in the entire range."

Ingrihild stood tall as she popped something into her mouth. Dried fruit? Snow's mouth watered. The matriarch and the dwarf who'd answered the door both had wrinkles and grey streaks in their hair and the same high arches in their noses.

"You already spoke with Uncle Karldorin at the door. He is Ingrihild's younger brother. He's a bit of a grouch. Don't mind him." Gertrild gestured to three others. "This is my husband, Wielbran, and our niece and nephew, Hildaruna and Fritzgrim."

The female dwarf, Hildaruna, looked to be about Snow's age. The dwarf held out her hand for Snow, and they clasped forearms. Hildaruna shifted her grip a bit, tilting Snow's hand upward. She glanced at Snow's fingers and raised a brow. Snow could've sworn the dwarf noticed the ring, but that was impossible.

"Only my mother calls me Hildaruna," she said. "Call me Runa, and call my brother Grim."

Karldorin rolled his eyes as Grim gave an exaggerated bow. "At your service, Snow. And how did a respectable lady like yourself get entangled with our friend, Maxie. I mean, we think he's better than apricot pancakes, but you're obviously too good for him."

"Fritzgrim Ironfist," Gertrild sternly warned before softening her tone. "My niece and nephew are here to learn the proper way to mine."

Runa laughed, "I'm here for the naps."

"And the snacks," Grim grinned.

"Don't forget the fluffy blankets," Runa added.

"And the snacks," Grim said.

"And the teatime breaks," Runa said.

"And the sn—"

"We can add more chores if you prefer," Karldorin cut Grim off.

Grim shrugged innocently. "What? The snacks are really good!"

The youngest dwarf wormed her way to Snow's side and tugged on her dress. "I'm Lielinda. I'm ten years old. Sapphires are my favorite gem. What's yours?"

"Oh, um . . ." Snow fumbled, not sure she had a favorite gem.

"You only love sapphires because our mountain doesn't have any," Karldorin said. "Emeralds are better. Stronger."

Lielinda pouted, and Grim took her hand. "Who likes emeralds? Boring! They're so common that I just throw the little ones into the refuse. Who wouldn't?"

"Agreed," Runa said, moving to stand on the other side of Snow, mumbling just loud enough for her to hear. "Definitely not good enough for royalty."

Snow sucked in a breath. Did her father say that no one could see the ring—or no *human*? How did they feel about the human royals? She knew dwarves paid tribute to the throne, but she had no idea what complicated relationships or tensions existed. Snow found herself edging closer to Max. She reached for his hand but realized she was overreacting and stopped herself. She brushed the back of his fingers and hoped he didn't notice her nervousness.

Then, surprisingly, he grasped her hand in his. The warmth radiated up her arm, calming her yet sending her heart pounding. The reaction caught her off guard, and she reinforced her inner walls, but they were already firmly in place. The emotion came from within *her*. Part of Snow wanted to pull away, unsure of herself, but another part wanted him to stand closer.

Taking a breath, Snow reminded herself that her ring was invisible, and her paranoia was understandable but unwarranted. All the same, she didn't pull away from Max as the dwarves led them through the massive double doors. Inside, Snow stopped short. Instead of dim lanterns and rough walls, they walked onto one of many sturdy, crisscrossing walkways and bridges. The warm stone cave soared overhead, light coming from the radiant veins flowing through the wall. Sconces burned at the many entrances, leaving no corner in darkness. Besides the illuminated veins, Snow caught glimpses of reflective chunks of stone far overhead—unclaimed gems?

The dwarves led her across a bridge to a cozy room where the walls were buffed smooth. Glowing stones cast the overstuffed, low-slung couches and tables, decorative vases, and cut flowers in soft light. Along the opposite wall, three trees grew with unfamiliar yellow fruit. To the left, the walls pinched slightly inward, creating another space just beyond with a long table, cupboards, and a sink.

Max ran his thumb across the back of Snow's hand, and she realized she was crushing his fingers in her grip.

"Sorry," she relaxed her hand. "This isn't . . ."

"What you expected. I know." Max gave her a tight smile.

"I'll be fine. This is good," she tried to convince herself as much as Max. Yes, the dwarves were friendly and welcoming, but they hadn't agreed to let her stay. Snow hadn't even asked.

For days, she'd been focused on their destination. But now that they'd arrived, their plan meant she'd be cut off from Max, no matter what the dwarves decided. The day she met Max was seared into her memory—she had been exhausted, and everything was foreign; her childhood mind couldn't stop flashes of the creature from popping up every time she'd closed her eyes. But Max had brought her breakfast on her bed. His bed, she'd found out later, as the Hunts hadn't planned on

Snow staying with them. She had lain there, unable to sleep, but after he coaxed her into eating a few spoonfuls of cooked oats, he sat next to the bed and held her hand as she'd finally drifted off. He'd been her island of safety, and they'd hardly been apart ever since.

She'd taken those days for granted, but now they were at an abrupt end. He'd leave her. If he were caught helping her, he'd pay the price in blood.

Max grasped her hand in both of his, and she realized her vice-like grip had only grown stronger. She took a deep breath and forced one finger at a time to release him, letting go. Snow wrapped her arms around herself, bracing for the inevitable. Her emotions swam, but she swallowed and tried to focus.

"Maxie, are you going to stand there all day?" Grim said before guiding Snow to a comfortable chair.

In a snap, Gertrild situated a tray on the table in front of Snow with a steaming cup of tea and a scone.

The matriarch, Ingrihild, perched on the edge of the chair next to Snow, leaning forward, her brows drawn together. She didn't look cruel, but she didn't look friendly, either. "Tell me, my dear, why is a daughter of the royal Albrecht line gracing our humble mountain?"

Stunned, Snow recoiled. Had Heinrich revealed her existence to the dwarves?

"How did you know?" Max's brow scrunched.

"The ring," Ingrihild said, looking at her daughter. "You recognize it?"

"Of course," Gertrild said, sitting on the couch opposite Snow. "It's dwarven made. Probably by the Goldfine clan. May I see it?"

Max tilted his head, and Snow averted her gaze, dread crawling up her throat. She had sensed Max's confusion at her parentage in the Wildwood. The betrayal, loss, and mourning crashed over her, and she had pulled up her inner protection. Not for herself but to give him privacy. She was willing to brave any emotional storm with him, but he would hate her capabilities.

Years ago, when Rosalind had taken her to visit the witch, Snow sensed the two women's animosity toward each other. However, both had agreed on the necessity of the barrier and the purpose: to protect Snow from overwhelming, unwelcome feelings. But Snow had also heard them whisper of how Snow's power would ruin her relationships. No one could ever truly love her when she wielded an unfair advantage—an unseen, dreadful weapon.

"My father gave me the ring and said it would be invisible." Snow lifted her hand to show the dwarf but didn't remove the banded signet. "He demanded I keep my paternity a secret." Her excuse sounded small and pathetic.

Ingrihild pursed her lips, giving Snow a hard look. "Until when?"

"Until I am nineteen, in two springs." Snow didn't dare look directly at Max, but he hadn't moved, his feet planted in place, his body rigid.

Please don't ask more about the ring.

The elder dwarves all looked at each other as if in silent, knowing conversation.

"I can *see* you all thinking. Just say it." Runa put a hand on her hip, shifting her weight. "No reason to skirt the obvious."

Snow squeezed her eyes shut as if she could stop the coming fallout. The king had thrust her onto this destined path. No, her father was dead, and Snow had never questioned deviating from his instructions.

Max was the most loyal friend the Abundants could have put into her life. Snow should have told him the whole truth in the Wildwood—that she was the heir. There had been opportunity. She'd lied to Max by *not* telling him everything.

Snow dimly heard Ingrihild speaking. "We'll hide her. For now," the matriarch said. "Out of respect for the peace between her family and ours that has persisted for generations. But the ring won't be visible for over a year—and trouble will come looking. We won't sacrifice ourselves for an outcast even if she is the king's chosen heir."

An awkward silence fell as Snow slowly opened her eyes and looked up at Max. His face had grown pale, his hands curled tight at his sides.

"Looks like maybe it *wasn't* obvious to everyone?" Runa sucked in a breath through her teeth, cringing. "Sorry."

"That's why they say, 'Never assume,'" Grim said. "It makes an—"

"Fritzgrim!" Gertrild cut him off before turning to Max. "We'll leave you two while we prepare rooms for the night. How long will you be staying?"

"I must return immediately," Max said.

Snow gripped the sides of the chair, the room spinning.

"Of course. I'll have the younglings prepare food for your journey," Gertrild said.

She ushered the others out of the room, Grim and Runa shoving and teasing each other as they went. Soon, Snow and Max were alone, and Snow wasn't sure she could find a way to explain her lies in the little time they'd be afforded. Snow pushed to her feet but found herself stumbling forward to the chair next to Max.

"I understand if you're upset," Snow began, unable to look at her best friend.

"The king wanted to protect you," Max said, rooted in place. "What else is there to explain?"

His words cracked the stoic resolve she'd clung to for moons, revealing the harsh reality. She was the chosen future queen. Her father's closest friend was the royal huntsman. She'd told herself that the huntsman standing before her would be her steady, trusted best friend forever. But would he?

Snow reached for his sleeve, but his shoulders tightened, so Snow held back, not touching him. He didn't smile. He didn't reach for her hand. And in that breath, their relationship fissured. Like an uncut gem shifting in the light, the movement revealed a truth buried deep in the mineral. A flaw, a dark speck within the valuable treasure.

From the day they'd met, Snow had kept secrets. She couldn't hide from that truth. So, she hadn't stayed silent because of the king's demand. Snow hadn't wanted Max to know.

She'd feared losing Max, his familiar comfort she wrapped herself up in every day. But they weren't children anymore. Max had grown up, and whatever her intentions, she'd pushed him away, and he might never come back.

"Travel safely, Max," Snow said then chastised herself for standing awkwardly and for sounding so hollow. But she didn't have time to fret before the dwarves stepped forward for their goodbyes at the cave entrance.

Young Lielinda tugged on Max's trousers. "Next time, you have to stay longer. I miss your stories."

Max got on a knee and gave her a hug. "I miss you, too."

As each dwarf returned to the inner cave, Snow's anxiety grew. Her time with Max was ending, and she couldn't leave their broken words hanging between them. She could smooth things over. She had to. Between the queen and the Wildwood, nothing was guaranteed. What if she never saw him again?

Finally, just Grim and Runa remained. Snow bit her lip, practicing what she might say. *I don't know how long I can survive without you.*

Too much? She remembered the warmth of his hand, which felt like a lifetime ago. Runa offered Max a bag of food. He put the gift into his bag, and the muscles of his forearms shifted with the movement, drawing Snow's attention.

"I'll escort you until sunset," Grim said. "I already have permission. Ingrihild just advised that I don't get us killed with my chatter. But she is hoping for more news from Clarus. I'll fill you in on local gossip—"

"When will we see you again?" Snow blurted.

Grim raised a brow at the ensuing stilted pause.

"After the spring hunts," Max finally said.

His curt tone combined with the coming weeks stretching out before her felt as if the cave was crashing around her. Max wasn't abandoning her, but he wouldn't be back for a full season. She counted in her head, taking a slow breath. *I can do this.*

Max closed the distance between them, and she could breathe again.

"I'll check on you as often as possible." He didn't touch her, but he looked at her, holding her eye contact. It was the only time he'd met her eyes since he'd learned she was the heir. "While I'm gone, I'll gather what information I can. I'll be alert to trouble just in case I need to fetch you sooner. This spring, we will make a plan for your return."

"Princess Elisabeth and High Judge Helene know of the ring," Snow said. "I don't know if they'll dare resist Queen Agnes, but they may help."

Snow longed for him to wrap his arms around her in one of his usual hugs. She wished she could shrink like a fairy and travel in his bag. Not long ago, she would've buried her face in his neck without a thought.

Their easy familiarity was gone, swallowed by a beast of her own making. But Max would return. He promised. Snow held that hope, a quiet flicker in the recesses of her soul.

CHAPTER 10: MAX

YEAR 9 OF THE MAIDEN COMET, SPRING

After the falconry hunt, Max led the successful hunting party to his favorite resting spot. Wild daffodils grew in sunny patches of light, and the breeze cooled the weary group after the long ride. The lovely spring weather had enabled the party to travel deep into the forest, merely a two-hour ride from the Wildwood border. Everything about this place reminded him of Snow.

Though he hadn't seen her in two moon cycles, he thought of her every day. He was working to move past his hurt, processing his misperception of their relationship. He was torn between needing more time apart and, at the same time, scheming ways to return without the queen's notice. He reminded himself that, of course, he'd want to help Snow. And not just because the kingdom needed her but because he would be a loyal friend. His feelings for her had nothing to do with it.

While Max's thoughts wandered, servants tended to the horses and falcons as nobles joked and complimented each other's training. The relaxed atmosphere was a stark contrast when compared to the hunt two weeks earlier; the queen had joined, and everyone walked on eggshells the entire time.

According to rumor, the queen's mood calmed after Snow "left." Agnes hadn't approached the Hunts since, thank the Abundants, even during the hunt.

Heinrich had told the servants that Snow mourned the king's death and had decided to take a position with a household in the south. No one seemed to question the explanation except for Dottie. The cook expected a personal letter, which she would never receive.

At least, Heinrich's excuses for Max had worked. The Hunts had secured the queen's trust when Max delivered the ghost crocus bulbs to the royal healer, who created a precious tincture from the plant.

Max turned his attention to the group as he noticed Princess Elisabeth breaking away from several nobles and approaching him. "Well done, apprentice. Your father would be proud. I hope he's feeling better soon."

"I appreciate the compliment, and I'll pass on your good wishes to Heinrich." Max bowed, hiding his discomfort. His father had left the cottage in the middle of the night, mere hours after Max had returned from taking Snow to the dwarves. If he'd known his father was leaving so quickly, Max would've told him that Snow was the chosen heir. Max would've said a lot of things.

Heinrich had never been gone this long before. And when his father returned, which could be any day, Max would rectify everything.

The princess lowered her voice and put a hand on his shoulder. "I miss Snow, too."

Max sighed, not hiding his sadness from the princess. Just hearing Snow's name aloud brought a wave of emotion: a mixture of loneliness, wistfulness, and a little embarrassment at the latter. She patted his shoulder, lingering in case he wanted to share his feelings. Heinrich had left a secret message for the king's fae asking for help, but even *if* Reinhold wanted to reveal himself, the huntsman had disappeared. If Max couldn't talk to the fae, he would need help from inside the court to return Snow to the throne. Would Elisabeth have the political strength to make the change?

Elisabeth flashed a sad smile before adjusting her sleeves and turning to greet the other nobles.

"Gather the hares destined for the queen's kitchens," Max directed the two kitchen staff servants who'd accompanied him. "The cook will want the game cleaned and dressed before they come through her door."

"I'll bring the baskets to the river," Johann offered.

"No, you ain't. Not after last time," Ottilia countered. "You took off for hours and left me all the work. You'll clean, and I'll fetch the baskets." She tossed him a sack with their tools.

While the nobles ate their lunches, Max and the servants cleaned the hares. Several other servants from nearby estates also cleaned, preparing to take the spoils home to the accompanying nobles' households and their local Blessed Houses. As he worked, Max eyed the princess. He'd never noticed before, but the older nobles curtailed conversations with her and appeared less animated. Perhaps what his father had said about her was true—Elisabeth's childhood mistakes still followed her, and they couldn't rely on the princess for substantial help against the queen.

But if the queen was a witch, it meant she had harnessed fae magic. So, how much should he trust Reinhold? Could the king's fae have gone against fae law to collude with Agnes? Was there anyone from whom he could seek aid?

An hour later, most of the nobles had wandered off to negotiate private deals, and the servants began sharing their own gossip.

"Is it true that most of your noblewomen got themselves large mirrors?" a visiting lord's servant asked.

"Take a good gander at every lady here. They *all* got one," Ottilia responded with a snort. "Plus, half the lords. And the mirrors ain't large. They're *massive.*"

"Queen Agnes made them popular," Johann said. "I remember when she first arrived. Mama was still taller than me then."

Ottilia grinned. "I remember how sweet and cute you were as a child. What happened?"

Johann stuck his tongue out at her, and the visiting servant balked but didn't ask questions.

"Actually, mirrors have been fashionable for ages," Ottilia added as if she were a court historian. "The old ones had words carved around the edges—self-motivation gibberish."

"Really? You're tellin' me there be rubbish like, 'You are beautiful and smart and can do anything you put your mind to'?" Johann joked, "Pish. We all know the stacks of gold they're born with don't hurt."

The visitor shook his head, likely getting more gossip than he'd bargained for. Before Max could interject and change the subject, the high judge approached them. Helene never joined hunts, and Max had been surprised by her request to join this time. According to Snow, the judge knew of the king's intent to make Snow the heir, but it was too soon to reveal that she still lived. And when the time arose to include Helene, the information would be carefully relayed—not in the open forest.

"May I have a moment?" she asked Max. "I'd like to compliment you on the hunt, and I have questions. I am afraid I'm in need of some tips for next time." Helene probably meant it as a lighthearted joke about her poor skill, but the servants all quieted and suddenly focused intently on their work.

"Of course." Max quickly wiped his hands and led her several paces away, out of earshot. "What can I help you with?"

"I was hoping your father could, um, help me with my training." She shifted uncomfortably but kept her head held high. "He's been absent too long. I do hope when he returns that he stays healthy and present for a few seasons."

Max paused, watching the forest in his periphery. "Did he promise to help you with any specific type of hunting?"

The judge pressed her lips together and began walking. Max joined her, but soon realized she was headed for her horse and attending servant. Perhaps that was all she wanted to say.

"I'm glad you joined us today," Max said, in case anyone was watching. "We'll have one more spring hunt in two weeks."

And then I'm off to check on Snow.

"Heinrich must stay close to home," she hurriedly whispered. "Give him my warning."

Helene cut off their conversation as she mounted and rode away without another word. Max stood staring after the judge, wondering what more the woman knew but didn't dare say.

Before the sun set, Max huffed up the mountain to the castle, a crumpled note in his hand. Focused on the kitchen side door, he didn't notice the royal visitor in the courtyard until it was too late to change direction. The queen stood on a step stool inspecting the buds on the limbs with one hand while a servant held the other, balancing her. Seeing Agnes, Max gave a low bow, hoping she'd dismiss him quickly.

Instead, she left him bowing for a lengthy period. Her footsteps crunched on the rocks as she strolled closer to him with an uneven gait. He held his breath, the rumors of her instability swirling in his mind.

"You may rise," she finally said.

As Max straightened, he tucked his hands behind him along with the note. This close, he noticed how much the queen had changed. Her cheekbones had grown more pronounced, and dark circles bagged under her eyes. Servants had said she was often heard mumbling to herself even in her sleep. Some said her homesickness was driving her to insanity without the king's constant care.

Max had brushed off the gossip as the queen had always sufficiently entertained herself when the king was away before. But then again, Max was on edge being away from Snow, and he knew he'd see her again. Soon.

"Have you eaten one of my apples? One is missing." The queen's words were harsh, but her eyes seemed distant.

"I would never eat from the queen's tree without permission," Max said, unnerved by the accusation.

"That's good. I would hate to see you hanged." She nodded as if sincerely relieved.

Max swallowed as his instincts blared for him to exit the conversation as quickly as possible.

"I never wanted to be queen, but I love Friedrich." She looked beyond his shoulder and pressed her hand against her belly. "I thought I was pregnant once. Then I got sick. If I was with child, I wasn't after that."

Her servant shrunk in on herself, unsure of what to do. Royals rarely shared their personal lives with anyone, let alone Max. In his periphery, he caught movement on the balcony overlooking the courtyard, but he didn't take his focus off the queen. Agnes straightened, her face hardening. Defying the morning light, the queen's eyes dilated, the black swallowing her hazel irises.

"You're dismissed," she said, waving him off before turning to her handmaid. "I'm tired. Take me to my rooms."

Max struggled to remain composed as he continued across the courtyard. Whoever—or whatever—had been on the balcony was gone, and the note from the cook was now a sweaty piece of parchment. Inside the castle, Dottie grabbed his arm and took him aside, asking for the note. It merely said, *'Kitchens. Now.'* Even so, she threw it into the fire.

"Yer father, bless his soul, brought me boar organs two moon cycles back. Cooked it up for the queen, she was all pleased-like. Ain't thrown a tantrum since," Dottie said, grabbing his shoulders tight. "But this morn, there be chaos in the castle. Queen was fuming and got everyone rattled, even the princess. Then, not four hours later, I heard the queen caught yer father on the road, not the King's Road, mind you. Some small trail southwest of Caston. Impossible to know where he was, but she did. And I hate to tell you this, but. . ." The cook dabbed her forehead with a cloth.

"Just be out with it," Max hissed.

"Word around the castle is, the royal huntsman's been tossed into the dungeon."

Max reeled. Dottie had made the connection of calm to the boar, but she didn't understand the reason. Max did. Had the queen figured out that the meal wasn't what she'd hoped? Wasn't Snow's heart and liver? Max's stomach roiled at the queen's depravity.

Beyond his disgust, the warning from the high judge blared in his mind. For all the judge knew, Snow was dead. So her warning was out of respect for Heinrich. Helene probably discovered that the huntsman was protecting the other children and had hoped to warn him that he'd skirted too close to danger.

More importantly, Max had to assume that the queen suspected Snow still lived. This revelation made his conversation with the queen even more strange. Why didn't she arrest him instead of asking about apples?

Because she either didn't believe Max was involved or the queen hoped he'd lead her straight to Snow. Max let out an uneven breath, sickened by this critical revelation. To save Snow, he had to stay away from her.

"I need to see my father," Max said.

"That's a bad idea." Dottie shook her head.

"I should go, but thank you for the information." Max spun and marched to the back rooms before servants noticed their intense conversation. No reason to draw Dottie into this mess. He pretended to count the remaining stores of meat. But in reality, he was scheming on how he'd ask for a favor from the one person who *could* get him a visit to the dungeon: High Judge Helene.

CHAPTER II: SNOW

YEAR 9 OF THE MAIDEN COMET, SPRING

The wagon trundled through the mountain pass away from the trading post, the back laden with fresh supplies. Snow sat between Grim, who was holding the reins, and Runa as the dwarves argued. After a season of mining, Snow's hands had blistered and popped many times over. And without the innate link to the earth nor the strength of the dwarves, Snow was sore and exhausted.

Ingrihild, the matriarch, had allowed Snow to tag along on the supply run. But as much as Snow relished her first trip in the fresh air, paranoia had set in. She felt like everyone was watching her. Snow told herself the villagers appeared too busy to pay her much mind, other than perhaps a few children who were as curious about her as they were with any travelers.

"Vermillion is a bright red," Runa said again.

"Verdant. *Green*. Verdure. *Green*." Grim spit out a sunflower shell. "Verdancy. *Green*."

"You're verbose," Runa rolled her eyes. "Which has nothing to do with green."

"Well, vermillion rhymes with chameleon. They're green."

"Chameleons change colors. Besides, 'rhymes-with' doesn't indicate the meaning or definition."

"What do you think, Snow?" Grim asked. "Don't you think 'vermillion' sounds 'green'?"

Snow grimaced, knowing the word was probably one her tutors had insisted she know and use. But she was realizing more and more that her education, while better than most of the lower classes, was lacking. The dwarves had extensive education and were especially good at accounting ledgers and witty insults. Not necessarily in that order.

"Don't make her pick sides," Runa said, reaching around Snow and flicking her brother's ear.

"If she can't rule on colors, how will she rule a kingdom?" Grim joked.

"In this case, I'd defer to my high judge. Helene knows the law. Certainly, there's a subsection about 'vermillion,'" Snow teased sarcastically, but inside, she squirmed.

She was supposed to be training to rule at this very moment, not running errands and practicing mining techniques. Snow had learned about supply and demand, thanks to the dwarves; their families agreed to control the gems and metals allowed into the market each year. But that drop of economics knowledge was minuscule compared to the sea of needed royal education.

As her doubts began to creep in, she remembered what she'd seen in the trading village. The dwarves had expected the same small post they'd always visited, remote and tucked into the higher reaches of the mountain range. But the village had grown significantly, pushing up against the rocky face of the encompassing mountains. Many farmers, crafts folk, and even city guards had fled Caston, wanting distance from Clarus. The citizens were tired of ever-increasing portions of the taxes in the form of bronze, crops, or physical labor to the queen, not to mention the ensuing disappearances if they refused.

Seeing the changes wrought by the queen's rule only strengthened Snow's intent to visit her childhood home, which was only another day's travel east; she knew in her bones that a Shadow Beast hadn't wandered into her village by accident. If she could figure out how the queen manipulated a magical beast, perhaps that information would help Snow dethrone her.

The Attuned from the Blessed Houses dedicated their lives to the worship of the goddesses, and they spent their days in study and service to the community. In Isolzing, the local Attuned would remember the beast's attack; perhaps they'd even recorded it. A detail or a rumor from that night could help her learn a weakness or an insight into the queen's abilities.

Once the trio turned onto the unmarked path at the base of the mountain, brushing up against the Wildwood, they were alone, well away from other travelers. For the first time ever, Snow calmed entering the wood knowing the forest blocked fae magic.

"Did you feel like you were being watched today?" Snow whispered, not wanting to garner attention from within the wood.

"The queen can't search for any one person at all times," Grim reminded her of what Ingrihild had already pointed out. "Queens are busy, and magic has limits. Even fae magic."

"Especially fae magic," Runa grumbled.

Grim paused, considering his words before continuing. "Aunt Gerty warned this might happen."

"What?" Snow asked.

Runa patted Snow's shoulder, truly sympathetic. "It's natural that you'd feel anxious. It's the first time you've left the safety of the cave in several moons. And someone with magical resources is hunting you."

Snow sat for a moment, recalling Ingrihild's reassurance—that even if the queen were actively looking, quickly pinpointing a location took masterful skill, which humans couldn't fully develop within their short lives.

"You're right," Snow said. "Logically, the queen had little chance of finding me in two days. But what if I want to travel farther?"

"Let's just take it one trip at a time," Runa said.

"Your aunt talked about visiting Isolzing in the fall," Snow pressed. "I lived there as a child. I'd like to see my home again."

"It won't look much the same," Grim said quietly. "It's a sprawling city now."

"According to the gossip in the messenger station," Runa began, "for those abandoning the lands surrounding Clarus, Isolzing is a favorite destination."

"Which could garner the queen's special attention—so it's safer to stay away from Isolzing. For now," Grim said, giving Snow a sympathetic look.

"In a tragic way, it will work in your favor that the people hate the queen," Runa said, her nose scrunching. "They're much more likely to accept you as their ruler."

"They'd probably take *anyone* at this point," Grim said. "How do you think I'd look in a crown?"

"Ridiculous." Runa rolled her eyes, but then she hunched closer, a conspiratorial grin forming. "But it gives me an idea. What about a disguise—for Snow?"

Grim raised a brow at his sister but didn't say anything. None of them did. They fell into focused quiet, listening to the sounds of the darkening wood.

Snow didn't know how the queen searched for the unfamiliar faces of the late king's children, what spells she used, or who taught her. Snow needed to understand more, and she knew answers lay just out of reach. She could travel to Isolzing at any time, but it would be a fool's errand. She could imagine trying to talk Karldorin into letting her back into the cave.

Hi, remember me? The human who everyone bent over backward to help? I flitted off over the mountain and gave the queen plenty of opportunity to find me. And now I'm leading her straight back to your home because I'm selfish and short-sighted. Do you think I'll be a great strategist? Snow inwardly groaned.

At the cave, Snow helped Runa and Grim carry supplies. Grim sought out the family, and Runa sorted through the small bag of missives she'd picked up from the local messenger service. Snow put tulips into a vase and chopped the fresh mushrooms and wild greens for dinner. She had gotten used to the clang of pickaxes, but the oddly comforting pings had stopped a week ago. Apparently, the clan only mined while snow blocked the passes. The rest of the year was focused on trading, food storage, and a lot of relaxing and traveling. And snacking.

Grim returned, hurrying into the living area. "Aunt Gerty asked for a hot pack for her face."

"Another episode? Poor auntie." Runa put down her missives and rushed to help.

"What's wrong?" Snow asked.

"Aunt Gerty suffers from painful shocks in her jaw and cheek," Runa explained while she poured hot water into a leather pouch. "Healers say it's a lifelong ailment, unfortunately. Auntie is a bit young for the onset, but she says, 'The Abundant Ones give her what she needs.'"

"Uncle said the attack came on last night, mid-sentence," Grim said, grabbing lavender and peppermint oils from the cupboards. "I'll make massage oil for her to use later."

"What can I do to help?" Snow asked.

"You're doing plenty already," Runa said. "But I think they'll cancel their excursion to visit my parents. Gerty's pain can be triggered by the smallest things, even just smiling."

"Poor Gertrild," Snow said.

"Our aunt and uncle enjoy serving and socializing within our community, but Gerty's jaw pain has kept them home," Grim explained. "Though, they're experimenting with different regimens to keep the attacks at bay."

Snow wondered if they'd asked a fae for help, but she knew well enough to keep thoughts of *their* powers to herself. Dwarves in the mountain range had learned to harness magic from the Wildwood and pull it like a blanket over vast portions of the mountains, shielding them *from* fae magic. What that meant, exactly, Snow didn't know.

Runa handed Grim the hot compress, and he hurried off to Gertrild's room, leaving the vials of oils on the table. While he was gone, Runa delivered the mail and packages from the trading post to the dwarven recipients in the cave, leaving Snow alone. She wished for a letter, for news, but the table Runa had worked at was now empty, every missive accounted for. Though Runa and Grim had taken her in like a sister, she missed her friends at Clarus. She missed Max.

He had promised to visit her after the spring hunts, which would be soon. Any day. When she let her mind wander, her thoughts generally landed on questions about Max. Was he in the forest? Tracking a rabbit? Was he missing her half as much as she missed him?

Snow shifted the vase of tulips, recalling how the flowers signaled better days for Max's mother; her delicious cakes were often proof of her happy mood. Maybe Max would bring a slice of cake for Snow's birthday? She brushed off the thought along with the crumbs she swept from the floor, only caring that he was still safe.

Runa reappeared, directed Snow to the sofa, and threw her a blanket. The dwarf pulled out a wooden game with too many little pieces to count. "Let's play."

"Sounds good," Snow said, having learned not to argue. She sat forward, wrapped the fluffy blanket around her shoulders, and strategized her placements on the board. She was used to working long days, every day. But the dwarves were different. Ingrihild preached her three tenants: being, doing, and relating.

Mining was "doing." According to Ingrihild, life was bigger than work. Exercising the mind was good, too. The dwarves read everything from philosophy to adventure novels. But they also slept or just sat with their thoughts—the "being." And, as Grim said, they ate the *best* food. Maybe that was "relating." Snow hadn't quite figured the culture out, yet.

Runa made the opening move, just as Lielinda skipped in.

"Ruthless," Lielinda said to her cousin, before loudly rattling off tips to Snow.

Snow grinned, moving her game piece, thoroughly enjoying the game already.

"What did you think about the trading post?" Snow asked Runa as Lielinda leaned into the game board, her brows furrowed in concentration.

Runa made her next play, but her attention slid to her cousin. "I think the dwarves will help them with their planting. They'll need a good harvest in the fall."

So, she'd noticed that the people looked half-starved. Had she also noticed their thin clothing and worried faces? Snow hadn't learned much from her royal tutor about the commoners, but she had learned plenty from her mother. When people went hungry, they grew angry.

"There's usually an early planting around my birthday," Snow said. "Maybe we could travel to Isolzing to help?"

"Are you sure that's how you want to celebrate?" Runa's gaze dipped to the ring on Snow's hand, though it wouldn't be another year until it appeared.

"I can't think of a better way to spend my day than with farmers who provide food for everyone, including those who moved."

Who fled.

"That's a generous idea, but I don't think we will be able to travel the pass that soon. . ." Runa's voice trailed off, and she jumped to her feet. "Wait right here. I have something for you."

Runa ran off, giggling to herself. While she was gone, little Lielinda moved one of Runa's pieces one square over. Lielinda was more devious than the other dwarves, but Snow didn't sense any real maliciousness. Snow moved the piece back, tsking at the young dwarf just before Runa hurried into the room.

"This is for you," Runa said, handing over a letter to Snow.

Snow immediately recognized the handwriting. Max had sent it.

"It's addressed to you, Hildaruna, not to me," Snow said. Because the seal was broken, the missive unfolded of its own accord and a smaller, sealed letter inside fell onto Snow's lap. The back of it read, 'On your birthday' with a hand-drawn sketch of a delicate anemone flower on the back.

"This makes *so* much more sense now," Runa said. "Besides the fact I have an autumn birthday, Max has never sent me a letter before.

Heinrich has sent several letters addressed to our whole family, which Grandmother reads over dinner. But never Max."

"My birthday," Snow said quietly, mostly to herself.

"So, I guess you won't have to wait long to open it," Runa said with a wink before returning her attention to their game.

Snow's hands shook. Max wasn't returning for her birthday. Runa didn't know it, but Max would only risk sending a letter if he couldn't come in person. Snow pressed the missive to her chest, the little flame of hope inside her blown out, leaving behind a thin spire of smoke made of disappointment and more than a bit of worry. Snow tucked the note into her belt while she glanced at the pieces, which jumbled in her mind.

Lielinda held a hand over her grinning lips, and Snow sensed her glee. Snow paused and scrutinized the board, spotting the piece that Lielinda had moved while Snow and Runa had been distracted. With one piece shifted, the entire strategy of the game tumbled in a different direction. The opposing player would lose everything if they didn't notice the smallest change behind their back.

CHAPTER 12: MAX

YEAR 9 OF THE MAIDEN COMET, SPRING

High Judge Helene had coldly refused to help Max see his father. When Max asked a second time, she threatened to send him to the dungeon where they'd have plenty of time to talk. Frustrated, Max held his tongue, knowing his mother and Snow needed him. So, he was surprised when the judge pounded on his door only two weeks later.

"I'm glad I caught you," Helene huffed, out of breath. "Do you still want to see your father?"

Max quickly invited her inside, grateful that his mother was out of earshot in their small garden, prepping the soil. The high judge moved to stand in front of the stone fireplace, which staved off the spring morning chill.

"Would you like some porridge and jam?" Max offered her breakfast

"We don't have time for pleasantries," she said, waving off his offer. "I didn't dare be seen with you, not after Heinrich was thrown into the dungeon," she launched into an explanation of why she'd denied Max's request. "Queen Agnes has spies everywhere, and she is scrutinizing all of the huntsman's closest allies in the court, including me." Helene began pacing in front of the fire. "I switched my riding to today, and I hope the change doesn't raise any suspicions. Everyone is paranoid these days, but we need to talk. The queen is in one of her fits."

"She's been having more *trouble* of late, from what I hear," Max said.

"She's throwing whatever she can lift and yelling at anyone who dares enter the royal wing. But I realized this brings us an opportunity," Helene continued. "After the queen's volatile episodes, she sleeps long and hard. She'll probably crash sometime tonight or in the early hours. She'll sleep all day tomorrow. It's risky, but if you slip out of the kitchens after your morning delivery, I'll make arrangements for you to sneak into the dungeons." Helene went on to give detailed instructions, telling him she'd watch for his arrival. "If the cook is arranging breakfast for the queen, the plan is off."

Max debated telling Helene that Snow was alive. But, for all he knew, Helene was a spy herself. He had to assume the queen knew Snow still breathed, which is why his father was in the dungeon. But what if the queen didn't know for certain? What if she had sent Helene here under some sort of witch's spell? Would he be able to recognize a bespelled human?

"You should know," Helene said, dropping her voice, "Princess Elisabeth promised to petition for Heinrich's release to be set for one year from his arrest, which is very generous as the punishment for treason is death. To be honest, I expected the queen to demand he hang within the week, which was common in generations past."

"Treason?" Max gasped, hearing the accusation for the first time.

The judge nodded, continuing, "Elisabeth must have made good on her word because, the next day, she and the queen requested my presence. The queen seemed agitated, and Elisabeth was calm. At first. Until Queen Agnes sentenced Heinrich to a year in prison . . . and then he's to hang."

Max's mind spun, and Helene's words of sympathy swirled into a buzz of nonsense. He shook his head and forced himself to listen.

"Elisabeth became livid. She literally shook, her hands fisted like she used to do as a child," the judge said. "Obviously, the queen must've changed her mind about whatever they'd privately agreed to. The queen could barely string the sentences together, almost like her tongue was tied. But she did and then spat a command for us to leave. Then she signaled to her guards. As if *I'm* a threat." Helene's brow scrunched at the memory of the insult. Then her attention caught on the huntsman's heavy winter boots resting by the door. Boots Heinrich would never need again. She cleared her throat and smoothed her riding cloak, sobering. "I'm sorry about all this, Max. I'm willing to take a risk for you to see your father, for both your sakes. Heinrich was a loyal friend to the king. This shouldn't be his end, but there's nothing we can do."

The back door squeaked open, and his mother hummed in the kitchen. Helene scurried out the front door without a word, leaving Max feeling as if he was sinking, his world turning to dirt and ash. He gripped his family amulet in his hand, the metal cutting into his palm. It protected the wearer against injuries from iron but was impotent against a rope.

Before Max could think, he had ripped the pin from his jacket. He threw the amulet on the floor, the clasp snapping. With a swift kick, the heirloom skittered across the wood planks and under the couch. Made of gold and spun with magic, it was worthless if it couldn't save someone he loved.

Max caught his prey early, but he waited to ride up the mountain until his customary time. He kept his usual subdued greetings, though his heart raced at the prospect of sneaking into the dungeons and speaking with his father. On his way to the back rooms, his three pheasants in hand, he glanced at the two trays being set up for the royals. One for the princess and one for the queen.

His heart sank, and he dragged his feet on the way to clean his catch. Behind him, a servant spoke in low tones to Dottie.

"So, just one tray, then?" Dottie confirmed with the servant.

Max glanced behind him in time to see the servant nod in agreement.

"I'll be preppin' a pot of soup to send once she's on the mend," Dottie said, putting a tray away.

Heartened, Max hurried to the back rooms and started working. After a half hour, Max scrubbed his hands and arms. He generally wasn't disturbed, but if anyone noticed him missing, they'd assume he went to use the privy. However, they'd get suspicious if he was gone for long. Moving to leave through a side door, Max found a guard's uniform hanging on the hook. The scrawled note pinned to the chest said, "Hunt."

Thank you, Helene, Max thought.

He ripped off the tiny paper and shoved it into his mouth, swallowing it as he dressed. He'd almost felt naked, walking the corridors without the amulet pin he'd worn since becoming his father's apprentice. Leaving it behind was foolish, but the relic his mother's family had prized for so long couldn't help his father. Where were those family members now? Not petitioning to save his father, that was for sure.

As he walked the halls, he realized the cleverness of the disguise. Most of the servants dropped their gaze when they noticed the uniform marching down the hall. And Max could move quickly as if on an important task. At the entrance to the dungeon, the guard wasn't stationed, which only happened on rare occasions when they were needed elsewhere. Max sent another silent 'thanks' to the judge for whatever she'd done to draw the guard away.

Hurrying inside and down the steps, another guard approached in the darkness broken only by slits of light high in the wall. Max stood straighter as he approached. The guard barely acknowledged Max as he strode past on a task of his own.

Taking a breath, Max marched by the first set of cells and stopped at the second section, third door, recalling the judge's instructions. But the man in the cell didn't look like anyone Max knew.

Checking over his shoulder, verifying he was alone, he crouched down next to the bars. "Heinrich Hunt?"

The prisoner looked up, tilting his head in the near darkness. His voice croaked as he spoke, "Son?"

Max nearly broke hearing his father's voice. He leaned his face against the bars, whispering. "I had to see you."

His father scooted closer, his hiss barely audible. "You shouldn't have come. It's too dangerous. Leave. Leave before you're caught."

"I'll be quick. I promise I've been careful." Only as he spoke the words did he realize that it may have been the princess who skipped breakfast, not the queen. Sometimes, Princess Elisabeth wanted complete solitude. Was the queen actually awake and aware? Max swallowed, realizing he should've verified before running off. His father was right; Max did need to go. But he was here, and he wouldn't squander these few precious moments. "Obviously, the accusation is a lie. I'll always be proud to be your son."

Heinrich's shoulders slumped. "Technically, I did act against the queen. I didn't bring back Snow's heart and liver, and I moved two children while the king was sick and one more afterward. Somehow, Agnes figured out what I was doing."

"Did anyone question you about Snow?"

"No. Not yet." Heinrich suddenly reached through the bars, grabbing Max's jacket. "You may need to move them. I trust no one else, and the queen doesn't suspect your involvement. Go to the Attuned in Caston. I was careful, but the queen is resourceful. Hopefully, Agnes won't discover their locations for a few years, but you must take my place as protector. Their lives are in your hands."

Max opened his mouth to explain he feared he was being watched as well, especially considering that Snow was the chosen heir. But a prisoner sneezed, interrupting them. This place wasn't secure, and he'd already lingered too long. Still, Max reached through the bars one last time, gripping his father's weathered hands in his own. His father felt like bones, his skin gritty with dirt, the flesh loose.

"I love you, son," Heinrich whispered, squeezing his hands one last time before shoving him back, hard. The movement must have cost him precious strength, but it shook Max's senses. Heavy footfalls approached. Max jumped to his feet just as the guard strode into view. Straightening and marching forward, Max acted like he'd been doing his rounds. With every step, another crack fissured through his heart, threatening to break him completely.

CHAPTER 13:
SNOW

YEAR 9 OF THE MAIDEN COMET, SPRING

S now awoke to the pinging of axes in the mines. She sat up and
stretched before moving aside the curtain and allowing veins to
lighten her room. The dwarves had hinted at a birthday surprise today,
but there was only one thing she wanted. Snow picked up the letter
from Max and curled up on her bed. She had no idea if the tulips had
faded, and today was as good a day as any to celebrate. Snow took a
deep breath and then eagerly snapped the wax, hungry for a single
syllable from her friend.

Dear Runa,

It's been too long since we've seen each other. I hope this letter
finds you well. The winter frosts linger, but the crocuses have
come and gone. Though, I did find a special species that I had
hunted for as a special gift to the queen. You would be proud
of my knowledge of flora and fauna, which is much better
than Grim's. Let him know I said so.

Snow bit her lip, reminding herself that he couldn't say anything personal in case the letter was intercepted. She was grateful to know he'd successfully found the ghost crocus, but she wished for a personal sentiment.

My mother sends her well wishes. She longs for warmer days,
and she misses you, especially now with my duties as the royal
huntsman.

Snow sucked in a breath, not finishing the letter. Only his mother was mentioned. And Max was *the* royal huntsman. Something had happened to Heinrich. This letter was a warning. Did the queen suspect Snow was alive? Or worse, did she *know* she was living with the dwarves?

She lowered a shaking hand to her belly, telling herself that if the queen were an imminent threat, Max would've made that clear. He would've come himself. For now, Snow's whereabouts were unknown. It was more probable that Heinrich was waylaid by natural causes. Snow tried to console herself, but worry about the man who'd rescued her mounted. He was hurt. Or worse. She wished she was at the cottage with the Hunts to console them and lighten their load. But would they want her?

Her stomach twisted at knowing she was the likely source of their troubles. Snow didn't know how long she stared into nothingness before she was drawn back to the letter.

> *With all the laborers and their families moving south, Clarus is experiencing a bit of an upheaval. You may see troubled souls in your travels, so consider staying close to home when possible.*
>
> *Sincerely,*
> *-M*
>
> *PS: I hope you have been able to reconnect with your mother and get the answers you have been looking for.*

Max had sent a warning to the dwarves to stay out of sight, but the very last line was hers.

Max knew of her goal. This was the closest she'd ever been to returning home, and he knew what he was asking: Stay away from Isolzing. But safety wouldn't get her the answers she needed. She knew a Shadow Beast had killed her mother, but how had the queen directed the creature to Snow's home? How had the queen brought it to Isolzing at all?

Hints to Agnes's magic might still be recovered, but someone needed to look. Snow fiddled with the ring on her finger. If the queen knew Snow lived, she couldn't wander outside the Wildwood without bringing back danger to the caves. Snow longed to act, to bolt over the mountains. But without a plan to take the throne shortly thereafter, she'd reveal herself and lose the element of surprise, all in one swoop.

While considering her options, Snow hurried to the kitchen for breakfast. The entire dwarven family was waiting with grins on their faces—except Ingrihild, who looked as unruffled as usual. Runa, Grim, and Lielinda gave Snow a gift. Unwrapping it, Snow found a finely woven purse with delicate stitching.

"Thank you." Snow's fingers whispered over the top, not wanting her calluses to snag the satin.

"Grim is known for his design," Runa beamed, "but all three of us worked on it."

"It's fit for a queen," Grim said with an exaggerated bow.

Ingrihild stepped forward and gave Snow a small wooden box with intricate carvings. Inside was a gift wrapped up and tied with green satin. With a tug, the ribbon fell away, revealing two small, uncut gems.

"Emeralds?" Snow raised a brow, taken aback that they'd give her part of their quota. "This is too generous. You've already done so much for me."

"You've more than earned it," Ingrihild said, a happy glint in her eye.

The matriarch wasn't one to lavish unwarranted praise, and Snow's reservation melted away at the matriarch's reaction.

"The emeralds aren't the real gift, anyway," Runa smiled. "You said you wanted to go to Isolzing."

"Grim and Runa are taking you," Wielbran said, putting his arm around his wife as he spoke. "The morning before the next full moon when the strawberry season should be at its peak."

Snow didn't know what to say. The gifts were more generous than she'd ever expected. But, the trip to fill in the gaps of her past made her eyes sting. Their offer was everything Snow had wanted since she was torn away from her mother, but she had to refuse. Snow blinked back the tears and handed over the letter to Ingrihild, unable to speak. The matriarch read the letter twice before letting her brother scan it.

"The queen may know Snow is alive," Ingrihild announced.

Grim's jaw dropped, and little Lielinda gasped. Everyone knew that Snow's permission to stay in the caves would change if the risk to the dwarves increased.

"We're not sending Snow out into the Wild." Runa folded her arms and jutted out a hip.

"No one is suggesting that," Gertrild said, though she looked to her mother for confirmation.

"What is your plan?" Ingrihild asked Snow as she returned the note. "How will you take the throne?"

Snow had intended to present her plan to Max and perfect the strategy together. If her scheme was terribly flawed, would Ingrihild still protect an ill-prepared ruler? Or would the risk outweigh the benefit?

Snow lifted her chin, hoping to project more confidence than she felt. "When I turn nineteen, my ring will be visible to humans. With the high judge's papers and the princess's word as a witness, I'll have the proof I need to convince the captain of the guard to swear allegiance to me. With the guards on my side, I can command them to restrain the queen."

"The guards should take Agnes to the dungeon for breaking a dozen Solinsel laws," Runa muttered under her breath.

If anything went wrong, *Snow* could end up in the dungeon, or on the run forever, or hanged. And the queen had magic Snow didn't yet understand.

"What do you know of fae magic?" Ingrihild asked, cutting right to the core of Snow's biggest concern.

Snow clutched the emeralds in her fist. "Fae have differing abilities and strengths. They give Giftings to royal-born humans."

"When it suits them." Karldorin tightened his arms across his chest.

Snow continued, "Some fae are masters of glamour. Spies."

"Glamour, yes," Karldorin grumbled. "Spies, not so much. Why would they bother?"

"Let's review what we know," Ingrihild said. "Based on what you and Max have told us, the queen likely bargained for fae magic. When humans bargain with fallen fae for magic, the result is potentially an abomination. A witch."

Karldorin piped in, "The only way a *human* can possess magic is by absorbing dark magic from a fae. It goes against all the Abundants' laws!"

Snow had been around King Friedrich long enough to know he didn't have any magical abilities. Reinhold used his own magic to assist the king because of their Bond; she'd heard the link was stronger than even a familial bond between siblings. It had to be. Otherwise, the fae would be more prone to torment rather than help the humans in their care.

Unless, of course, the fae were plied with the best food, fawned over, and treated like royalty—then they *might* grant a human a favor. According to Karldorin, if Reinhold had *imbued* the king with the ability to perform magic, the bequest would go against not just fae law but nature itself. Snow shuddered.

"We know because Karldorin and I have been researching. And . . . I see your face, Runa. Yes, I keep a few books about witches. No, I won't lend them to you."

"Pft!" Runa said, rolling her eyes.

"The tragedies began about five years after Agnes arrived, so the timing makes sense," Ingrihild continued. "Assuming she is a witch, she has spent her time and energy perfecting her preferred spells. It sounds like she has learned what's called a 'tracking spell'."

Karldorin added, "Using a pond, glass, a blade—"

"Anything reflective," Ingrihild interjected. "The queen can spy on one person or place at a time, using the reflective surface. I suspect she *was* focused on you, Snow. Until she thought you were dead."

"But if Agnes suspects that I am alive, she could potentially track me back to the cave, and I wouldn't even know," Snow said.

Ingrihild pursed her lips and raised a brow. "For argument's sake, even if she did occasionally look for you, potentially wasting her time, she'll need talent and a pile of luck to find your location. Even if she was *incredibly* fortunate, she would only be able to track you back to the Wildwood. She'd have no idea which cave you're in, assuming she could even find the doors. And, inside our home, we have ancient protections." Ingrihild glanced at her brother. "Besides, there is another way to hide you."

"Mother?" Gertrild's whispered interruption was filled with surprise, warning, and more than a little curiosity.

"Overthrowing a ruler is no easy task." Ingrihild's voice hardened. "It's not going to happen from a place of safety. It benefits no one, not even the dwarves, for you to stay holed up in the cave. Our ancestors didn't risk the seas to escape the wars of the north for us to let peace slip through our fingers. If you're willing, we will help you. But we won't be foolish, either. Why go to Isolzing?"

Snow's mind spun. Ingrihild wouldn't risk discovery by delivering a lackluster solution, but the matriarch needed a good reason to trust Snow's ability. She gave Ingrihild the simple truth. "Isolzing may hold answers to help us fight the queen."

Ingrihild tilted her head, considering. Then, she turned her attention to the elder dwarves, but Snow didn't dare look at their expressions. Didn't dare *feel* anything either. She didn't want to repeat any of the drama she'd experienced as a child by misinterpreting or, worse, understanding more than they did about each other's intentions.

Finally, the matriarch spoke. "Put your faith in us, Snow. We will make the necessary arrangements before the winter snow blocks the pass."

"I'll call a clans meeting," Karldorin said, hurrying from the room, Grim on his heels.

The remaining adults rushed to follow, already in deep discussion, leaving Snow and little Lielinda. The youngest dwarf reached up and took Snow's hand. Snow slowly closed her eyes and took a deep breath. Ingrihild wasn't kicking her out. She was extending even more assistance. Before winter, Snow would finally return to her childhood home.

CHAPTER 14: MAX

YEAR 9 OF THE MAIDEN COMET, AUTUMN

Max's two hunting companions finished field-dressing the roe deer they'd caught that morning while Max rode to the castle. The irony wasn't lost on him that he was doing one of the things he was angry at his father for doing: spending time indoors rather than in the forest. But, like his father, he needed to know the gossip.

In the kitchens, low conversations of frustration rumbled. The autumn harvest season was usually a time of celebration. Not this year.

With the field laborers fleeing, farmers were forced to leave many fields fallow. And of what they planted and harvested, half was shipped to the northern kingdoms. The blacksmiths and tanners worked overtime, sending blades and saddles for distant wars, receiving too few bronze coins for their efforts. Guards became enforcers and tax collectors—and the queen seemed to know if a single horseshoe or bag of grain was "missing."

Max was as paranoid as everyone else . . . more so knowing the sickening request for Snow's heart and liver. At the slightest hint that the queen knew where Snow was hiding, he'd get to her first.

"Me sister took off yester eve," one kitchen servant said, her eyes rimmed with red. "We scrabbled like stray cats, but I do miss me little nieces and nephew summat fierce."

"But your sister's husband is the best cobbler in Caston," Dottie said as she pounded a ball of dough.

"Aye, but folk be desperate. They'd chew their shoes rather than mend 'em," she grumbled. "They be headin' south for better fortunes."

"Nay, they don't sup as well as us in the castle, that's for certain," another servant added.

Dottie lowered her voice, just loud enough for Max to hear, "With the new steward, we may be starvin' like the rest of them."

They shot each other knowing looks. The new steward was the queen's lap dog, according to rumor. That, or he was severely under-trained.

On Max's last two hunts, nobles and merchants had complained that the new steward didn't understand requisitions, and several accounting errors had already surfaced. Merchants who'd delivered cloth for the queen's dresses hadn't been paid. More alarmingly, guards grumbled that their pay had been reduced, and all the captains' permissions to hunt in the royal forest had been revoked. Max realized he was tapping his jacket where his amulet once sat. With the guards disgruntled and the people on the verge of anarchy, the kingdom teetered at a tipping point.

Dottie asked him to fetch some fresh herbs hanging on the opposite wall, giving him a chance to eavesdrop further without suspicion. Dottie didn't ask why Max was lingering in the kitchens, but she'd started giving him excuses to stay as long as he needed. As he moved around, he heard more troubling news. And then one surprising piece of new gossip.

"Prince Leopold de Bourbon from across the sea sent his emissary to talk with Queen Agnes, but she's been tucked away in her bedchamber since he arrived," the queen's maidservant said. "She's usually babbling or hollering like a loon. But she's been peaceful of late, thank the Abundants. The emissary has been patient, especially with the queen staying locked in her chambers, refusing to come out. I'm praying Princess Elisabeth will return soon, for mayhaps the prince is aiming to wed her. And the princess is the only one able to coax the queen out of her rooms these days."

"Aye, if the princess marries him, we could eat," another kitchen maid said as she carried a basket of potatoes to the table. "The prince's got a load of gold, and who knows what else he might offer for her hand."

With the pressure of a visiting emissary and without Elisabeth to use as a crutch, the queen would finally be distracted. There would never be a risk-free time to approach his father's contact in Caston, the Abundant Heinrich had mentioned. But this was the best opportunity he'd had since he'd visited his father during planting season moons ago. Max had to take it.

"Dottie," he said, handing over sprigs of rosemary, "when did the queen last deliver a donation to the Blessed Houses of Caston."

She raised a brow. "Not since the king passed. Been a long while. The deer ye brought in be a blessing from The Abundant Ones. We'll salt and smoke it to last and send a share of the meat next week."

"It might be prudent to deliver food sooner. Perhaps tomorrow," he suggested, hoping she'd go along with it. "And I'll deliver the donation on behalf of the queen. I'm happy to do it."

"Of course, that's a better plan," she said as if her first idea was ridiculous. "We just finished smoking and drying the last bit of roe deer you brought in last moon. Will that do?"

The kitchen staff swirled around him like a well-choreographed dance, none the wiser to his plan. Perhaps this would work.

"Perfect," Max grinned.

Max trotted his horse into Caston, a heavy pack strapped to both sides. In the city, somehow he felt even more exposed without his amulet, unprotected from attack. He only had enough meat for two of the three Houses, so he had to choose wisely, and he had to avoid robbery along the way. He stopped by the oldest and most well-respected Blessed House.

The Attuned gladly took the meat, her eyes misting as she told him of the needs of her House. Nearby, a younger group attentively sat in a circle while an Attuned told them a story, and an older group silently scratched a lesson on parchment with their quills. The children were dressed in simple though worn clothing with their hair pulled back into tight ponytails.

"Did Heinrich Hunt make a delivery here in the last year?" Max asked.

"You're the first royal huntsman to visit. Quite the unexpected honor. Usually, castle servants make the deliveries," she paused and cleared her throat. "I have never asked the crown for supplies," she began, her cheeks flushing. "But I beg of you to tell the queen of our need; proper meals in the Houses means fewer thieving orphans. Please, help us."

"I'll do what I can," he said, knowing that the cook would need to ask the steward's permission for a second delivery. On the heels of this one, the request would not be granted, especially not until the third House had received a donation.

"I received more charges than I could care for over the harsh winter season. I even had to turn a few away as I didn't have a mat to spare." Her voice trembled. "Harvest season is upon us, and I fear the coming cold."

She could've put other children on the floor, but he bit back the thought. He'd learned what he needed—she wasn't the type to bend the rules. Even the children sat in perfect circles around their instructors. This Attuned wouldn't be his father's choice for hiding the king's indiscretions.

Leaving, Max changed his tactic. He guided his horse to the poorest district. This part of town reeked of desperation and simmering anger, prompting Max to find a guard to escort him to the Blessed House. Inside, Max delivered the second pack of meat to a grateful attending.

While he waited to speak with the Attuned, he scanned the children scampering in the large central area. Max was sure the space was intended for meditation, but the children giggled and ran around, playing games together. Their clothing was patched and frayed, their hair cut short and a bit wild.

One particular child caught his attention. The girl had the same dark complexion as the king, framed by messy, dark curls. Something in her mannerisms reminded him of Snow. He clutched his chest, his heart pounding. He'd thought he'd put Snow in the recesses of his mind, but in a flash, she overtook his thoughts, flooding him with memories. He wished Snow could be with him, seeing her half-sister for the first time. Then his lungs deflated; if Snow had come to find her sister, she wouldn't have invited Max. Another portion of her life she'd kept from him.

When the Attuned appeared, Max felt like the world around him tilted. The young woman looked similar to Snow, just a few years older. The same black hair but pulled back in a practical bun. The shape of her eyes was different, and her nose was narrower, but her gait . . . the deep blue color of her eyes—Snow. She gripped Max's arm and helped lower him onto a bench.

"You're Heinrich's son," she said simply.

Max had known that Snow had half-siblings, but seeing them still made his head spin. Kings and queens did as they pleased, but this part of King Friedrich's past sickened Max. The king's behavior was irresponsible for many reasons, but especially for a king whose children could be leveraged against him. His progeny had no protection unless they were lucky enough to find each other.

"My father sent me to relocate children who are in danger. He would've come himself, but he's been . . . detained," Max said.

Her shoulders tightened, understanding the dire situation without further explanation.

"I'm not leaving." She lifted her chin. "Ever. The queen won't see me as a threat, anyway."

The Attuned swore to a life of service, dedicating themselves to the Abundants. They kept themselves out of political affairs and took in the orphans, earning the undying support of many. Blessed Houses dotted all the seven kingdoms, and not even Agnes was likely to violate their unspoken amnesty. In many ways, this sister's oath was her best armor against the queen.

"What about the girl?" Max asked.

The Attuned pressed her lips together. "If she's in danger, send me a signal. Deliver nine candles to the House; one for each of the children born to the same invisible father." Bitterness edged her voice. "At dusk that same day, I'll have Nora delivered to the northern gate."

Was it foolishness or brilliance to hide the king's child in plain sight? Or had Heinrich wanted Nora within easy reach for relocation? Or had his father calculated that no one would look after her as well as her own sister, an Attuned. Perhaps he assumed the queen didn't consider this little girl a threat. Yet.

"Where are the others?" Max asked, masking the crack in his voice.

She looked Max up and down, scrutinizing him before continuing. "Two children are beyond the kingdom's borders. The youngest was adopted, and I do not know where the child resides. That's all I can say for now."

She was a good liar, but not good enough to fool Max. She knew of her sibling's locations. "If I recognized you both, others will, too. At least, attempt to disguise yourselves."

The Attuned escorted him out, not responding to his suggestion. Outside, Max marched to his horse, the scent of onions and cooking meat already filling the street. Though he respected this Attuned, she was stubborn. When the queen was done with her negotiations to marry off Elisabeth, she might track down Nora. His father had been right in urging him to find the Attuned.

As he trotted through the merchant's quarter at the main gate, he glazed past criminal "wanted" posters but jerked to a halt when he saw the massive notice nailed higher on the wall than all the rest.

> *Missing Person: Snow, the queen's ward*
> *Reward: ten gold pieces if it leads to the recovery of the ward*
> *Report sightings to the Captain of the Royal Guard.*

Max's stomach dropped at the drawing of Snow on the notice. Every criminal in the city had ample incentive to pull the city apart, looking for Snow, stone by stone. And every merchant traveling the kingdom would know her face, eager for the reward and the queen's favor.

CHAPTER 15: SNOW

YEAR 9 OF THE MAIDEN COMET, AUTUMN

On the second afternoon of travel, Runa, Grim, and Snow crested the rocky mountain and trundled downward toward Isolzing. As Snow and her companions' wagon rode closer, she squinted, evaluating the town in the distance. The houses in the center were arranged in a circle around the central square, constructed of wood and stone with proper thatched roofs and painted shutters on the windows. But the homes on the outskirts looked haphazardly cobbled together. Beyond the dwellings sat vast tracks of harvested fields, yet all the travelers were thin with hard eyes and grim expressions.

"Ready?" Runa asked as they neared Isolzing.

"Are you?" Grim elbowed his sister in the ribs.

Snow secured her braided black hair under her cap, and she tucked her chin under her thin scarf. Snow had grown strong from her weeks in the mines, and she trusted the strange sigils Wielbran had stamped inside the band of her ring, but she didn't want to draw unwanted attention, human or otherwise. The sigils were enough to bring a piece of Wildwood magic with her, hiding her from distant fae magic. But, it didn't hide her from those around her. However, the only wicked person she truly needed to avoid was far away at Clarus castle.

Yet, there was one person at Clarus she wished to see. Though, the memory of Max's expression when he'd discovered her secrets soured her stomach with guilt. Had she destroyed their friendship? She barely dared let the thought flit through her mind. Snow never allowed her thoughts to quiet long enough to ponder the recent events—her betrayal—otherwise, her emotions threatened to drown her like an ocean current too strong for her to stay afloat.

The road turned from rock to dirt, and horses' hooves thumped on the uneven ground. In a pumpkin field adjacent to the town, a lone raven sat on a post, a beady black eye on the trio as they trundled into town. The sound of clucking chickens filled the air, along with the earthy scent of the dirt roads mixed with the fragrance of hay and manure. Sheep in nearby pens were growing their wooly coats, preparing for winter.

Villagers with rounded shoulders went about their daily business, wearing patched clothing, the fabric worn thin with ragged hems. It wasn't uncommon for the lower classes like herself to wear rougher work clothing at home or in the fields, but not while running errands in town, especially not with the cooling weather.

Wood smoke from open cooking fires and chimneys choked the road in some places. Taking a closer look as they passed by the quickly constructed residences, she noticed several people staring at the trio with guarded distrust. Grim and Runa kept their caps down. Steering quickly to the central market, the three travelers were greeted with the aroma of preserved fruit, fresh vegetables, herbs, and wild honey.

The merchants' offerings were scant, considering the size of the city, and markedly smaller compared to what Snow was accustomed to in Caston.

"This town is on edge," Grim mumbled. "Let's get our things and get out at dawn. I'll prepare our lodging."

"But the market will close in a couple of hours for the evening. The mood is a bit tense, but a few humans are no threat to *us*." Runa flexed her arm with a grin. "We aren't leaving until we get everything on auntie's list. I don't want to stress her any more than necessary. And Snow needs time to pick herself out a gift."

The dwarves had told her the emeralds were hers to bargain with. They thought it would be good practice, and apparently, it was common for dwarves to select their own presents. Snow had no idea what to get for herself, as her goal was to talk to the Attuned.

Snow had been taken to the Blessed House after her mother was killed, so it was the best place to start her investigation. And after the less-than-warm atmosphere of the town, Snow agreed with Grim—they should leave as soon as possible. Which meant she needed to talk to the Attuned that night.

"We'll evaluate the vendor offerings tonight and buy in the morning." Runa elbowed Snow, edging her out of the wagon. "Stay where I can see you."

Snow nodded, and they hopped down and watched Grim trundle away. Snow followed Runa through the stalls to where the dwarf perused the vendors and products. Snow stopped in her tracks, spotting a massive mirror at the end of the row. Snow recognized the style, and she slowly walked toward it, a nervous tingling running down her spine. The vendor, a middle-aged man with a young helper, called out.

"A lovely mirror, is it not?" he asked.

Snow glanced behind her and realized he was talking to her. It made sense, actually, because her clothing was in much better condition than most. She tip-toed closer, barely noticing the handheld mirrors on the table, her attention on the large one behind him.

"This one is quite nice," he said, trying to re-direct her to a small mirror in a wooden frame.

Snow nodded, ignoring his tight smile. Apparently, she didn't appear wealthy enough to afford the large display. Likely a correct assumption.

"The exotic wood is from a distant kingdom across the sea," the merchant continued.

The massive mirror behind him drew her attention. Along the edge, bright words were etched, 'Anything is possible with a positive attitude.'

Snow grimaced at the sentiment, too sweet and naïve for her taste. She wished Max was with her to joke about the mirror, but it was yet another experience she hoped to tell him about later. She missed experiencing the little things in life together. Max made everything more fun. Runa jogged up behind Snow and looked at the table. The vendor brightened, seeing the dwarf.

"This is a replica of the princess's mirror," he boasted to Runa as he pointed to the large mirror. "And just as fine."

Snow rolled her eyes. She'd seen the princess's mirror. She didn't recall any sickly-sweet phrases along the edges. It had a sophisticated, curving design. Admittedly, the two mirrors were about the same size. The queen's mirror was easily three times larger than anything on display.

"Though the princess's mirror is *fae* crafted," the merchant's helper said, her eyes bright.

"Well, it was a birth gift from the fae," the merchant said matter-of-factly, "I heard all about it. The detail is worthy of a queen."

"Or a princess," the little helper continued.

"Or for anyone ridiculously flamboyant," Runa muttered under her breath.

Snow thanked the merchant and walked away, not wanting to spoil Runa's evening with talk of fae. As the pair continued on, a woman with a small cart trundled in their direction.

The peddler stared at Snow for a moment before abruptly stopping and unveiling her goods. A sumptuous red material displayed carved combs, all delicate and beautiful. Something about the woman seemed familiar. Had Snow known her as a child? Did the seller think Snow looked familiar? Perhaps the woman knew Snow's mother, Rosalind? Though, the peddler would've been much younger than her mother a decade ago. Snow nearly walked over to the woman when Runa interrupted her thoughts.

"I'm hungry," she said. "Let's find Grim. He's probably already eaten. The nincompoop."

Snow continued past the peddler, feeling the woman's attention on her. As Snow and Runa walked through the town center, Snow wracked her memories, trying to remember anything about Isolzing. But only the town square and communal well looked vaguely familiar.

They turned the corner, and between two structures stood a rounded house with a spire on the top—the Blessed House. She smiled, remembering this structure. Would someone there remember her? Remember her mother?

"Runa, go to the inn, and I'll meet you later," Snow said. "I need to visit someplace first."

"Oh, no," Runa said. "I'm not letting you wander around alone. So, make it quick because my stomach will start growling, and I'll get grumpy. You don't want to see me grumpy."

Snow snorted, grateful for a friend. They hurried to The Blessed House and were graciously greeted by an elderly attending, one of many servants who dedicated themselves to supporting the good endeavors of the Attuned. Everyone in the Houses worked to honor the goddesses. After explaining that Snow had once lived there and retelling the story, the attending nodded in understanding.

"I remember you," she said with a wavering voice. "So will the Attuned. I'll fetch him for you."

Shortly thereafter, the Attuned greeted them. The petite man was younger than the attending with delicate features and sharp eyes. He wore the subdued robes of an Attuned and a cap pulled down over his ears, ready for the coming evening chill. He carried a leather-bound book under his arm, and he practically glided as he led them to an interior room. One wall opened to the darkening sky, framing an inner courtyard with modest plants and two stone benches in the center. It was simple but peaceful.

"I must attend to the children. You know how some need an extra story at bedtime," the elder attending said, leaving the three of them.

"Snow White," he said. "What a blessing to know what happened to you after you were taken away."

Relief flooded Snow. He *remembered*. He explained that Snow's mother was buried in an unmarked grave beyond the fields. His words were soft and compassionate as he expounded on how Rosalind must've distracted the Wildwood beast long enough for Snow to escape.

She wasn't sure if it was the smells or the elevation, but she remembered the keening of the beast. The black fur and long muzzle. The flash of glowing red. Snow took a sharp breath in, and Runa gripped Snow's forearm.

The Attuned quieted, and Snow realized that tears rimmed his eyes. She dropped her attention to her hands, her own emotion welling. She could lose herself to grief later, but not now. She needed to know everything he could remember.

"Have I shared too much?" he asked softly.

"No, not at all," Snow said, clearing her throat. "Anything you've learned about that night, I want to know."

On his lap, he opened the book, the binding falling on one particular section as if it had been studied often. Even upside down, the drawing sent a shock down her spine. The beast from that night.

Snow was at a loss for words, her memories already flooding. A distant part of her longed to have Max with her. He would know exactly what to say and do. He always did.

"Maybe we should come back tomorrow," Runa said gently.

"No," Snow said, both eager and fearful. In all of Addy Hunt's books, no image of a Shadow Beast existed, hardly even a footnote. "I don't want to wait another moment to hear whatever the Attuned have discovered."

"We study all creations, good and evil, because the Abundants allow us to learn and grow from both." The Attuned slowly turned the book around so Runa and Snow could study the image as he spoke. "A Shadow Beast is as vicious as it is strong. Few have survived to describe its attacks; everything I have is compiled from their stories. These beasts have a signature keening, and their fangs and claws are poisonous, but it's the eyes you must avoid. Their magic is fear, and their red eyes are their greatest weapon. Never let them pin you with their gaze."

Runa raised a brow. "Your record is quite remarkable. Some of these entries are over a hundred years old. Have you ever faced one of these beasts?"

"I'm merely a record keeper of others' experiences," he said, pressing a graceful hand to his chest before changing the subject. "The creature can be controlled, to some extent, but only with a certain kind of magic."

"Fae magic?" Runa interjected.

The Attuned nodded. "But I imagine only a witch would attempt to control one. I've never heard of one leaving the Wood. Yet, even with great magical strength and close proximity, the hold is tenuous. With a sharp distraction, the bond to the beast is broken."

"So, the witch must have been near Isolzing when the beast attacked," Runa pressed.

"Or even closer." His words sank in, leaving Snow's stomach roiling. Agnes was close by when she'd set the beast on an innocent child. "The city was smaller then, and a few villagers did mention a stranger. Their descriptions matched — a woman in a fine cloak, but she kept her cowl low. That's all I was able to discover."

"You said that my mother distracted the beast," Snow said slowly.

Runa stiffened as they both finally understood; Snow's mother had thrown herself in front of the bloodlust-driven creature, supplying easy prey and providing the *distraction*. She had given her life to protect Snow. Snow gagged, covering her mouth and shooting to her feet. The Attuned rang a bell, and an attending rushed Snow to the privy where she heaved into the bucket. She wanted to scream. To cry. But her emotion was bottled up deep inside in a place she couldn't reach.

"How would one defeat such a beast?" Runa asked when Snow returned.

"If you're unfortunate enough to run across one in the Wood, and you don't look into its eyes," he paused, "you can only pray to survive if you aren't alone. Everyone must split up so after one person is killed, the other is too far away for the Beast to dare leave his prey."

"You can't fight it and win?" Runa asked.

"No one ever has," he shook his head.

Snow numbly pulled out the dwarven-carved wooden box from her old satchel. With a shaking hand, she pressed a rough emerald into the Attuned's hand. He protested that the jewel was too much. Snow insisted he keep it as Runa pulled her out of the House. As she walked away, she wasn't sure why she didn't give him both gems. He'd given her everything she'd wanted to know. And more.

"We'll go by the graves tomorrow morning," Runa said before Snow had a chance to ask.

Runa guided Snow to a well-kept part of the town with two-story homes settled next to each other, practically sharing walls. The dwarf tenderly shuttled Snow up through a back entrance to where Grim waited. Soon they had her tucked into bed, and Grim gave her a warm bottle to slide down by her feet. As Snow curled up in a ball and turned her back on the pair, she overheard Runa whispering to her brother.

"We met with an elf who is posing as a human Attuned. I trust his knowledge, of course," she said. "Coming here was the right choice as he's studied first-hand accounts of Wildwood creatures. He confirmed that most certainly a fae or a witch controlled the Shadow Beast. But they must be quite powerful and nearby. How creepy is she?"

"Definitely twisted," Grim whispered back, "probably by the dark magic she invited into her soul. Foolish woman."

"She's absolutely depraved."

"We need to get out of this city."

"For once, I couldn't agree more."

CHAPTER 16: MAX

YEAR 9 OF THE MAIDEN COMET, AUTUMN

Max delivered pheasants and quail to the kitchens shortly after dawn. He brought in a smaller catch because Dottie only wanted enough for the day. Servants busily preserved meat from earlier in the season, their burdens heavy as several others had returned home to harvest their family's farms.

"No hunts planned today?" Dottie asked him, confirming the schedule for the nobles who requested the use of the royal forest.

"No one other than me for the rest of the week," he said.

"Could ye kindly take them two lads down to the valley?" Sweat beaded around Dottie's face while morning loaves of bread cooked nearby. "The blackberries be ripe as can be, and the queen's asked for a berry posset. I'll be needing them afore the sun goes down."

"Very kind of you to gather from the queen's forest rather than tax the market," Max said.

"I help where I can." Dottie didn't say as much, but the local farmers would struggle to feed their families through the winter, let alone support the appetites of the castle, too.

"Wait, wasn't posset Reinhold's favorite?" Max asked.

"Aye. The dessert hasn't been requested since the king's passing," Dottie said before shooing Max out of the kitchen. "I'll have the servants ready with their baskets in a half hour."

While Max cleaned his hands and forearms, a plan began forming to confirm if Reinhold still dwelled in Clarus. Max needed to know if the fae had helped the queen. Perhaps he regretted his choice? Or was he still helping her? To find out, he'd need Dottie's help. Thus far, he'd avoided involving her directly, for her own sake.

His mother had taught Snow and him about fae bargains, including how fae only bothered to bond with the most influential humans. Bonds increased the power of both the fae and the human, making the union appealing for both parties. And the magic was exclusive; no fae could be bonded to more than one human at the same time.

If fae magic was involved in the conspiracy against Snow and her siblings, Reinhold would have a much better understanding than Max ever could. His knowledge was crucial and could help them find a solution. Or he'd turn Max into a bumbling idiot who might dance his life away in the woods, never to be found again. It was difficult to say for certain.

But Heinrich had never whispered any suspicion about Reinhold. He'd trusted him. Was his father wrong, and Reinhold had betrayed his master? Elisabeth's Bonded fae had done the same, so perhaps disloyalty between bonded souls wasn't as uncommon as the stories told.

Finished with his work, Max lingered in the nearby hallways as servants, merchants, and lower nobles proceeded about their business. As he waited for Dottie, he strained to hear gossip about the queen. Agnes had bouts of productivity over the summer and was busy entertaining guests, specifically Prince Leopold's emissary. The emissary's continued presence could be a decent distraction when he moved Nora.

Max had consulted his father's map, and the kingdom seemed to shrink. It became clear why his father transported two older siblings to a port. What was safer than putting the entire sea between the queen and her prey?

Max planned to hire a transport to take Nora to a mountain village as soon as snow started to fall; any pursuit would be difficult until the following summer. By then, Snow would be queen. That, or she'd have to flee, and Max and his mother would run away with her. And his father would be hanged. Max's mouth dried, and he shoved any possibility of him not succeeding from his mind.

Princess Elisabeth strode down the hall, headed toward the main stairs to the upper courts. Noticing Max, she smiled and changed course, greeting him.

"I haven't seen you in ages, huntsman," she said. "How are you?"

"The cook is pleased with my daily catch, so all is well," he said, forcing a pleasant expression.

"It will be better if Snow returns," she said encouragingly. "I hope she is safe. Your father said she wanted to return to her childhood home, but I didn't expect her to leave."

Elisabeth paused as if conflicted. Did she want to confess to Max—truths he already knew—that Snow was the heir? More than anyone, Elisabeth would suspect something was amiss. Max wondered if his father's decision to not ask for help from the princess was a wise one.

"I saw the announcements in Caston," Elisabeth said, lowering her voice. "The queen is using the people to help her locate Snow. I hope she is safe. Have you heard from her?"

Max evaluated the princess, debating on how much to tell her.

"I wish I had," Max said honestly. He hadn't gotten a single letter from her, as was expected. Any correspondence could lead back to her whereabouts. Neither Max nor Snow were naïve—servants could share news of any letters directly with the queen.

She bit her lip, her expression darkening. "The queen has found a match for Snow."

"What do you mean, 'a match'?"

"To wed," Elisabeth said. "The queen noticed Snow's beauty and sent her painting to eligible nobles and royals in other kingdoms. A prince sent his emissary."

Max shook his head, realizing the servants' gossip was wrong. The prince wasn't interested in Elisabeth. He wanted to marry Snow. It made sense. Max's father had hinted at Snow's engagement long ago when he'd told Max to stay away from her. When the king made Snow his heir, of course, he arranged a strong ally to secure her future.

"If the emissary approves Snow, he's authorized to offer a substantial dowry, plus a lucrative trade deal. Prince Leopold is the third child born to the king, unlikely to inherit the throne, but he's a prince. "

Max didn't care if this Leopold owned all the land across the sea. He hated the idea of Snow with anyone who wasn't *him*.

"Can you imagine Snow marrying a prince?" Elizabeth asked.

Max wondered what the prince would offer if he knew Snow was the true heir of the kingdom. The thought of any amount of coin for Snow sickened him.

"Does Snow know she's betrothed?" Max asked.

"Of course. She sat for hours with a painter."

Another secret Snow hadn't shared with him. But why would she? They were just friends.

Elisabeth quieted, her face turning sympathetic, which Max hated.

"Your friendship with Snow was real, but she's on a different path," Elisabeth said kindly, which was insufferable.

Elisabeth knew Snow was the chosen heir. He wished the princess would hint that Snow might not leave the kingdom to wed; with a foreign kingdom's support, it would strengthen her case for taking the Solinsel throne. But Elisabeth gave no such hint.

If Snow stayed, could Max remain her best friend while he watched her live her life with someone else?

"With the queen's spending and inability to balance the royal budget, the wedding contract would save our kingdom from financial ruin," Elisabeth continued in conciliatory tones. "Furthermore, if Judge Helene publicly agrees to a reasonable use of the treasury's influx, especially if done in front of other nobles, the queen will be coerced into helping her own people."

"We can hope," Max stuttered, barely able to speak.

"I've known the prince since he was a child," Elisabeth said. "He's a good person. I know you care about Snow, and I do too. I think they could grow quite fond of each other. He's taken with her already."

He's in love with her face. Not with her.

Max gripped his hands behind his back, hiding his tension. "Snow deserves the very best."

"Let us hope that we can find her, for everyone's sake," Elisabeth said before heading toward the stairs. "I've convinced the emissary to stay until spring, but he grows impatient."

Max stormed to the kitchens, jealousy coloring his vision. He shoved away the image of Snow kissing a strange prince from his mind and focused on what he could control: setting a trap for Reinhold, the fae skulking around the castle who might have answers.

The autumn's crisp mornings were a welcome respite from the long summer. Instead of missing Snow less, Max's temper was raw, worry and longing wringing him through. But he'd watched the kingdom deteriorate and knew Snow would be a good queen. He loved her, but for him to stand in the way of not just happiness for the people of the kingdom but for Snow wasn't right. He'd heard the prince was an excellent hunter and had a lightness about him—humor—that would likely soften Snow's hardships.

When Max fetched Snow to escort her back to the castle in the spring, he was determined to keep his distance. To be her friend, but nothing more. He couldn't even allow himself to touch her as it would only add to his torture, if not to her own. Though, perhaps he was too worried because, for all he knew, she barely gave him a thought. She was to be queen, after all, so where would a huntsman fit into her life?

He wouldn't.

At least the plan was set to whisk Nora out of Caston; the transport's down payment was already given, reserving their services. He and his mother had dipped candles, reserving nine extra to deliver to the Blessed House when snow began to fall. He grew more anxious about the departure as the leaves fell, grateful that the queen hadn't yet seemed to notice Snow's siblings hiding under her nose.

Even so, Max had finally retrieved his amulet from under the couch and dusted it off. With the pin broken, he'd need to have it repaired. But a fae amulet was worth more than everything else he owned, and he didn't trust anyone to fix it. So, he'd sewn the heirloom into his belt, an inelegant solution but a practical one.

Max trundled up the hill with his wagon, two servants aiding him. The kitchens were tense, and Dottie barely acknowledged him as she worked. Several fairies had been invited to dine at the castle. Pure foolishness. The queen demanded the finest foods, half of the delicacies out of season, shipped from surrounding kingdoms at a heavy cost. But the queen didn't care. She wanted to ingratiate herself with the fae. But why? Was this a ploy to curry favor with Reinhold? Or was she after something else?

To help, Max stayed late and dressed the roe deer for the feast. When he was done, he was surprised when Dottie pushed him into the back pantry where herbs hung, drying, in the shadowed corner.

"When we set the trap," she whispered after checking over her shoulder. "I thought you were daft."

They'd left out posset topped with blackberries, Reinhold's favorite, leaving a light dusting of flour or powdered sugar. They found no prints, but one of the goblets of posset was missing. One might've assumed the culprit was a hungry servant, but Dottie had secured the room, including the windows, and put a trustworthy guard at each door, promising extra rolls for their families.

"It worked, but are you *sure* about tonight?" she continued.

With all the food, Reinhold would certainly visit the kitchens before morning. And Max would be waiting.

He just gave a sharp nod. They were running out of time, and intercepting the clever fae would never be easier. Dottie shoved him out of the pantry, not bothering to discuss or explain anything else. Practical as ever.

Max left the castle and rode his horse back to the cottage to help with the chores. With his father gone and winter coming, he and his mother were busy with their own preparations. And Max looked forward to mindless wood chopping and thatch repairs, letting his worries fade to the back of his mind for a moment before he returned to Clarus.

Unfortunately, when he got home, a simple card of paper erased the fae from his mind. The thin, cream-colored paper had a hand-drawn symbol of the Blessed House. The Attuned was summoning him. And there wasn't even a dusting of snow on the mountain.

CHAPTER 17: SNOW

YEAR 9 OF THE MAIDEN COMET, AUTUMN

G rim, Runa, and Snow were up before dawn, debating.

"Our home is secure," Grim said, gesturing to the rooms where they'd slept. "Snow will stay here while we pick up the supplies."

"Safe from human thieves. Not witches or dark fae," Runa retorted.

"Not that witches or fae would even know I'm here." Snow waved her ringed finger through the air. The last thing she wanted was to be cooped up alone. She had figured out that the dwarves owned the house and rented out all but the back rooms, which they stayed in when visiting. "Let's go together. We'll be able to leave town faster if you don't have to return to this house."

"Best to obey the queen," Runa smirked.

The three of them frantically packed and hurried to market street. They shopped before the vendors finished setting up, not bothering to haggle as the dawn faded. With the wagon half-full and their bellies grumbling, Runa signaled for them to finish up.

Snow stood a few stalls down from the mirror merchant, whose young assistant was unveiling the large mirror. In her periphery, a peddler trundled near, a red cloth vibrant against the dull neighbors. Settling in place, the peddler quickly pulled back the cloth, revealing the carved wooden combs. Snow realized she hadn't purchased a gift for herself. Lielinda would definitely ask, and Snow was embarrassed to tell the little dwarf she was too nervous to shop. Snow scurried over to the seller, never out of the dwarves' sight.

"Is there any particular design you prefer?" the peddler asked. Her words were kind, but Snow shifted uncomfortably, sensing the woman's eagerness.

"They're all beautiful in their own way." Snow looked over at Runa, who signaled for her to hurry.

"Perhaps you like clouds and the sun," she said, pointing a gloved hand to one comb with a long row of short teeth. "This one is made from deer antler."

The seller tugged at her sleeves then pointed out different designs of birds, flowers, and stars made of ivory, boxwood, and maple. The tips of the woman's gloved fingers settled next to a narrow comb with long teeth, the top curved in a crescent. Ivy leaves decorated the top and vines curled down both sides, the carving deep and detailed. Snow gasped, remembering the design.

"You have good taste," the peddler commented, leaning forward as she plucked up the comb, turning it over so Snow could inspect the craftsmanship on the back.

Snow was speechless. Her mother had worn a similar comb. She had forgotten the memory until now. Could the very same artisan have made this one as well?

Snow pulled out her wooden box and handed over the rough emerald. The peddler took the payment without noting the generosity but smiled as she held out the comb.

"Let me help you put it in your hair." The vendor lifted the comb, and Snow caught a vague sweet scent.

"What is it made of?" Snow asked.

"A fruit tree." She shifted, and the shadows seemed to blur unnaturally across her face. Snow blinked, and the woman looked perfectly fine. Between the rising sun and Snow's nerves, her eyes were playing tricks on her. The seller continued, "The wood is softer, which allows for the exquisite detail. Store the comb carefully, and don't drop it, of course."

Snow reached up to remove her cap just as the peddler leaned closer into Snow's personal space. Something about the woman set Snow on edge.

"Will you box it up?" Snow asked. "I'll take it home."

"I'm afraid I don't have the proper wrapping. But your hair can hold it under your cap."

The woman reached for Snow's hat, but Snow leaned out of her grasp. Back at the wagon, she sensed Runa's impatience. Snow grabbed the comb from the peddler and shoved it into her old bag. Quickly thanking the woman, she turned to jog to her friends when she felt the woman's grip on her forearm.

The peddler jerked her back and smacked Snow's face. A sting pinched above her lip, and Snow gasped.

"A bee," the woman said, her words flat. "I tried to brush it off."

Grim was at her side, his hand on his hip, near a dagger. "Is there a problem here?"

"No, just a bee," Snow said, her lip starting to tingle. She wanted to get away from the woman and out of Isolzing.

Grim walked with Snow to the wagon, climbing up after she was settled.

"You look terrible," Runa said as the wagon jerked forward. "Your face is swelling up."

Grim glanced back over his shoulder at the woman at the cart.

"I didn't see a bee, but the vendor tried to help, and I think she frightened it into stinging me," Snow said.

"I have some ointment in the wagon that will help," Grim said, "Let us know if your throat starts to itch."

Snow had been stung on her arm once before, but the wound had barely swelled. This felt different, and already the tingling in her face was starting to ease, though strangely, the fingers on her right hand buzzed. Even more bizarre, her skin didn't feel tight and stretched thin, but when she touched her cheeks and lips, they felt swollen.

As they trundled through the town, Snow couldn't shake the odd encounter with the vendor. She wanted to love the comb, but the woman unsettled her. Snow pulled up her inner defenses like a comforting blanket, chastising herself for not doing it sooner. At least she wouldn't suffer more awkwardness that morning.

Snow distracted herself by watching the streets fill. Children scrambled to school or their apprenticeships, and laborers made their way to the outlying fields. The cart slowed behind the growing line of farmer's wagons headed for the main gate.

"What did you buy?" Runa asked, more relaxed as the gate grew closer. "I can smell it through your bag."

Dwarves had a heightened sense of smell, which helped some dwarves locate minerals.

"A candied apple, obviously," Grim joked.

"It does have a touch of caramel," Runa said. "Too sweet for my taste, though."

"The scent should fade," Snow said. Her mom's comb didn't have a smell, at least not that Snow remembered.

"It's not bad. Don't worry," Grim assured her.

Near the guard house, a city guard was replacing a faded notice on a wall. He stepped back just as the trio neared.

"Dung on a stick," Grim said.

"Shut your pie hole," Runa punched him in the arm.

On the notice, a drawing of Snow stared back at them. She was a wanted woman, a reward and all. Several townspeople were already inspecting the notice, whispering amongst themselves. Several turned and stared at the wagons leaving town, and the dwarves and Snow were stuck in the line of farmers taking turns to leave through the main gates.

Snow tugged her cap lower, and Grim sat forward, blocking her the best he could.

"That bee had good timing," Runa said under her breath. "No one will recognize you now. Finally, some good luck!"

Between her swollen face and tingling fingers, Snow felt anything but fortunate.

CHAPTER 18: MAX

YEAR 9 OF THE MAIDEN COMET, AUTUMN

Max had a decision to make. He could go to the Blessed House now, or he could catch Reinhold. He had to choose between Snow and her sister. Snow would want him to choose her siblings. But Snow was the legitimate heir, and putting her on the throne would ultimately save her siblings. Or that's what he told himself as he ran to the castle. He had to attempt to make contact with the fae—to find out exactly how powerful the queen might be. The task was dangerous, but Max had to try.

Unable to stable his horse at the castle on the off chance that it would tip off Reinhold to a trap, Max huffed up the mountain. Dottie sent the other servants to their rooms early with an excuse that they needed their rest for the extensive feasting on the morrow. Max stayed behind and helped Dottie bar the windows, and Max locked the doors from inside the kitchen.

The scents of winterberry pie floated through the castle. And Max waited in the shadows, keeping the pies in his sight.

As the moments slipped by, Max's anxiety grew. Why did the Attuned summon him? It must've been urgent, or she wouldn't risk the message. Was he wasting his time at the castle when he should be in Caston?

A dusting of soot fell into the empty fireplace. From the chimney, a fairy appeared, wings fluttering. The small creature flew past the window, and the moonlight revealed Reinhold. Seeing him was almost surreal, but the relief was temporary as fresh nerves washed over Max.

The fae approached the fruit in his natural, small form and paused, reading the note just as Max had planned.

Reinhold, esteemed fae, I need your help.

The wording let the fae know that he was both expected and welcomed. It also alerted the fae to the presence of someone else in the kitchens. In a flash, Reinhold turned, swirling into his larger, human form. He stood on the table, a foot crushing two pies, the violet color spilling across the wood.

Reinhold's hands splayed at his side as he searched the room, his attention falling on Max, and he lifted his arms. "Young huntsman? You lured me here?"

Max held out both hands, showing he wasn't armed. Not that it mattered. A fae could bind him with invisible rope, turn his feet to lead, or any other number of ghastly things. Every fae had a different set of skills, and Max didn't know Reinhold's. Nor did he want to find out.

"I won't break the law and save your father. It would damage relations between our kind," Reinhold said, turning back into his smaller form.

Max waited for the fae to eat, knowing they hated being kept from their quarry. But he also wanted to ask his questions before Reinhold grew annoyed and left. Or murdered Max in some magical way because the fae was allied with the queen.

"I understand why you can't free my father, despite his friendship with your master," Max said. Though he'd never expected the fae to help his father, pointing out the loyalty between the king and Heinrich didn't hurt.

Reinhold turned to go, so Max hurried to speak, "One question, honorable fae."

"Make it quick. I've blocked my presence here, but the astute will notice that part of the kitchen is invisible, which will invite scrutiny. I haven't hidden for this long to be undone by pie."

"What happens to fae after their bond is broken?" Max asked gently, knowing Reinhold had just suffered this very thing.

Reinhold's expression crumpled. "You question why I'm still at the castle." The fae set down his food, and he looked almost vulnerable. "It's not your place to ask, but I respect your attempt to ascertain if I'm a danger. Though, I assure you, I'm not the one you should fear."

"You mean, Queen—"

"Do not speak her name. I fear drawing her attention," he said, returning to his food. "But to answer your question, a break is . . . difficult."

"Difficult?" Max prompted.

"No word in the human language can adequately describe the feelings. So, yes. *Difficult.*" Reinhold's nostrils flared. Even small, the fae was quite intimidating. "Before the bond, all fae know a natural break is inevitable as humans are short-lived. However, we don't really have any comprehension of what that means until the death arrives."

"What about an unnatural break," Max dared press, remembering what had happened with Elisabeth. Could her fae lurk like Reinhold? Could he cause mischief around the castle?

Reinhold's eyes narrowed. "I cannot pretend I don't know to whom you're referring, so understand that the fae council took the princess's situation seriously. I hate to imagine how painful the severing was for her Bonded. The offending fae was locked away between realms where he could never hurt anyone again. No human is capable of releasing him. In fact, a great deal of magic would be necessary to even communicate with him. Though, if a—" he stopped himself, tapping his chin, and then seemed to wave off the thought. "Be assured, huntsman. He cannot hurt Elisabeth any longer."

Reinhold turned, signaling he was done with the conversation before taking another unrefined mouthful.

The fae dabbed the edges of his lips. "Tell me, is *she* alive?"

Apparently, the Wildwood had hidden Snow well. Max kept his expression neutral. "Do you want to know?"

"No," Reinhold cut him off. "Actually, it's better to be safe and not speak of her. The queen has proven to be both insane and a master manipulator. I concede it seems she wields dark magic, and I fear she's more clever than both of us." The fae shook his head. "She outwitted me. The king was my charge, and I failed him. The queen pretended to protect him, and I believed her. She betrayed him after she begged him to trust her—that she was his best chance at recovery. And now, I'm stuck here. So I have advice for my young charge."

Snow, Max thought.

"Tell *her* I hope she's learned to use her fae gift."

Max quieted, shocked that she'd received a gift. But, of course, another secret she hadn't mentioned.

"The gifting might be the key to her and her family's survival," Reinhold said. "It's her one edge against the queen."

"Will you stand with,"—Max stopped himself from saying Snow's name aloud—"*her* and witness she's his daughter when she comes forward?" *She'll need all the help she can get.*

"I'll do whatever I can to put the child on the throne. But if you figured out how to find me, the queen will, too. I will do my best to see this to the end, but I must leave the castle. With dark magic and even darker intentions, even a fae can be killed."

CHAPTER 19: SNOW

YEAR 9 OF THE MAIDEN COMET, LATE AUTUMN

The veins of the cave glowed extra bright, and light overhead shown down on the youngest dwarf, Lielinda, showcasing her wide smile. The cave was warm and welcoming, and Snow enjoyed the undercurrent of excitement.

On the bridge, Snow stood among the dwarves for the family's Name Giving Ceremony for Lielinda. She'd turned twelve years old, and her parents had selected her surname. Everyone dressed nicely for the event, including Snow. Lielinda had even insisted on braiding Snow's hair into fanciful loops, and Runa helped pin them in place. Snow added the carved comb from the marketplace and wore a simple red dress the dwarves had procured for her moons ago.

"Because of your tenacity," Lielinda's father began.

"Her deviousness," Grim whispered.

"And like your grandmother, you have an innate link to ore," her father continued.

"Though she wishes it was to sapphires," Runa whispered.

"You will hereafter be known as Lielinda Orespark," her mother said.

Grim and Runa whistled and cheered, along with Karldorin, as Lielinda beamed. Snow clapped, happy for the dwarves. Her stomach churned. A single burble, but Snow stiffened, worried. Was a third bout of illness coming on?

After returning from the trading post, Snow had struggled with nausea. Karldorin, the most knowledgeable healer in the household, suspected her sickness was due to the bee sting. Snow's health eventually improved enough to help with housework. But only a few weeks later, she had made herself presentable and joined the dwarves in an informal summer solstice celebration. Grim and Runa's parents visited, and though wary at first, they welcomed the human stranger. By the time the visitors left a few days later, Snow's nausea and fatigue had returned with a vengeance. Karldorin was never able to pinpoint the cause, but he had tended to her—while complaining about weak human constitutions—until Snow felt better.

Grim leaned against Snow, pulling her out of her thoughts.

"I hope Lielinda figures out how to filter that ore-smelling nose of hers," Grim joked just loud enough for Runa and Snow to hear.

"Agreed. She had me digging after an infinitesimal ribbon of ore last week," Runa said. "Quite literally would have missed it if she hadn't *insisted* it was there. Too small a deposit to bother collecting, let alone digging *forever* to get to it. Complete waste of a good afternoon."

Grim's laugh turned to a snort as he swallowed his mirth back, catching a glimpse of Ingrihild's warning glare.

"Sheesh, brother," Runa said, keeping a smile on her face and barely moving her lips. "You show a lack of decorum."

Lielinda's smile widened when her parents presented her with a gift—a headband topped with small, sparkling sapphires. They must have planned the gem-encrusted accessory seasons ago because no one had left the cave in moons. Another reminder of how the dwarves accommodated Snow and put her safety first.

Sweat beaded on Snow's forehead. Was she tired after standing for a short period? Or was the sweat a reasonable reaction to any hint that her mystery affliction had returned? The waves of illness frustrated Snow. She didn't even feel like studying when her stomach churned. Karldorin had assured her that the ailment was unlikely to return, *again*, but had it?

Perhaps she'd been cooped up for too long, and that's why she felt weak. Maybe humans needed natural sunlight on their skin. Yes, that could be the problem. Deep down, she doubted that was the case, but no matter the cause, Snow would grit her teeth and endure.

Karldorin pushed past Snow, Runa, and Grim, and grabbed Ingrihild's shoulder, not bothering to lower his voice. "Someone's at the door."

Gertrild gasped. No one was expected until spring. In a flurry of action, the dwarves hurried toward the vaulted entry. The pre-rehearsed choreography smoothly unfolded as the five dwarves and Snow stopped at the thick wooden doors separating the entry space from the rest of the house.

Ingrihild and Wielbran continued together to the main entrance and the stone door, pickaxes in hand. Karldorin bolted the wooden double doors behind them; Snow and the others were trapped but safe in the cave, nervous and waiting. Karldorin shifted to the side, his face pressed to the wood of one of the doors.

Seeing Snow's confusion, Runa explained, "There's an archaic spell on the door. Karldorin can look through to see and hear what's happening in the entrance."

"Wielbran is signaling that it's okay," Karldorin said, but his shoulders stayed tense. A moment later, he relaxed and stepped back, flinging open the doors.

"Max is back!" Lielinda shouted, running into the entrance.

The huntsman stood in the center of the entrance, and Snow's heart leapt at the sight of him. He held the hand of a girl about Lielinda's age—a miniature version of the king. Snow froze, her stomach flipping. She'd never met any of her half-siblings.

"Nora, this is Lielinda," Max said, squatting down next to the little girl.

Nora's eyes were wide as she huddled close to Max, probably just like Snow had done when she first arrived in the caves. The dwarves ushered the girl into the cozy living space where she relaxed enough to eat fruit and cheese.

Max signaled to Snow to speak with him privately. A sudden, giddy excitement fluttered in her chest but faded when she realized he'd also asked the elder dwarves to join them. On the other side of the room, Max spoke to them with a quiet voice. "I cannot stay. I'm sorry."

"I guess we are housing all the king's brats now?" Karldorin mumbled.

Snow might've been offended, but his words contained no real bite, and the dwarves had unfailingly protected her.

"I'm sorry I didn't warn you. It's only for a few weeks," Max said, while Lielinda and Grim distracted Nora at the table. "I have transport paid and ready to take her to another location, but I had to move Nora earlier than expected. I'll return to fetch her when I adjust her arrangements."

"Too risky. Just leave instructions about where to take her and when." Ingrihild paused and tilted her head. "Why did your timetable shift?"

"Two of Snow's half-siblings fled the kingdom. But the queen found them," Max said, his expression falling. "One was killed, but the other escaped. He made his way to a Blessed House in Caston and alerted a trusted Attuned. That Attuned contacted me because she feared Nora was no longer safe. Fortunately, the queen has important visitors, and I took advantage of her distraction. I grabbed Nora under the cover of darkness and moved through the Wildwood, barely stopping to rest."

"The queen will notice you've been gone," Snow said. Who would cover for Max the way he'd covered for his father?

Max winced. "It's a fae feast."

"That event could be a full moon cycle with those ravenous wolves. And they say dwarves are greedy." Karldorin huffed, his complaints turning into incoherent mumbling.

"Agnes will be focused on pleasing the fae. It is a good plan," Ingrihild said. "The queen must want a favor from the fae. I can only guess what."

"You must rest, Max," Wielbran insisted. "With the queen distracted, a few more hours won't matter."

"Unfortunately, the sibling that survived the queen's recent attack has gone after the king's youngest child," Max said. "His name is Ludwig, and because he's survived this long, he's under the impression that only he can protect the youngest. He would've taken Nora, but the Attuned refused. Anyway, he left only a few hours ahead of me. I think I can catch him because the Attuned gave me specific instructions on where to find the youngest child; information Ludwig doesn't have."

"There aren't many places to protect yourself from the fae's prying eyes," Karldorin grumbled.

"I don't think Ludwig realizes he's being watched with magic," Max said. "The Attuned tried to explain, but his mind was already made up—he is convinced he was sold out by dockworkers."

"Bring the young man here," Ingrihild said.

"What's one more?" Karldorin shrugged.

"Thank you," Max said, a hand to his chest.

"I'll come with you," Snow said.

Karldorin shook his head, and Wielbran placed a hand on her wrist. Not restraining her, but it drew her attention all the same. "No, little queen. Take a risk in the spring when your ring is visible. Don't throw away the kingdom's chances when you're only a few moons away."

Wielbran had never referred to her as anything other than 'Snow'. She wasn't sure what to make of it, but his words were delicate, like she was a flower to protect. But Max was exhausted and thin. He needed help. And this wasn't the dwarves' fight. She had to do it.

"I must help my family." She grabbed Max's arm, gripping it tight. He flinched as if revolted by her touch. The reaction stung, but Snow pressed on. "Promise not to leave without me."

"I agree with Wielbran," Max said. "But I do as you command."

His words were a punch to her gut, and her grip slackened. Max was distant, treating her like a vaulted queen. She didn't want him to feel obligated to her out of loyalty to a crown. Did he no longer feel tied to her as she did to him?

Swallowing the bitterness in the back of her throat, she jogged to her room. She removed the pretty comb from her hair but left the braids and changed into dark, plain trousers and a tunic. She secured her dagger against her waist and grabbed a woolen cloak, another gift from the dwarves. Before leaving her room, she stepped back, taking in her pallet bed, soft blankets, and clean clothes, feeling a warmth from the dwarven generosity. This place had become her sanctuary. But it wasn't her home.

She hurried through the cave corridor toward where Max awaited. Snow missed their past connection so much that it bruised her. They hadn't seen each other for eight moons, and it might as well have been eight years. As she entered the room, she immediately found Max in the kitchens, Wielbran helping him pack food in his satchel. She couldn't help but close the distance between herself and the huntsman out of habit, but also because she yearned to be near him. Seeing him brought up all the things she'd wanted to share with him, but they were overshadowed by the guilt and fear that he'd abandoned her. Not physically, as he was here. But emotionally, pulling back out of her reach.

Unable to control both her inner turmoil and the wall she constantly reinforced, it slipped. With her attention on Max, she felt a cold, yet prickly wall—one that hadn't been there before. A warning to stay away.

Snow could barely breathe, desperate for his touch. Wanting him to assure her—and his withholding made her want to crawl out of her skin. Where was the comforting hug, the one he'd offered too many times to count? Not one, even after the long desert of affection. Their easy friendship had been ripped away, and Snow was desperate to have it back. But she couldn't. And she knew exactly why she didn't deserve it.

"Surely the queen knows Snow couldn't have survived the Wildwood for this long. Agnes must know that Snow has taken refuge somewhere," Karldorin was saying to Max. "It's possible someone from Isolzing or the trading post recognized Snow with Grim and Runa."

"Agnes may suspect Snow is with some dwarf clan, but she wouldn't know which one," Max said. "Even if someone identified Grim and

Runa, Agnes wouldn't know where they live. But, it's only a matter of time before she starts banging down all dwarven doors."

"We'll go and warn the others," Grim said, and Runa nodded. "Starting with our parents."

"If I'm spotted away from the mountains," Snow said, "it will confuse the queen. It will benefit you if she isn't positive where I'm hiding." *Then I'll live in the Wildwood. It'll be better for everyone.*

As if sensing Snow's thoughts, Ingrihild spoke up. "When you're done with your mission, return here. We all have a vested interest in your survival now. We need you on the throne."

"I literally do not care who is on the throne as long as it's not Agnes," Karldorin grumbled.

"Snow has no loyalty other than to justice," Ingrihild said. "With humility, she can bring peace to the kingdom, which means peace for the dwarves."

As the matriarch, her word was final. Snow would return to the dwarves. But as soon as her ring was visible, she would take her fight directly to the queen.

"Well, as I cannot seem to stop you from coming along," Max said, "I insist you wear this." Using his knife, he cut his amulet from the inside of his belt. But instead of giving it to Snow, he gave it to Gertrild. "Between your arcane magic and your husband's skill in the forge, will you help me? I broke this family heirloom, but I think the Abundants had a different purpose for it. Please, turn the amulet into a bracelet for Snow."

Snow gapped, her jaw dropping. She knew what the amulet meant to Max and his family.

"I can't accept such a generous gift," Snow said.

Behind Max, Runa made a face and shook her head as if saying, 'of *course*, Snow couldn't accept it.' Despite the pin's fae origins, even the dwarves could see the magic for what it was—priceless.

"If you don't wear it, I won't bring you. *That*, I swear by, my queen," Max said.

Behind him, Runa shrugged. Snow snapped her jaw shut, unsure of what to say. Even though Max had drawn boundaries, unable or unwilling to be what he was to her in the past, he was finding new ways to support her. And Snow wouldn't refuse him. She gave a solemn nod of her head, accepting.

Wielbran cradled it carefully. "I'll do my best to make a chain and clasp of dwarven craftsmanship matching the quality of this relic."

"And I know just the spell to layer on top," Gertrild said, evaluating Snow.

As the two dwarves disappeared farther into the caves, Ingrihild insisted that Max and Snow rest. It wouldn't take the dwarves long, and soon Snow and Max would be hunting down her brother in the darkness.

CHAPTER 20: MAX

YEAR 9 OF THE MAIDEN COMET, LATE AUTUMN

The huntsman led Snow west, through the Wildwood. He had felt comfortable enough—or desperate enough—to ride his horse to the dwarves' cave this trip, but not through the pitch-black night. After two hours of careful walking, the wood stopped at the King's Road. He took a breath, knowing that, as soon as they stepped out of the Wildwood, they could be watched by an unscrupulous fae.

Maybe even Reinhold. The fae seemed to genuinely want the queen off the throne, and another fae could've given Agnes dark magic. Perhaps an unknown fae in her native kingdom. Even so, Max couldn't rule out Reinhold completely. Fae were clever, having lived for hundreds of years. Despite his distrust, Max felt obligated to tell Snow what the fae had advised.

He grabbed Snow's wrist, accidentally clasping the familiar amulet she now wore. It was the first time he'd touched her, and Snow instantly stopped. She looked at him, the moonlight streaming through the thinning trees highlighting the curve of her lips. Max focused on her eyes, but that was torture in and of itself.

"Wait," he whispered, forcing himself to drop her wrist. "I spoke to Reinhold, and he asked me to give you a message."

"This should be interesting," Snow said, drawing her cloak around herself.

"He said for you to use your fae gifting to your advantage," Max said.

"He rarely spoke to me when I lived at the castle," Snow said. "And now he wants to advise me?"

"So, you *do* have a gifting?" Max asked, deflated. Part of him had hoped Snow didn't know what he was talking about.

Snow bit her lip, her chin tilting like she did when she was deep in thought. He didn't think she was conjuring up a lie, but she might be coming up with strategic wording to hide the truth. It wouldn't be the first time.

"Never mind," Max said. "You don't have to tell me." *I'd rather not deal with more deception.*

Max stepped toward the road, and this time, Snow grabbed his sleeve.

"I didn't know that's what it was. But it makes sense. I wish Reinhold had told me." She dropped her hand away, her fingers slowly brushing the fabric in the process. "My mother *should* have told me."

Max sighed. "If your mother had told you, you'd have asked why a fae had given you, a commoner, a gifting. You were a child, and if villagers found out, questions would have followed. At the very least, they'd try to leverage your gift."

He could understand why Rosalind hadn't told Snow, just like he understood Snow's lies. But they still stung. And Max wasn't a child—he'd lost his innocence the moment his father began training him in the Wildwood.

"Max," Snow began. "I'm so sorry. About everything. I should have told you. I wish I could make it up to you, but I don't know how."

"Snow," Max turned to look at her, longing to hold her and hating that he did. "You don't owe me anything. Not even an apology."

"I promise I won't keep any more secrets," Snow said. "Unless I absolutely must."

"For the security of the kingdom?" Max tried to grin, but it felt empty.

"It's the best I can offer," Snow said, taking a small step toward him.

"Before we leave the Wildwood, if you have anything else pressing, anything you want to share," Max said, thinking of her betrothal. "We can talk here."

Snow licked her lip, leaning closer. Her presence half-drove him to madness. He straightened, wishing she'd just spit out the truth—she was engaged. He understood the necessity of political marriages. It didn't mean he liked it, but why not tell him?

"I already told you about my trips from the cave and the ring with the additional dwarven magic," Snow said softly, now so close he could feel the heat of her body. Snow reached out and gently gripped his sleeve again, the tension thick between them. Last year, he would have comforted her. An easy, familiar act in the past. But, now, his feelings had become a torture.

"Nothing else?" he asked.

Snow slowly shook her head, her attention dropping to his lips.

"We should go," Max ripped his arm from her grip and hurried across the road, his heart pounding.

In Rosewood, Max entered the nearest tavern, which was about to close for the night. With Snow's image plastered all over the kingdom, she opted to wait in the stables. The Attuned had given him the name of the city and the couple who'd adopted the youngest of the king's brood, but the town had grown, and her instructions for the location no longer applied.

"Do you know where I can find the Hohenberg household?" Max asked the man behind the bar.

The barkeep kept wiping a mug, but his brow furrowed. "You mean Lord von Hohenberg?"

Not revealing his shock, Max smoothly pulled a coin from his pocket and placed it on the counter. "The very one."

After getting directions, Max found Snow, and they warily crept down the street, avoiding drunkards and any other trouble. Snow paused at a sign outside a shop, her own face staring back at her. The notice was nailed to the wall with instructions, but this time, they were different.

"Before, the posters wanted me 'recovered', dead or alive; it wasn't specified. Now I'm in distress, and the reward has doubled. Good to know I'm increasing in value," Snow said sarcastically. "I wonder why she wants me alive, though. What changed her mind?"

"I'm guessing because of your prince. The agreement could be voided if you're never found. Contracts generally require both parties to be alive—even for a political marriage."

"A marriage?" Snow shouted. "What?"

Max paused, listening for anyone alerted to their presence and rushing toward them before continuing, his voice barely a whisper. "You know, your prince? He offered the queen a lot of coin and a valuable trade agreement for your hand in marriage."

"So, you're saying I'm worth a lot more alive than twenty gold coins," Snow's sarcasm had a bitter bite, but at least, she was quieter.

She pressed a hand to her stomach, her face hardening. Then she marched forward, Max at her side as his mind spun. He'd thought Snow knew about the agreement, but apparently not.

"Why didn't you tell me?" Snow hissed.

"How was I to know the engagement wasn't another one of your secrets?"

Snow frowned. "The king commissioned my portrait, but he died before the painting was completed. My introduction to royal families ended before it began. The queen must've sent my likeness overseas, but I doubt my father intended to marry me off without my consent." She lifted her hand and wiggled her fingers, showing off a ring only she could see. She slowed, swallowing. "I confess I suspected my father was fishing for suitors, but courting anyone was on a long list of bridges I'd cross *later*. Much later. So, I understand why you assumed I knew about the engagement. I apologize for snapping at you."

"I'm relieved to have it in the open," Max said, happier than he should've been that Snow hadn't known about Prince-Third-Son. Though, it didn't matter if he was upset or elated over the news. It was Snow's life, and it wasn't his place to give his opinion on it. Though, he'd dearly like to. Besides, she was the future queen. Once she secured her throne, every eligible bachelor in the seven kingdoms would want to court her. He was a fool for her, but not an idiot—queens didn't marry huntsmen.

Snow quietly fumed, as he navigated through the streets. He wondered if she'd ever mourned the fact that they couldn't be more than friends. Then he pushed away the selfish thoughts and envisioned strategies to put Snow on the throne after her ring appeared.

"Now that you know Reinhold is at the castle, does it change your plans?" Max asked.

"If anything, his presence will potentially help if he supports me."

"I don't trust him," Max said. "He never said why he's lurking in our realm."

"Do you think he's waiting for me to return?"

"He didn't indicate as much," Max said. "But he didn't want to talk about you. Spying fae magic in the castle and all."

"Well, he cannot oppose me. The fae council won't allow him to go against our laws, especially not one he signed. He will have to support me. I've been reading about laws, the fae, and Solinsel history, thanks to the dwarven library," Snow said, poking him in the ribs with her elbow as they jogged forward.

"Ouch!" he said, rubbing his side. "That actually hurt."

"With all my mining, I could beat you in an arm wrestle."

I'd like to put you to the test. He stopped himself from saying the words before he came dangerously close to flirting. In the past, their banter had been innocent fun, but those days were gone.

"The people will celebrate your return," Max said instead. "The queen put an extra tax on imports, which added to her treasury. So the merchants increased their prices to cover the tax. But, the people can't afford the goods they need because Agnes also added taxes on every transaction in the market. She's even taxing personal gardens; my mother had to send half her herbs and flowers to the castle. So the nobles, royals, and visiting fae eat themselves sick while everyone else starves."

"That's terrible," Snow said, hurrying faster.

"The queen spends coin on youth tonics, and she's constantly babbling to herself in her room. Her servants say she's talking to the dead king. But I think she might be talking to a fae."

"Reinhold?"

"Possibly, but she's entertained other fae since you left. It could be any of them," Max said. Hopefully, the queen was still too distracted with the current group of fae visitors to track anyone. It was certainly the largest party she'd ever hosted. "One servant said the queen was raving about you last week. She requested a crowbar. And a hammer. She made quite a racket, banging away and crying. No one dared approach her rooms."

They fell silent again, discomforted with the queen's obsession with getting rid of potential threats. But as long as Snow was hidden from fae magic, Agnes was blind. Even so, Max didn't want Snow with him on this task. Yes, she was the future queen, but he loved her. Not in the way he loved being outdoors or hunting or in the way he loved his parents. He loved Snow in everything she did and everything she was. He would spend every moment with her, never tiring of her company or her smile. But he couldn't ever be with her. Not in the way he wanted. The least he could do was protect her.

He glanced at her wrist, feeling some tiny amount of peace at knowing the amulet would protect her from metal blades.

As they turned up the walkway to a well-appointed estate, Snow gawked but didn't ask questions. It wasn't long until Snow and Max pushed their way past the steward and entered the reception room where they found a tall, disheveled man with dark hair arguing with the nobleman and his wife. The room was opulently furnished with plush chairs, ornate chandeliers, and masterful paintings on the walls. A fire crackled in the fireplace, casting flickering shadows on the walls and reflecting orange flames in the massive window that overlooked the estate.

"We've been careful," the noblewoman said. "We're not leaving."

The nobleman turned, spotting Snow and Max, and called to them, "And who are you?"

The servant began, "I'm sorry, M'Lord—"

"I'm Snow, and this is Max," Snow said. "And I think that's my half-brother. We're here to help you escape the wrath of the queen."

The man, presumably Ludwig, turned and faced them, his eyes wide with fear. "The queen's men are after me," he said, not denying that Snow was his relation, though he barely spared her a glance. "They killed my brother, and I'm next. She'll find you, too."

The von Hohenbergs looked nervous but resolute. "You're safe here tonight," the nobleman said, trying to calm everyone. "But you'll have to leave in the morning. All of you. Our son is the future lord of the estate and cannot be associated with an unseemly spectacle."

Suddenly, a howl cut through the night, sending shivers down Max's spine.

"I must check on my baby," the noblewoman gasped, stepping toward the nearby corridor.

Her husband stopped her, pulling her close, but his voice trembled. "Stay calm. Our son is old enough to train with blades."

"Blunted blades," she countered. "I must alert the night watch."

"A wolf cannot enter our home, my love," he said. "The doors are locked, and all the windows are ten feet off the ground. We'll all go to bed, and things will look better in the morning."

Another howl started low and slowly built in intensity. Max froze, horrified by the slight wavering quality of the beast's cry. It was just as the stories described.

"That's not a wolf," Snow said, her voice cracking.

"It's a Shadow Beast." Max pulled his bow from his back, notching the string.

As the howl crescendoed, it took on a keening quality, as if the creature lamented some deep sorrow. The wail subtly signaled injury or weakness, and it might've disarmed another hunter. But Max knew this was no ordinary creature—he wouldn't be tricked.

"We're going to die," the steward screamed, bolting away through the same direction they'd entered.

Snow drew her dagger, her hand trembling. The noblewoman pushed away from her husband, crying about her baby, but she stopped short of the hallway, gasping. She tripped back, falling.

In the same instant, Max noticed a dark form *in* the hallway beyond. A growl, deep and guttural, sounded from the shadows. The very foundations of the floor seemed to shake. The Shadow Beast emerged, stalking through the hall past an open window, moonlight illuminating its shimmering fur. A bald scar extended across its muzzle, wrinkling as the beast snarled and bared its razor-sharp teeth.

Max pulled back his arrow as tight as every muscle in his body. Von Hohenberg drew his sword, sliding to a stop in front of his wife, his stance wide, blocking Max's shot.

The Shadow Beast lunged, and von Hohenberg sliced his sword through the air, anticipating its path. And missing the beast, completely. The creature's attention was focused on Snow's brother, and the creature easily maneuvered past the blade. Snow threw her dagger, but the angle was ineffective, and it bounced off the fur and clattered to the floor. Max took aim with his bow and let loose an arrow, striking the Shadow Beast in the hip, the metal sinking into the flesh. The beast roared and turned its attention to Max.

Max had already put himself between Snow and the beast, careful not to look directly into the beast's glowing, red eyes, thanks to Snow's research. Unless that information was wrong. Which would be bad because it would be very helpful to look directly at the beast about now. He took another shot, this time hitting the beast below the shoulder. The beast stumbled but was far from incapacitated.

Snow's brother grabbed a nearby candelabrum and charged, swinging the paltry flames at the Shadow Beast. On impact, the candles tumbled, and the weapon bounced off the creature as if it had hit a stone wall. The beast shifted and kicked Ludwig with a paw, sending him flying across the room. The smell of singed fur stung Max's nose, but the beast didn't falter. The nobleman moved to strike the Shadow Beast with his sword, but he was too slow, and like a child's stick, the beast batted the sword out of his hand.

The trajectory sent the sword flying through the air—toward Snow.

Instinctively, Max moved to tackle her to the ground, but as he did, the blade cut across Snow's back. She cried out and stiffened, her eyes wide with fear, knowing the blade had struck. Max's momentum took him and Snow to the floor next to the Lord's sword. In the firelight, he saw the blade was bloodless. He grabbed her wrist, her amulet under his fingers.

"You're okay," he assured himself as much as Snow. "The magic."

Snow blinked, her breathing fast and shallow.

Max rolled off of her, grabbing his bow and an arrow, just as Ludwig smashed a chair against the side of the creature's face. The Shadow Beast roared, shaking the room. A framed portrait clattered onto the floor. The creature shook its head, dazed. Seeing the opening he needed, Max fired another arrow, hitting the Shadow Beast in the chest. A perfect shot.

The beast let out a howl of pain and fled toward the corridor where he'd first appeared, but the huntsman wasn't done yet. He shot one more arrow, hitting the Shadow Beast in the back. The beast yowled, but this time, it was different. The beast spun and faced Max and Snow. A crimson line stained its chest. Instead of retreating the way it had come, the creature raced toward them.

Max braced for a direct assault his dagger in hand. But the creature leapt over them both to its quickest escape route. In an exquisite shattering of glass, the beast crashed through the massive window revealing the moonlit gardens beyond, bounding away, leaving the room filled with only the sounds of heavy breathing and the crackling of the fire.

Max turned back to find Snow curled up on the floor, her face pale as she stared, unfocused.

"Snow is in shock," Max said, sliding on a knee next to her. "Bring a blanket!" Snow's breathing was too quick. Of course she'd be in shock. She'd been attacked by a Shadow Beast as a child. The sights and sounds of one of these creatures were forever linked to her mother's death.

"She was struck with a sword," the nobleman said, his voice tight, but seemingly unharmed, as was his wife. "I'll send for a healer, but I don't know how much can be done."

The noblewoman rushed off, probably to her baby, shouting for her servants and household guards. The attack was over before they'd even had a chance to respond.

"The blade didn't strike her," Max said, wiping the sweat from his forehead. The blade had passed through Snow as if she wasn't even there.

The nobleman neared and picked up his blade. "Odd. From my angle . . . Well, never mind. I'll have the servants bring you whatever you need. I must check on my family."

"Thank you," Snow whispered to Max.

Snow's brother approached, limping, and a hand pressed against his back. "I worked for a healer for a short time. Let's take Snow closer to the fire, and I'll evaluate her. You'll need to calm her down while I fetch a few things."

"You're the healer," Max said. "Maybe you should help her. I can find whatever you need."

"She doesn't know me," he said. "Clearly, you're friends. Talk to her. Calm her. It's the best thing for her right now."

Max went to scoop up Snow when a shooting pain coursed through his leg. Fortunately, Snow's brother steadied Max and helped carry Snow across the room.

"Your trouser is torn," Ludwig said to Max as they settled Snow on a lounge near the fireplace. "I think you caught the tip of the Shadow Beast's claw. I'll get supplies from the kitchen to stop infection. Assuming the queen hasn't taxed the pantry down to the spider webs. I'm Ludwig, by the way."

"I'm Max Hunt, the royal huntsman."

Ludwig's attention fell to the gold chain with the amulet on Snow's wrist. In the firelight, Max noticed the tiny dwarven markings etched into the metal chain, though they would merely look like scratches from wear to the casual observer.

Snow's brother raised a brow. "Well-well, have you got a story to tell? Another time, perhaps." Ludwig jogged off toward a servant entering with a blanket, calling back over his shoulder. "Then again, the queen could have another assassin at the gate, and we won't live until dawn."

The servant threw the blanket to Max before running after Ludwig, redirecting him so he'd actually find the kitchen. Ignoring the warmth that oozed down his leg, Max tenderly tucked the blanket around Snow, telling her how brave she was and what a good job she'd done. He kept his words soft, but he positioned his back to the wall, watching the entrances, keeping his weapons at the ready. Mid-sentence, Snow reached up and grabbed his hand, and a warmth ran up his arm. Snow pressed her lips together into a hard line and blinked back tears.

Fighting through the searing pain in his leg, he scooped Snow up and held her against his chest, stroking her hair away from her face. As he held Snow, her body softened, and her breathing deepened. She trembled and tucked in closer, one of her hands gripping his. He brushed away a silent tear with his other hand as it tracked down her cheek. The moment both broke him and brought him resolve. Keeping his distance from Snow for the next five moons until her nineteenth birthday would be brutal. But he would use that time to move past his feelings. They were of no use to him, especially when Snow still needed him—so very heart-wrenchingly close.

CHAPTER 21:
SNOW

YEAR 9 OF THE MAIDEN COMET, LATE AUTUMN

B ack in the dwarves' cave, between her shock and the exhaustion of the endeavor, Max's goodbyes blurred by too quickly. No hug. No squeezing her hand. Just a formal bow at the cave entrance.

Snow sensed his loyalty, but his heart was shut. Why wouldn't he after all the secrets she'd kept from him—but still it pained her. She stared at the door long after he left, feeling like half her heart had been ripped away. Having him back for a day should have eased her ache, but instead, it only intensified her longing to be near him. She fiddled with the amulet he'd given her and consoled herself that she'd only have to suffer through the winter before Max returned. And then, for better or for worse, everything would change.

A few days later, Snow sat on a couch, trying to ignore Ludwig pacing the floor behind her. She wasn't the only one. Grim meditated on a mat, his back to them all. And Lielinda relaxed on the floor with Nora, both engrossed in building a tower made out of translucent marble blocks and tiles. Runa plopped down next to Snow, striking up a conversation.

"Feeling better?" she asked.

Snow realized she was pressing a hand to her belly. Yes, she was still upset about seeing the Shadow Beast, but the nausea that had appeared the day of Lielinda's Name Giving still lingered. It wasn't nearly as bad as the previous bouts, so Snow didn't mention it.

"Yes," Snow said.

"You're just sulking about Max, then," Runa teased.

"What?"

"Don't think I haven't noticed the way you look at him."

"Like a lost puppy," Grim piped up.

Runa threw a pillow at his head, her aim perfect.

"You're ruining my concentration!" Grim said sarcastically.

Ludwig finally sat in a cushioned chair across from Snow, but his leg bounced up and down as his heel tapped the floor. Snow had taken to heart Reinhold's advice and had tried lowering her inner defenses, allowing herself to feel others. Ludwig was a ball of nerves, the very opposite of the dwarven family. She hadn't recognized the calming influence of the dwarves until she'd spent time around her half-brother. He'd been on edge since arriving.

"Ludwig," Grim said, getting to his feet. "If you're feeling up to it, please tell us more about yourself."

Ludwig bit his thumbnail but then spoke. "I didn't grow up like our youngest brother. No fancy estate. No adoptive parents."

Snow swallowed, feeling his bitterness swell. Unaware of Ludwig's building anger, Grim nodded, signaling his support.

"We shall see if the von Hohenbergs' coin will save them from the queen," Ludwig said. "Fools."

The von Hohenbergs had blamed Ludwig for bringing the Shadow Beast to their door, and they refused to leave. Snow didn't need to sense them to recognize panic and disbelief.

"You told them the truth," Runa said. "Deep down, they must know you're right. And, your brother's family has resources—he isn't alone."

"Alone like me?" Ludwig chuckled darkly. "Actually, I was raised with a sister. Of all the king's children, we are the only two full-blooded siblings. Our mother was the king's favorite—before Rosalind." He gave Snow a pointed look.

Snow fidgeted, not liking where the conversation was going. Their father's actions were not her own. But compassionate queens needed to listen to hard words. Besides, Ludwig was her brother. He was allowed complicated feelings. And he'd helped her after the attack in Rosewood; he and Max had worked together to transport Snow back to Darkstone Mountains.

"I'm sorry to hear Rosalind was killed when you were a child," Ludwig continued. "But, at least, the king sent for you. My tutor gave me a note, a warning from my mysterious benefactor. Though, I knew it was the king. My mother revealed his identity to my sister and me before a stranger appeared and moved us away. Little good it did us in the end."

Snow extrapolated that his sister was the sibling just older than herself, and Max had seen her alive. So Heinrich's strategy actually did help safeguard them. But Snow let her brother fume—he was understandably mourning the loss of a half-sibling Snow had never known.

Changing the subject, Snow turned to Runa. "Did you find out what these markings mean?"

Snow had asked Gertrild and Wielbran, but they had simply replied, "Strength." Snow easily sensed that they were keeping something back.

And of course, she'd asked Runa. But Runa and Grim only knew the basics of archaic dwarven magic runes. Whatever Gertrild had designed was much more advanced.

Runa winked at Grim, who was preparing food. He nodded and pulled a book out from inside a kitchen pot. Grim tossed the tome to his sister, both of them grinning like mischievous fools. Runa flipped through the pages, settling on one. Looking repeatedly from Snow's bracelet chain to the book, Runa pressed her finger next to a passage on the page.

"This rune is interesting because our uncle engraved the symbol on both the amulet and the chain, across the welding bond. It says 'strength'," Runa said. "It's strengthening the bond but uses a root variation meaning 'health'."

"An interesting choice," Grim said, chopping carrots at the counter.

"That symbol is engraved on both sides where the amulet attaches to the chain." Runa shut the book.

"Did you learn anything else?" Snow asked. She had pointed out another word in the middle of the chain to Runa, runes she'd missed until the day before.

Runa fiddled with Snow's bracelet, sliding it until the discrete etching was next to her thumb. "That's all I've discovered so far."

Ludwig spoke up, "You are fortunate."

"Is she?" Runa said, her tone challenging.

"The king took her into his own home," Ludwig said.

"You call that fortunate?" Runa snapped back. "Seems like Snow was brought within striking distance of the queen's fangs."

"The Abundants smile on her," Ludwig said, his irritation growing. "She found you dwarves, didn't she?"

The dwarves had been more than accommodating to Snow, especially considering the queen's relentless hunt. If Agnes found Snow,

Nora, or Ludwig in Darkstone, the dwarves would suffer. Snow's guilt flared.

With Snow's own troubled heart to contend with, the worry that emanated from Nora and the dwarves, plus the pounding anger from Ludwig . . . the storm of feelings escalated. Either the growing emotional toll or the attack in Rosewood unleashed long-buried memories of her childhood. Her mistakes from misusing her gift haunted her, and the amplified sensitivities rolling off others threatened to drown her again.

Beyond herself and her crumbling wall, Snow sensed a turbulent sea of emotions—a cacophony of pain. And it frightened her. So she stayed within what she could endure, not venturing for fear of being sucked into a riptide, knowing she could not take a drop more of emotion. For the witch's spell, Snow shouldn't feel grateful.

Yet she did.

She understood Ludwig's pain, but even so, she wouldn't be rush matting at an entrance, woven to absorb dirt and emotional detritus for everyone else's comfort.

"The king moved all of us after my mother was murdered," Snow pointed out, keeping calm but direct. "That's when our father realized something was amiss. He tried to hide us *all* in safe places."

Snow didn't take kindly to anyone speaking poorly of Heinrich's efforts. Yes, he acted on the king's orders, but Ludwig couldn't understand the risk the huntsman had taken to protect them all. And now Max shouldered that burden.

"I heard something about you," Ludwig said to Snow.

Next to her, Runa narrowed her eyes at him as if daring him to say another offense. Grim paused his chopping at the table.

"I'm sure you've heard many things about me," Snow said.

She sensed something beyond Ludwig's bitterness—jealousy. Had he heard about her fae gifting? From what she knew about the fae, Snow's endowment was a rare gift. The other children were unlikely to have recieve one. But only Max and Reinhold knew about it. Or were there others?

"Why did our father make *you* the heir to his throne?" he asked.

"You think the king should have selected you?" Runa asked.

Runa stood, and Grim gripped the knife, his attention darting from Ludwig to his sister. Dwarves didn't need weapons to be dangerous—compared to humans, they were three times stronger. Or more. Across the room, Lielinda and Nora had stopped to stare at the devolving conversation.

"Why would you think Snow was the heir?" Grim asked, his brow furrowing.

Lielinda flushed and dropped her head, a curtain of hair hiding her face.

"I just want to know what makes Snow special?" he asked.

Runa started, "As if you—"

"Nothing makes me special," Snow interrupted. "I'm not better than anyone else. Not necessarily." Snow didn't mention their sister, the king's first choice. Ludwig had never been considered, not according to Heinrich. But telling her brother would only hurt him.

"We both had tutors," Ludwig said, his anger still taut. "I have life experience. Wisdom. The crown doesn't necessarily go to the firstborn in Solinsel, but my age should count for something. Yet, the king chose you. Why?"

"I never asked for this," Snow said. "But I assure you, I will strive to be a good queen."

"Will you fight against your sister?" Runa asked. "Or support her?"

"I wish you'd just told me," Ludwig said. For the first time, Snow sensed a flash of sadness.

"I would have when the time was right," Snow said honestly.

He nodded. "I know you trained at Clarus to entertain fae and many other things."

Snow wasn't sure she wanted to hear more of Ludwig's thoughts, but she didn't interrupt.

"One of the older siblings would've been a better candidate," he said. "You're the convenient choice. Typical for King Friedrich, so I'm not surprised."

Grim dropped his knife and began to march toward Ludwig until Snow stopped him with a warning look. Ludwig was her brother. Her fight.

"However," Ludwig continued, his expression darkening. "The queen must suffer for what she did to our brother. She has relentlessly destroyed our lives. I will not just support you. I will fight by your side."

"And when this is over?" Runa asked. "And Snow sits on the throne?"

"Snow can have the throne," he said, and Snow felt his resolve, his bitterness, his hatred rise to a boil. "It is built on filth and dark magic. I want nothing to do with it."

Ludwig stood, looking down on Snow where she sat, and he stormed off into the mines.

"If we don't go find him, he'll be lost in the caves for days," Grim said, continuing to chop. "A bit of hunger might humble him, don't you think?"

Runa rolled her eyes, "He needs at *least* a week to meditate. It'll be good for him."

Snow barely listened to their banter because she realized Ludwig didn't hate her. His words were a deflection because, deeper down, he felt an unexpected kinship with Snow. The person he hated was the king, their father. Snow had endured all the painful emotions until she uncovered more—feelings closer to the core truth of why Ludwig lashed out.

As discomforting as wading through her brother's emotions had been, she had done what Reinhold had suggested. And she'd survived.

CHAPTER 22: MAX

YEAR 10 OF THE MAIDEN COMET, WINTER

Thick snow accumulated on the mountaintop, and the queen summoned servants to escort her to the valley for a horseback ride. Because the forest floor merely had a dusting in most places, her servants indicated the queen would likely ride for hours. The guard's uniform Max had worn the last time he snuck into the dungeons had been whisked away, but he was desperate for news from his father. While the queen was distracted, Max tracked down a guard on the lower level, an old family friend, at the dungeon's entrance.

"He's alive but weak," the guard said, not relaxing her stance.

Max handed her a bread roll from his own ration. Quick as a whip, she stole it into her pocket. The guards ate well, but their families only fared marginally better than everyone else. All the guards could do was keep their heads down, follow orders, and hope to avoid the queen's notice.

"Would you like me to give Heinrich a message?" she asked.

"Tell him we miss him. And not to lose hope," Max said, wishing he could give his father more. He was scheduled to hang in merely four moons.

"I will," she said, a note of sympathy in her voice.

Max's leg ached as he traversed the dungeons, winding his way toward the stairs to the servant's level of the castle. He'd hidden his limp and had not mentioned his injury amongst the servants, not wanting to draw attention. He'd been to a healer in Caston, without sharing his name, hoping for a remedy. After weeks of treatment, nothing helped, and Max stopped going when the healer grew suspicious of the wound.

Moisture seeped onto his trouser leg, and he limped along, breathing hard. He was far more concerned about his father's health in the damp dungeons than his throbbing calf. If the people were hungry, the prisoners were starving. When Snow became queen, she'd enforce humane conditions, though it brought Heinrich no relief at the moment. More importantly, she'd rescue his father from an unjust penalty. If Snow wasn't successful, Max would lose both his father and his best friend. And his own life, too, as he would undoubtedly be caught helping her.

Distracted, Max took a wrong turn. With only a few tiny windows and the heavy cloud cover outside, the lower floor was dim, and Max couldn't find his way back to the main stairs. The stones in this area were smaller and rougher cut with thick, bumpy mortar between them. An older part of the castle perhaps. He wandered fruitlessly, his concern mounting.

A sinister feeling slithered across his skin, and he soon passed by a narrow staircase that wound to a lower level. Max hurried past, feeling like the icy fingers of death chased after him. He forced himself to slow, taking a deep breath, attempting to calm his racing heart. He couldn't allow paranoia to rule his mind. He'd never escape without notice unless he stayed sharp.

Pressing forward, he realized the older corridor ended, running into a perpendicular hallway. He recognized the smoother stonework of the intersecting hall, and the tightness in his shoulders relaxed.

Guards' footsteps approached from the left, the direction Max needed to go. Wanting to avoid trouble, Max retreated to the old stairwell and hid, waiting for the guards to pass. He'd spent little time in the lower level, and he was grateful he'd found an exit; he just needed to exercise patience and ignore the way the hairs on his arms were standing on end.

The guards picked up their pace as they neared the intersection, and Max's heartbeat increased. He stilled, reminding himself that he couldn't be seen unless they turned into this older portion of the castle and actually explored the stairwell. The guards passed the entrance to the older hallway and slowed to their normal pace. Were the guards avoiding the area Max was hiding in? Why?

Max's leg throbbed, and his instinct was to flee the derelict old coffin. This place reeked of danger. After his injury from the Shadow Beast, he couldn't afford another mishap. But, Snow couldn't afford any fetid surprises held inside the bowels of the castle. Refusing to be frightened off by the creepy atmosphere, Max gritted his teeth and stepped down the spiraling stairs. Yes, it was foolish, but it was necessary. This vile corner that even the guards avoided needed to be explored.

Besides, he felt helpless most of the time, like a performer on a stage with a mysterious witch as his potential audience. With the queen currently riding along with a horse trainer and a servant, Max couldn't pass up the opportunity to do spying of his own.

The heavy scent of burning herbs and pungent potions alerted him to the alchemy lab long before he reached it. The room was illuminated only by a guttering torch and jars filled with glowing substances. A cauldron sat on embers, a film of slime left along the edge. Shelves lined the walls, heavy with glass jars and bottles, each labeled in a mysterious language. Tables choked the room, cluttered with various implements, including a mortar and pestle, a decanter of wine, a worn doll wearing a dress, and an array of knives and scalpels.

But no dust.

The foreboding atmosphere and foul odors clearly marked this as a witch's lab. A fae didn't need these tools to cast spells. But a human did.

Witches went against the natural order of the Abundants, humans imbued with fae magic. But even a witch needed training and accouterments of their craft to create magic. This place confirmed Max's suspicions that a masterful witch with coin was behind everything, and she resided inside the castle: the queen. Perhaps Reinhold had given the queen magic, believing he was doing the king a favor, and now the fae regretted it. Guilt might explain why he hadn't left for the fae realm.

Having seen more than enough to unsettle him, Max turned to leave. As he did, he noticed a tree in the corner, an eerie green light cascading from a hanging glass jar onto the plant. Deprived of true sunlight, the tree grew at awkward angles, the branches twisted. Careful not to bump anything, Max moved closer, near enough to recognize the bark—an apple tree. Surely it was too sickly to produce fruit. Perhaps it had been healthy enough once, but it didn't even have leaves anymore.

From where he stood, he realized the green light was actually centered on another pot next to the dying tree—a thin apple tree growing from the soil. It was small, but not necessarily unhealthy. Just young, less than two years old. Without touching anything, Max shifted and inspected the larger tree more carefully. Stretching to look at the back, he discovered a deep gash in the trunk, almost cutting it in half, about as wide as his thumb and as deep as his hand. A sap-like substance had settled at the bottom as if its defenses had attempted to stem the wound but lost. Up close, he couldn't help but catch a whiff of the overly sweet scent.

Max's stomach roiled, and he jerked back away from the dying plant. Whatever the queen was doing, he had more than enough proof to condemn her. He tip-toed up the winding stairs, pieces of the puzzle coming together. The queen was a witch. She was well-practiced with spells and potions. Was her beauty a glamour? She could have entrapped the king, knowing his weakness for attractive women.

Ignoring the pain in his leg, he hobbled up the stairs and rushed in the direction the guards had departed. Orienting himself, Max found his way out of the dungeon, racing to alert the high judge. She'd maintained her distance, but this information was too important to keep to himself.

As he made his way to the judge's chambers, doubts about Reinhold's involvement began to grow. Witches could bargain for magic from any willing fae, though if their fae council discovered the depraved action, the guilty fae would be punished. Cast out. Reinhold was unfeeling toward humanity, even for a fae, but he seemed to genuinely care for the king. Max couldn't picture him betraying his Bonded's trust.

Furthermore, from what Max knew of fae, they wouldn't blink at getting rid of a pesky witch who might threaten their lifestyle rather than risk discovery. The queen was sloppy, going mad and ruining Solinsel. If an influential human made a fuss about the situation, like a high judge, the fae would have reason to investigate. Would Reinhold take that chance? Reinhold had just completed a fae milestone in concluding his Bond with a royal human. No fae would jeopardize newfound status and power. Frankly, Reinhold would've killed the queen the same hour the king died rather than risk losing power. Whoever the queen garnered magic from, it wasn't Reinhold.

At High Judge Helene's door, Max knocked. A man's voice bade him enter. Inside was a stranger wearing the robes of a high judge.

"Who are you?" Max asked, wondering for a moment if he'd entered the wrong room. The shelves were half empty, and a box sat on the desk.

"I'm the new high judge," the man said in a lightly accented voice. "You must be the royal huntsman. Can I help you?"

"Um," Max fumbled for an excuse; the pain reverberating through his leg made quick thinking difficult. "I wanted to ask about land use, but I'll return when you're settled."

Max hurried away, straining to hide his limp as he walked among the merchants, courtiers, and servants. *What happened to Helene?* He hadn't thought it prudent to ask a judge, whom Max didn't know or trust. Max dimly heard the princess call his name, and he pivoted as she hurried up from behind him. He bowed and apologized for not paying attention.

"It looks like you're moving around better. Is your leg healed?" Her smile faded. "What's wrong? You look like you've seen a wraith."

"Did you know that High Judge Helene has been replaced?" he asked.

Her face darkened. "The queen sent her away. A sudden move. It's been kept quiet, but the judge's replacement took over Helene's duties last week. His family is close with Agnes's, though he's lived in Caston for years. Agnes has him wrapped around her finger."

Perhaps Agnes's family knew she was a witch. Helped her with these elaborate plans. Overtaking a kingdom was much easier when the attack came quietly from within. Almost without shedding a drop of blood. Almost. With Agnes and the High Judge loyal to another kingdom, they'd nearly reached their goal.

"That's concerning," was all Max said, keeping his conspiracy to himself.

"I'm worried, too. Our people starve while Agnes and her associate lose coin like water between their fingers."

A realization dawned. Without the judge, Snow had no papers to prove she was the heir. The queen had undoubtedly destroyed any evidence of Snow's lineage.

"I'm sorry, princess," Max said, knowing he was acting very rudely, "I have to go. I don't feel well."

When Snow returned, everything would hinge on her ring—it was the only proof that she was the true heir to her father's throne.

Max waited each night that Dottie cooked one of Reinhold's favorite meals. In the darkness of the vacant kitchen, as the winter winds made the shutters rattle, the huntsman began worrying his plan wouldn't work a second time. Fortunately, fae loved the power that came from food more than they feared interloping humans.

"I need you to heal my leg," Max said as soon as Reinhold flitted through the fireplace one night.

Reinhold didn't bother to respond until he'd landed near the caramel cakes. "Why would I help you?"

"Because this injury is a result of rescuing the king's youngest child," Max said.

Reinhold was bound to the king in life, but how deep did that loyalty go? Would Reinhold do a favor for someone who had assisted the king's child? The fae kept his back to Max and glutted himself on the cake. After what felt like an hour, Reinhold turned, fluttered from the table, and transformed into his larger form, towering over Max. If he was trying to act imposing, it was working. Without taking his eyes off the fae, Max lifted his pant leg, revealing his red, swollen calf, and the ugly black slash.

"A Wildwood creature," Max said, leaving it at that.

Reinhold paused then flicked his wrist, and a wand appeared in his hand. The fae ran it over Max's leg, never touching the limb, but his leg burned as if he'd been branded. Max cried out in surprise before biting back his scream. The pain left him sweating. When he dared look back at his leg, the wound was closed but redder than a cooked beet.

"Magic responds to magic," Reinhold said, "I've removed what little was there, which will allow your leg to heal now. Next time, go to a healer who deals in magic."

"Can't humans only deal in dark magic?" Max asked, revolted at the thought.

"Correct. But did I specify a *human*? No, I did not. Many magical creatures can create healing elixirs. Brownies are often generous with their talents." Reinhold muttered something about 'this backwater kingdom' but didn't expound.

"I appreciate your help," Max said, careful not to say the troublesome words 'thank you' to a fae.

"No one can object to me removing a bit of thorny magic, but don't call on me again." Reinhold stepped back and grabbed another cake. He took a bite as he sauntered across the kitchen, his head held high.

"The king has been gone a long time," Max said, speaking before the fae reached the chimney. Reinhold stopped short, glaring a warning at Max. Still, Max continued. "I can't help but hope you might be waiting for *her* to appear . . . with her ring. She needs you." Max couldn't imagine another reason a fae would remain in the realm for so long.

"Your wound festered because it was caused by magic. Now you have an inkling about what I'm suffering." He paused, his face twisting in displeasure. "But you are an ant trying to understand a giant—you have no idea how it feels for a fae, in all our greatness, to be trapped."

Reinhold spun, transforming into his natural form, and disappeared up the flue, out of sight.

CHAPTER 23: SNOW

YEAR 10 OF THE MAIDEN COMET, SPRING

Snow awoke in her dwarven room, wondering if this spring morning was the one when her ring would finally appear. Though her return to Clarus was fraught with dangers, she was anxious to plead her case. After her morning ablutions, Snow grabbed her pickaxe and prepared to sweat off her building anxiety. In the kitchen, Snow and Runa sat down with nuts and dried fruit while Grim meditated nearby. While they breakfasted, Runa quizzed Snow on trade at the ports and sea routes to the northern kingdoms, nodding encouragingly when Snow answered correctly.

"Thank you for tutoring me." Snow's knowledge of trade had grown tremendously.

"Well, if you asked me which petty nobles not to irritate, I'd have no idea," Runa shrugged.

"I struggled so much at Clarus, even learning basic commerce," Snow said. "You're a great teacher."

Grim snorted but didn't open his eyes.

"Literally, no one has ever said that before." Runa laughed. "I don't know what tutors your father found for you, but they were terrible." Runa checked over her shoulder and then lowered her voice. "I snuck into my grandmother's personal library last night while she was eating supper. I finally found the archaic magical word my aunt used on your chain."

All lingering sleepiness vanished, and Snow sat up straighter.

"So, the 'shield' symbol my aunt and uncle added to your ring specifically hides you from all fae. But the amulet's chain marking is different." Runa pointed to the tiny engraving. "This symbol means 'illumination,' and it repels dark fae magic with old dwarven magic. And this extra line allows the marking to combine with another spell."

"With the 'strength' rune across the weld?" Snow asked.

"That's my guess," Runa said.

"Meaning she has no idea," Grim interjected.

Runa rolled her eyes, but then sobered as her fingers grazed the amulet itself. The *fae-made* charm. "All I know for certain, is the rune magic is built on top of another spell. Not impenetrable—don't act like a brazen fool—it's a layer of armor."

"Are we talking boiled leather or black metal chainmail?" Grim asked.

Before Runa could snap back a retort, Nora shuffled inside, dragging a fluffy blanket behind her. Grim opened an eye and offered to fix breakfast for Nora. But, of course, she sidled next to Snow instead. Nora picked off Snow's plate, which didn't bother her as she barely had any appetite anyway.

"Oh!" Nora tilted her head. "Who gave you a ring?"

"What ring?" Ludwig asked, entering the common area.

"Um . . ." Runa said, sharing a look with her brother. "Happy Birthday?"

Ludwig's eyes grew wide, and he ran to inspect the king's signet on Snow's finger. The symbol of her destiny officially called her to action.

"It's time," he said, his tone somber.

Within the hour, Runa and Grim rode to the trading post, a missive for Max in hand.

While awaiting the huntsman's arrival, Snow's generous friends presented her with another gift: a blue satin gown fit for a queen. The sleeves puffed into rolls, which were slit to allow the fine white underdress to peek through. Tiny stitched pearls weighed down the fabric, and a high collar framed her neck.

Snow couldn't fathom the expense, but Ingrihild insisted that appearing like she owned the palace would help her secure it; Snow would be taken more seriously in the robes of royalty rather than in servant's aprons. Now she was ready to present herself to the high judge, the captain of the guard, and the people.

After six days of waiting, nerves bubbled to the surface when Karldorin signaled Max had arrived. Unable to afford distraction, Snow ignored Reinhold's advice and reinforced her walls before she laid eyes on him.

Max's face was determined despite the dark circles under his eyes. He greeted Snow with a stiff bow, his quiver strapped to his back and his hunting knife at his side. Grim and Runa updated him on the dwarven security within Darkstone Mountains. The clans were waiting, supportive of a mystery heir attempting to take the throne but wary of the queen and her dark powers. Snow was tempted to pry for Max's feelings, but he deserved his privacy.

While the dwarves packed Snow's food for the journey, Max took her aside, though still close enough for Grim and Runa to hear and weigh in. In the semi-privacy, Snow found herself unable to take her eyes off Max, and she was grateful she'd closed herself off. She could barely stave off her own rising emotions, let alone someone else's.

"The High Judge has been replaced," Max confessed. "And your paperwork is lost. But Reinhold is at Clarus. He may aid you. Either way, with Elisabeth's word and your ring, you can secretly approach the captain of the guard and openly approach the new High Judge. With your ring, he can't refuse an audience with you in front of the court. You'll have a chance to tell your story."

Without the high judge's papers, her ring was her only physical link to the crown. Her plan was shifting before she even left the cave.

Max continued, "The captain will side with you, and so will the nobles. They're finally realizing that the trials of the commoners matter to their own well-being. And the high taxes on their estates aren't winning the queen any favors."

"It's frightening how quickly a ruler can push a kingdom into ruin," Snow said, reflecting on her own weaknesses.

Max grabbed her hand, his palm calloused and rough, and warm . . . so warm. Despite herself, she felt comforted by his touch. He pulled her out of the common room and across the bridge toward the entrance.

"You'll be a good leader." Max's voice was low, and the heat of his words brushed her skin.

Snow shivered at the upheaval of emotion within her. She tried not to notice the curve of his lips, nor the shadow of a beard growing on his chiseled jaw. How had he gotten more attractive? But she reminded herself to focus on the kingdom she needed to protect . . . and the queen who would happily kill anyone who tried.

Squaring her shoulders, Snow said wryly, "I can't be any worse than Agnes."

Max cocked his head to the side, his eyes narrowing. "Snow, something's off. What's wrong?"

"Nothing." Snow's ire flared. Why was he prodding into her personal insecurities? "It's not that I'm carrying the weight of the kingdom on my shoulders."

Max rubbed his thumb and forefinger across his tired eyes. Then he stared at her, and the moment stretched—as he took his measure of her—and his lips pulled into a frown. "Snow . . ."

Snow's mouth dried, and she dropped her chin. When she'd allowed herself to feel Ludwig, she had seen into corners of his heart and mind that she hadn't expected. But it had cost her. She hesitated to allow herself to feel that much again when it wasn't absolutely necessary.

Max tapped her chin, and her gaze shot up.

"I know when you're lying," he said plainly. Sadly. His face etched with worry and sorrow and . . . *pain*? "Even to yourself."

If she were to face down Agnes, Snow could not be weak. She needed mental clarity. She had to save her strength for that fight. Or was she just hiding from Max? Either way, didn't he deserve to know her truth? She'd kept too much from him in the past, and meanwhile, he'd done everything to protect her even after he learned how dangerous it was to align with her—to befriend the illegitimate daughter of a dead king.

The confession fell from her lips. "I . . . I feel *too much*."

She blinked up at Max, stunned that she'd revealed even this small sliver of truth. And somehow . . . she felt lighter.

"What do you mean 'too much'?" Max asked. His question held no judgment, nor did his eyes. No. In fact, while he still radiated all the intensity of a true huntsman, his expression softened as he continued to focus on her. He quirked a brow at her, questioning.

How much could she share?

If there was anyone she could completely trust—even more than herself—it was Max.

"I did what Reinhold suggested, but it drains me." Snow had kept her wall up and pulled it down with precision for years. She'd controlled it.

Hadn't she?

Snow bit her lip, readying her admission. "And honestly, I can't bring myself to completely lower my defenses. I haven't done that since I was a child. For good reason." She didn't remember everything from her childhood, but she remembered drowning in emotions, unable to breathe, and flooded with negativity. Snow shuddered at the memory. The shallow snippets she'd felt from the dwarves and her half-siblings were already challenging to bear.

Or had she never opened herself enough to actually understand the nuances? The intentions behind the emotions? How often had she misread a situation because she was too closed off? Her wall too thick?

Her real insights emerged when she allowed her instincts to influence her. Allowing emotions in.

How helpful would her gift be in detecting liars? How much more beneficial was a ruler who sensed when judges grew overwrought? Or if a guard silently suffered from melancholia? Her gifting could aid her in restoring her kingdom.

If Snow wanted to rule effectively, she needed more than an occasional slip of insight.

But *fear* kept her back.

As Snow reflected, she prodded the wall of bricks around her. Logically, this was her safe place. Concentrating, she heard the crashing of an emotional ocean in the distance, but the tumult was beyond her reach.

"The witch." Snow didn't explain. Max didn't demand more. He just waited as Snow frantically unraveled her thoughts, talking through her suspicions. "Her spell served me as a child, kept me safe, but I was never able to understand myself—never able to explore my magic."

Snow hadn't fully used her magic since she'd been a child. She wasn't even sure she could overcome the witch's spell and fully drop her walls. Something like that would take time and practice. And perhaps light fae magic. But the dawn of her return was here. She'd hidden from discomfort, wasting precious time. She was too late.

As realization dawned, Snow crumbled. Max braced her, keeping her upright. Without words, his piercing green eyes searched her face, reflecting his concern. Heat seeped from his palm to her back, and something about his small physical support helped her continue on.

"My gifting," Snow whispered. "I think it's too late."

"Your gift is feeling?" Max asked, his hand dropping from her back.

Her skin prickled as if an icy wind had blown over her. "Emotions, yes."

He flashed a half-grin, though there was no mirth in it. "I think . . . I've known for a long time." He glanced back at the bridge, but the walkway remained empty. Then he faced her, his expression hardening as he forced a swallow. "Then you must start practicing." He squared his shoulders. "On me."

"Max," Snow said, a mixture of terror and eager anticipation mixing inside her. After everything they'd been through, what would she find? Regret? Dutiful devotion? Something more? Did she really want to know? "I couldn't. Wouldn't."

"Snow," he sighed. His expression turned weary, but behind the exhaustion, his eyes were lit from within. For some strange reason, he was determined to have her do this, regardless of what it cost him. "It's for the good of the kingdom," he reasoned.

He was right, but what would it cost them both?

"Do it."

Snow's stomach clenched, but she would trust him. He'd never failed her before. He shared his books, his parents, and his home from the moment they'd met. He'd made sure she felt included. Listened like her words mattered. Let her know she was needed. Wanted.

Closing her eyes, Snow delved deep within herself, her thoughts like murky waters obscuring her path. As she navigated the labyrinth of her own mind, she felt the weight of the wall that guarded her gift. Trembling, she extended her hand, gripping the closest brick.

Max took her hand, his warmth and steadiness reassuring her that, whatever she found, their friendship would survive this. His grounding presence infused her with security, but would that be enough?

Snow took a breath, squeezing her eyes shut even tighter. She felt lost, trapped within the spell's hold, unsure of where to begin. Her last attempts had overwhelmed her and ended in failure. She had no idea how to rid herself of a spell, but she knew she could dismantle the walls, at least partly, brick by brick. Determined to try again, Snow smashed through a layer of her wall, and a surge of worry pricked her heart, sending a foreboding tremor through her being.

Yet, Snow pressed onward, pulling up her inner reservoir of determination, and envisioned ripping down the wall inside. She felt her internal walls crack, the sound so loud she could've sworn Max could hear it. Her ears buzzed, and an entire portion of the wall crumbled.

Instantly, a wave of adoration crashed over her, overwhelming her senses with its intensity. Panic rose, threatening to pull her back. Her ability was invasive. Max's private mind was his own. And she might have retreated, but Max's reassuring squeeze anchored her, urging her to stay the course.

The small action was his reminder—she needed to endure. The gift of discerning emotions in others was too powerful to rebuff completely. If she cared about her people, she had to risk drowning. She pressed forward, sensing Max's utter despair and his highest hopes. She didn't know his thoughts, but she felt his desperation to be with her. He longed for her, and he'd kept all his emotion coiled within. She opened her eyes and dared look at Max. Tears rimmed his eyes, his cheeks flushed. She reached up, cupping the side of his cheek.

"Max," she whispered.

A dam broke.

This man. He was all that was light and good. He was courage and strength. Patience and humility. He was her anchor. Her safe place. Her Northstar. But he was more than that. He was her heart.

He had stood by her side. Shared in her sadness and joy. Supported her dreams and soothed her most bitter disappointments.

But those were not just his emotions; they were hers, too. They were mirrored in one another—twin souls.

Max tugged her close and then wrapped his arms around her in a tender embrace, cradling her in comfort and adoration, as if she were the most precious thing to him. His scent of pine, leather, and crisp morning air filled her senses, grounding her with the calm of an immovable mountain. Resistance melted away, like butter under the hot sun, and she turned to a puddle, surrendering to the raw emotions laid bare between them. Max pressed closer, his warmth becoming hers, and she slid her hand up his chest, reveling in the dance of his heart beneath her palm.

Somewhere, in between their past horseback rides, shared glances in the kitchens, and teasing in the forest, Snow had fallen in love with

Max. How could she not? Their past was a tapestry of moments forever etched in her memory.

The ethereal glow of the arcane light of the caves danced in their surroundings, casting a delicate radiance that bathed the chamber in its enchanting hues. Within Snow's heart, emotions swirled like a tempest, a tumultuous mixture of joy, relief, and then strangely, vulnerability.

Snow didn't want to stay away from Max any longer. She didn't want to avoid him. Or her feelings for him. She was done hiding behind a wall of apathy. She wanted *more.*

Snow's breath quickened as the air between them charged.

Max trailed his fingers down her cheek and whispered her name, setting her skin aflame. Did he know how much she cared? Could he feel her emotions in her touch as easily as she sensed his?

Snow clenched his shirt and pushed closer, her lips parting.

Max's green eyes darkened, and his hand slid to the back of her neck, his fingers sliding into her hair as he tilted her head up. "If you don't want this—"

"I do," Snow whispered, her voice aching with the truth of it.

Max's embrace tightened, and his muscles grew taut beneath her fingers. She slid her hands up past his shoulders as he leaned closer. Her heart raced, and her breath came in short gasps as she rose up onto her tiptoes.

Their breaths mingled, and Snow's eyes fluttered closed.

The first brush of Max's lips was petal soft, a soft kiss that held within it the sweetness of a thousand flowers—an ephemeral taste of spring after a long, barren winter.

What Snow wanted was this. More of Max. More of his trust. More whispered adorations and tender touches. She wanted to spend her entire life getting to know everything about this man. All his secrets. All his feelings. And she wanted to share all of hers.

As he moved to pull back, Snow couldn't let him go. She wasn't ready for the kiss to end.

Moving on instinct, she threaded her hands into his hair and pulled him closer. "Max."

As if his name on her lips was another barrier shattered, Max swept her into his arms and pressed his lips to hers. Her walls were gone, and the difference set her ablaze. Where their first kiss was a question, this one was the answer. This kiss was a claim. That he was hers and she was his.

The weight of the dangerous throne and impossible tasks faded into insignificance. And Snow couldn't have been happier. She leaned back, a smile stretching across her lips.

"My queen is pleased?" he asked then pressed another soft kiss to her lips before pulling back.

Snow grinned and snuggled close, resting her head on his chest. The gallop of his heart slowed in tandem with hers. Any response was unnecessary, as the silent language of their emotions spoke volumes. In that exchange of warmth and tenderness, their connection affirmed the depth of their bond built on a foundation deeper than any of Snow's mistakes.

"I'm so sorry, Max," Snow said. "I never wanted you to find out about my father and family the way you did."

Max shook his head. "You were in an impossible situation. Your duty was to your family."

"You are my family," Snow said quietly, her words timid.

Max brushed Snow's hair away from her face, his eyes searching hers. She found comfort in Max's unwavering gaze, a refuge from the chaos within herself. His touch was a balm to her restless soul, a reminder that she was not alone in this journey. She hadn't been from the moment they'd met. The weight of the wall around her heart had lifted, replaced by a newfound sense of lightness. Freedom.

Yes, she was pulled out into the currents of emotion, but she could swim. She'd been pinned in place by fear, even when under a pounding waterfall. Now, she could navigate.

"I can take you to Anchor Bay," Max said, his voice rough. "With your ring, you're invisible to the fae. With a bit of coin, you can stay hidden for the rest of your life."

"And leave Solinsel in shambles? To what end?"

"To live," Max said, his grip around her waist tightening.

Snow pulled back from his emotions, knowing him and his feelings without needing to pry. "I have to try. But if you want to back out, I won't force you to stay."

She held her breath, letting him choose. Her path wasn't guaranteed, but he could step away and save himself, no matter what happened inside the castle. Max's expression softened, and his hand splayed against her back as he pulled her close.

"I'll cut down all of the Wildwood if you ask me to," Max said, his gaze taking her breath away.

"You'll do no such thing, huntsman," Gertrild said as she entered, ignoring Snow's reddening cheeks. "Sorry to interrupt, but you need to get going while the sun is up. You'll have plenty of time for all of that sappy talk later. *After* you seat yourself on the throne."

Runa and Grim approached, giving her hearty goodbyes, reiterating their offer to accompany them through the woods. Everything about Snow felt tender as unregulated currents of their warmth threatened to bring her to grateful tears. Sincere hope emanated from all the dwarves—even grumpy Karldorin. Like the humans, they too wanted better futures for their children.

Grim handed Snow her pack. "Don't eat all the snacks in one day."

"I'll do my best." Snow grinned.

Karldorin moved to the door, checking outside, then pressed his hand to the center. Lines of light blazed into the stone, the lock disengaging. Max and Snow finished their farewells, and Karldorin cracked the door open that would lead them into the Wildwood.

From outside the cave, a tremendous burst of air threw them all back, including Karldorin, sliding across the rough ground. Palace guards stormed forward, two at a time, spilling into the dwarven stronghold. A dark, evil feeling stunned Snow, making her sluggish with fear. Due to long instinct, she attempted to enforce her inner wall, but her mind froze, paralyzed.

Rough dwarven hands grabbed her, dragging her back into the deeper safety of the cave. The heavy inner doors slammed shut. Karldorin pressed his hands against the carved wood, his chest heaving. No one could enter or exit. A siege had begun. But not everyone had gotten to safety.

Behind the solid wooden interior doors of the dwarven cave, Snow and her siblings, along with Grim, Karldorin, and little Lielinda were breathing hard. But the others were trapped by the guards.

Panicked, Snow moved to Karldorin's side, who now had his face smashed against the door, watching the entry.

"What's going on?" Snow begged.

"You don't want to know."

Snow got on her knees next to him, pushing him to the side, and he let her. The sight took the wind from her lungs. The four dwarves were subdued, blades to their throats, and Ingrihild had a deep red slash down her arm. Max was on his knees, a guard tying a rope around his wrists behind him, his back arched at a painful angle.

The queen stormed in with deliberate steps, sending cold dread down Snow's spine. Agnes held her head high, more alert than Snow had seen since the king had died.

"You are under arrest for abducting the queen's ward," she said to the dwarves. The ethereal light overhead seemed to rake across her, distorting her features. Even her voice echoed incongruently in the cave. Snow tested her gifting, wondering if she could feel the queen's emotions through the door.

The queen's feelings were muted in intensity but distinct. Giddy anticipation and visceral hatred vied for Snow's attention, each one confirming that the queen would stop at nothing to get what she wanted.

A keening growl echoed from outside, and Snow stilled.

Please, no.

The howl vibrated ever so slightly, and Snow shuddered. The Shadow Beast. The queen controlled it—proof laid bare. The beast's howl began to crescendo. Even a few guards glanced out the open entrance door, nervous.

A guard dragged Max forward and cast him at the queen's feet. The huntsman was trussed like one of his catches, ready for slaughter. But the blades were the jaws of the Shadow Beast. The queen's expression was one of unrestrained delight. Whatever she'd planned, she would savor it. Max was set to be tortured first, just to make a point. Bile burned up Snow's throat, and she shifted away before she vomited.

Karldorin moved to observe the conflict again. His jaw tightened, his throat bobbing as he swallowed. "The queen says some prince has made her an offer. For you."

He moved, and Snow took his place, watching the horrific scene. The queen paced the entryway and coolly inspected the trees and veins of light as she spoke. "You will live a life of luxury in a far-off kingdom, Snow White. More importantly, if you don't appear, my pet will be unleashed on your captors here. The dwarves must let you go in order to save their little lives."

"Grim," Snow said, turning to the dwarf. "Take everyone deeper into the caves. Hide."

Grim frowned but did as she requested, guiding everyone away from the door.

"Karldorin, when I leave, lock the door behind me. And before you ask, no, I don't trust the queen. But I have to try." Snow hoped Agnes had weighed the trade deal with the prince and found the agreement valuable. The queen was strategic; if all Snow's friends in the entryway were slaughtered, she would sabotage her marriage with the prince and destroy the queen's reputation. And Queen Agnes knew it. The dwarves and Max were the queen's only leverage.

"Everyone out there is willing to sacrifice themselves to see you on the throne. You'd throw that away?" Karldorin asked.

"True queens cannot rebuild kingdoms on the bones of their friends," Snow said.

Perhaps she could still rally Elisabeth and Reinhold when she reached Clarus, just as Max had planned. There was a good chance Reinhold would find her. No matter what the queen had in store for Snow, she couldn't stay here. She had to take a risk.

"You can speak through the door, first," Karldorin instructed. "Don't throw yourself to the beasts without reason."

"I offer myself to this prince, willingly, if you let the dwarves go," Snow spoke into the wood where the dwarf had indicated. "Solinsel doesn't want war with their clans. Move them to the inner door, and keep your guards away." Snow spoke the truth, but nothing more. Now wasn't the time to try to convince the guards to side with her.

"A deal, then, shall we?" the queen said, signaling for the captain to put a blade to Max's back. "Face me."

Snow twisted her ring, hiding the signet. She felt like she was floating, but she forced herself to slip quickly through the gap in the door before Karldorin slammed it behind her. As the dwarves moved around the edge to the inner part of the cave, Snow stepped toward the queen, the one person who held the fate of them all in her claws.

On this side of the door, a sense of sickly sweet fermentation mixed with rotten leaves roiled in Snow's gut, an unexpected but familiar, ill sensation. The queen's sense of glee knocked away every other emotion, so intense that Snow struggled to think straight. To negotiate.

A growl sounded again from outside the cave, and Snow's insides turned to water. A memory of screams and breaking glass filled Snow's mind, blocking out everything else. Her walls were slippery, too hard to grasp, leaving her fully exposed to the queen's dark emotions.

"Snow," Max shouted, breaking her thoughts. "Don't do this. The kingdom needs you. Not this tyrant."

"What are your terms, exactly?" Snow asked the queen. Swimming through Agnes's oily emotions, Snow barely noticed the Captain of the Guard, loyally at Agnes's side.

"Your agreement to marry the man of my choosing." Agnes's hatred threatened to suffocate everyone in the cave. "And your ring as proof of your intention."

Snow struggled to breathe, shocked that the queen even knew of her ring. Who had told her? The signet was Snow's only proof of her bloodline and an indicator of King Friedrich's wish to make Snow his heir. Without it, Snow had nothing to show the judge and the courts. She truly would be trapped in an unwanted marriage in a foreign land.

Just as the queen had been.

Snow's heart shattered, all her hopes sunk in one fell swoop. She dimly realized she could step back, and Karldorin would yank her back into the safe cave. The dwarves were close by, too. No one would blame her. Max looked at her as if pleading for her to run. Why should Snow be Solinsel's sacrifice, a tool to bring money that the queen would spend on herself?

Snow twisted the ring displaying the sigil. "I'll do it, but I have conditions of my own."

CHAPTER 24: MAX

YEAR 10 OF THE MAIDEN COMET, LATE SPRING

M ax squirmed on the floor, but the captain had confiscated his knife when the guards tied him. His mind grasped for ideas to escape this situation, but he was trapped. He glanced up at the queen, who loomed over him, but she wasn't paying him any attention. Her focus was on her true prey, Snow.

"I want the Hunts to go free," Snow said. Her voice was firm, but her legs shook. "All three of them, with no retribution. You leave Max here. And I want the dwarves left alone. Safe. No human is to return here without the dwarves' permission. And my siblings—you will let them live."

Ingrihild gave a slight shake of her head, frowning. She didn't like this deal any more than Max did. He stared at Snow, willing her to look at him. Snow's breathing increased—too fast. She needed him, and Max hated that she stood alone. Finally, she glanced down.

"No!" Max mouthed. He would trade his life for Snow's without hesitation.

Queen Agnes lifted her hand, and a parchment magically appeared. As she spoke, red ink burned across the page. "As soon as you cross the sea with your prince, I'll release Heinrich from the dungeon. I will never seek the Hunts, nor will I darken the entrance to the dwarves' homes again. Their trespasses will have no retribution. I swear it."

Snow held out her hand, her sigil displayed. The captain didn't react, though his eyes narrowed as he scrutinized the symbol. Snow slipped the ring from her finger and held it in her open palm.

The queen practically salivated, leaning forward. At the captain's signal, two guards grabbed Snow at the same moment that the queen clawed for the ring. For a moment, time seemed to suspend. The queen clutched the ring, her nostrils flaring. She tilted her chin down to inspect her prize, and a corner of her mouth quirked in delight, the shadows oddly shifting on her face.

Boots slammed on the rocks, jerking Max's attention back to Snow and the guards. They dragged Snow past him, and he rolled over, desperate for a glimpse of her.

"I'm sorry," Snow said. Or maybe she only mouthed the words. Max couldn't tell.

The captain's boots marched toward Max, blocking what little he could see, closing the gap between them.

"Snow! No!" Max cried out, desperate. "*Snow* is your queen. She is the king's daughter. You all saw the ring!"

The queen called a command from outside the cave, muted by the blood thumping in his ears.

"Protect her!" Max pleaded as the captain he'd once respected kneeled next to him. Max strained against his bindings. They only tightened.

The captain's silence said volumes.

"I swear on the Abundants," Max growled, "if your guards hurt Snow, I will hunt *you* down."

"I'd hoped it wouldn't come to this," the captain's words overlapped with Max's.

"There's no place you can hide—" Pain exploded against Max's temple, and the cave went dark.

Max stood forlorn outside the dwarven cave, feeling like he might retch, and his head throbbed. The guards, the queen, and Snow had disappeared into the Wildwood along with the Shadow Beast. But distant keening sent chills up Max's spine.

After the dwarves had woken Max, they'd advised him to rest, but he needed to feel useful. The captain had shoved Max's knife under his unconscious body. A small gift to ensure he survived the Wood—the least he could do. Though, Max's travel would be sooner than the captain likely expected. He wouldn't stay with the dwarves long.

"Understand, first. Strategy, second," Ingrihild said, assigning the dwarves to scout the surrounding area, determined to understand how the queen had discovered them.

Everyone except Lielinda, Nora, and Gertrild searched. An hour later, Grim reported first.

"The queen's magic is enabling her guards to traverse the woods. All animals are staying away, though that may be because of the Shadow

Beast. She knows enough to avoid the worst areas, but she's headed west, straight for the King's Road, aiming to exit the forest as soon as possible. Her magic isn't completely protective. I found remnants of a few unlucky guards not far into the woods."

"Snow." Max clutched at his chest, hating that he wasn't there with her.

"She's fine," Grim said. "The queen put her in a small carriage. No chance of her rubbing up against poisonous plants or being caught unaware by a pouncing creature."

"Or gathering those plants as a weapon, either," Max grumbled.

"I found spy 'nests' along the mountain ridge, out of the Wildwood but near enough to report comings and goings," Wielbran said.

"I found a guard camp," Runa said. "I imagine several spies and guards were killed by poison and beasts while they waited all that time, half hidden."

"So, the queen figured that Snow was with the dwarves; she just didn't know which clan," Ingrihild said. "Based on what you found, they covertly stalked dwarven entrances. For who knows how long."

"Why didn't the queen assume Snow had died in the woods?" Max asked. "Between her ring and the wood, she has been protected by dwarven magic every moment."

"Well," Runa shifted, fidgeting, "We did take her to the trading post, but she was only out of the cave for a single day. Witches cannot magically find someone that quickly. Only a fae could. So that means Agnes was either very lucky or she is far more powerful than we assumed, and she constantly stares at the reflection, hunting."

"When did the queen sleep let alone attend to her other duties?" Ingrihild asked.

"Queen Agnes acts like she can barely function at Clarus." Max shook his head. "But tonight, she was completely different. Sharp. Focused."

"Is a fae helping her?" Runa asked. "Manipulating Agnes in one of their games?" The others muttered agreement about the possibility.

Max had no interest in arguing about the fae; the dwarves' prejudice skewed their judgment. Unless they were bonded, most fae couldn't be bothered with humans.

"When was the trip?" Max asked.

"Last autumn," Runa said.

Max swallowed back against the growing nausea. The timing matched with when the queen's fits began to flare again. "The queen had calmed for a time—when she'd assumed Snow was dead."

Runa frowned. "Agnes must've felt some amount of prideful victory every time she checked the reflection and *didn't* find Snow."

"Until she did," Karldorin said.

"The queen couldn't have known Snow survived until that point," Max continued. "Agnes would've easily spotted Runa and Grim. She figured out they were headed to the Darkstone Mountains. Agnes just didn't know which cave. When I arrived, it pinpointed the entry." Max felt sick, playing right into the queen's hands.

"I predict she'll stay away as she promised," Wielbran said. "I trust her greed more than her oath. She still wants the yearly gifts of gems and metals from the clans." He turned to Ingrihild. "I'm going to check on my family."

The dwarf stomped off, and Max felt a bit of relief that at least the queen wouldn't be back for revenge on the dwarves. However, the Hunts would not be so fortunate. When the guards returned with Snow, it would signal to Max's mother to flee to her cousin's estate for protection, just as they'd planned. Soon Max would no longer have a home. Agnes had left him behind, but if he returned to Clarus, she would throw him into the dungeon with his father in order to leverage Snow.

The queen would elevate a huntsman from another estate, and Max's family would be forgotten. At least, until Snow was married off; Max had no illusions that the queen would let him survive after Snow sailed away. He thought himself very, very lucky that she'd let him out of her grasp today.

The best hope for Snow now was that she would eventually grow to love Prince-Third-Son. As much as Max hated the idea of her with someone else, he would do anything to see her happy. Before she sailed away, Snow would be forlorn at Clarus, trapped and alone. Despite the utter foolishness of the idea, Max longed to see her again. Why should the queen's bitter, broken parting be their last? And if he was honest, he *had* to see Snow. Not just to console her, but perhaps he wanted someone to console him, too.

"What are you doing, standing there like a lost puppy, Maxie?" Grim asked. "Come back inside."

Max blinked, realizing that Grim, Runa, Karldorin, and Ingrihild were all staring at him.

"You didn't really think we'd lock you out, did you?" Karldorin asked.

Their offer of shelter warmed his heart, but he couldn't stay. "I'm going to Clarus. I have to try."

"I'm coming with you," Ludwig said, hurrying out of the cave with a stuffed satchel.

"I guess you can join us," Runa smirked, adjusting the pickaxe strapped to her back.

"What do you mean 'us'?" Max asked. "And why are you packed?"

"Runa and I are coming along," Grim said. "There's an old access point from the valley to the castle tunneled long, long ago."

"It's not that old. I helped dig that!" Karldorin said, offended.

"It's *ancient*," Grim said. "Runa and I played there as younglings. It's a bit creepy with the rumors of ghosts. But I much prefer it to storming the castle in the usual way." Grim pulled a finger across his neck and faked like he was dying.

"Snow doesn't need a ring to become the queen," Runa said, snapping her fingers at Max. "We just need another plan."

Max's goal had just been to reunite with Snow. Could they still overthrow Queen Agnes? Max shook his head. "We would need two witnesses to swear to Snow's identity just to get started. Powerful witnesses. I know of two, but one is a fae."

The dwarves groaned but, miraculously, didn't object.

"I don't trust the new high judge, so we need others present. Others from the court," Max said, recalling all the disgruntled high nobles. No one was happy with Agnes's reign, except the simpering judge she'd selected. "If Snow can convince them she's the stronger choice, she has a chance of winning the throne."

"So, we're depending on the best speech of Snow's life to save the kingdom?" Karldorin said, doubtful.

"Snow can win back the throne," Runa said, a hand on her hip. "We know she can . . . with a little help."

"I was thinking we'd just kill the queen and anyone in our way," Grim said. "A nice, simple plan is always best."

Max hoped things wouldn't get bloody. But chances were, it wouldn't go as smoothly as he'd hoped. Nothing ever did.

CHAPTER 25: SNOW

Year 10 of the Maiden Comet, Summer

S now rode in a carriage—flanked by guards—her eyes burning. She blinked back the emotion, not allowing herself to appear weaker. Not now. She hated how she and Max had been torn apart, but at least he was alive. He had blamed himself for her capture—regret and fear and *anger* consumed him. Would that vision haunt her forever? She gripped the carriage seat, shoving down her despair, and stared at the silken walls around her.

With every passing moment, the reality of her losses set in like spikes against her shoulders, leaving her bruised and raw. Two days passed, but still too soon, they arrived at Clarus in the middle of the night.

The moment Snow stepped out of her carriage, she felt the queen's stare bore into the back of her skull. Snow made the mistake of turning to meet her gaze and was pummeled by negativity. The queen's loathing, bitterness, and cruel victory had grown, burning like hot tar across Snow's skin and burrowing into her bones. Snow gasped for air. By instinct, she reached to pull her walls back up, but the incomplete, crumbling remnants did nothing.

Whatever the witch had once given her was gone. Snow had to swim or drown.

The cave had been demanding, but now without solace from a single friend, darkness consumed her.

Snow found herself curled on the ground, heaving. Crushed rocks dug into her side. Overhead, even the stars and moon hid from the scene behind the clouds. Snow had no such luxury; the bombardment of emotions didn't stop.

Forlorn and overwhelmed, Snow wished the Abundants would swallow her and deliver her to a distant corner of Fairen'la.

Her wish went unanswered.

Without words, calloused hands dragged Snow into the royal wing of the castle under the cloak of night.

Three weeks after returning to Clarus, Snow inspected herself in the mirror, wincing at her sunken eyes and how her clothing hung from her frame. Around her, the large, carved furniture pieces and mahogany paneling on the walls suffocated her rooms in an oppressive blanket.

What little sunshine found its way through the tall, slit window had been blocked by velvet drapes—until Snow pushed them aside and moved the mirror to strategically bounce the light. Not that it mattered anymore. This night would be her last before she sailed away with her fiancé, Prince Leopold, to a northern port.

If Max had hoped Reinhold would step in to help her, he'd be disappointed. The fae hadn't bothered to appear at all.

Max. Snow pulled her arms to her chest and gripped one wrist, feeling the metal pressing against her palm. A servant entered, and Snow dropped her hands to her sides. She feigned a stoic calm despite the amulet having left red indentations on her palm.

"Try to eat, my lady," the servant instructed as she tightened Snow's clothes at her waist. "Prince Leopold might notice your dwindling figure and refuse a sickly wife."

The servant was only trying to help, but Snow doubted the prince would notice if she grew horns and a beak. He had arrived on a ship two days after Snow was forcibly returned to Clarus; the queen had confidently invited him moons ago.

More than ten years her senior, Leopold was objectively handsome, but Snow was revolted by his sweaty hands and never-ending nasal voice. He had two favorite topics: fishing and fashion. And he had never asked for Snow's thoughts on either. Or anything else, for that matter.

"The queen will not be happy if you arrive late to dine." The servant closed the curtain in front of the mirror, darkening the room and interrupting Snow's thoughts.

Snow straightened, wanting to spare the servant trouble, no matter how much Snow dreaded eating with the awkward audience. She marched into the hallway, nearly running into Princess Elisabeth.

"Princess," Snow said, curtsying. "Are you on your way to breakfast?"

"Yes," she said. "I'm surprised you're not already there."

"Did you stop by to get something else?" Snow asked. Princess Elisabeth's rooms were now Snow's, per the command of the queen. Always gracious, the princess assured Snow not to worry, even as her things were gathered up and moved. Snow continued, "I'm so sorry you were rushed out of your rooms so quickly."

"You've already apologized. And besides, it wasn't your decision, now, was it? So no need to speak of it again," Elisabeth smiled pleasantly, but Snow sensed the princess's displeasure. "Besides, it's only rooms. And it's temporary. The queen robbed you of so much more."

Elisabeth's kindness never ceased. Snow found herself gravitating toward the princess—an island of calm. But too soon, Snow realized that, even within the princess, a bitterness festered. And indignation. Snow didn't blame her. Dottie had mentioned that when Elisabeth wasn't away on palace duties, she took the brunt of the queen's rough outbursts. Whenever Elisabeth returned to Clarus, she brought a sigh of relief to the new steward and castle staff.

Snow gathered her courage to ask a question that had plagued her. "What will happen to you after I leave?"

Elisabeth pulled Snow away from the nearest guard and lowered her voice. "I imagine there will be an uprising. Eventually. A powerful noble will take the throne. Whoever hires the largest army will win the crown."

Snow balked, worried. Citizens would inevitably get hurt in bloody grab for the crown, maybe even Elisabeth.

"But don't worry about me," Elisabeth said. "I'm like my ancestors. We always find a way to survive."

Snow was impressed with Elisabeth's confidence. Her calm and her foresight.

"I'll wait here, and we can go to breakfast together," Snow offered.

"Let's not give the queen any reason to be angry with you," Elisabeth said, giving Snow's hand a quick squeeze. "You go on. But I'll hurry so you're not so alone."

Snow squeezed back and hurried down the hallway. Approaching the Sunrise Parlor, Snow passed two guards standing sentinel at the doors. Both nodded respectfully as she entered, a look of pity in their eyes—just like other guards who were present when Snow was taken from Darkstone Mountains. But their sympathy did her little good. The queen had won.

In the parlor, a servant pulled out a chair for Snow, seating her next to her fiancé, Prince Leopold. She still felt odd dining with the nobles, but she knew the etiquette well enough.

"Here you are, Lady Snow," he said, flashing a wide smile.

He took her hand in his sweaty palm and brushed his lips across her knuckles. A hollow performance for the Solinsel court without a drop of real caring.

Across from the prince, Elisabeth had a reserved seat, for which Snow was grateful. Before the princess appeared, breakfast arrived. Platters piled with loaves of bread and delicately smoked fish with capers were brought in, along with yogurt, honey, and fruit. Snow forced herself to eat while trying to listen to Leopold's latest story and ignore the fact that the queen kept staring at her. After Heinrich Hunt's sentence had been suspended, Snow kept her distance from Queen Agnes, not wanting to give her any excuses to break her contract.

The stakes were too high: the Hunts', dwarves', and her sibling's lives.

Finally, Elisabeth joined them and politely asked Prince Leopold questions about his kingdom. It wasn't long until even Elisabeth began to lose patience with the boastful prince. Keeping her attention on her plate, Snow concentrated on one bite at a time. One breath at a time. Avoiding eye contact gave Snow much-needed respite.

"Don't you think, Lady Snow?" Prince Leopold asked.

"Of course." Though Snow had no idea what he was talking about. She'd learned he had no real interest in her actual opinion.

"The cook's tarts last night were the best I've ever tasted. Quite the unexpected surprise," he said.

"Oh?" Snow imagined Dottie pulling them from the oven with her apron, her cheeks bright red from the heat. Once Snow left their island kingdom, she'd never see Dottie again. The realization wasn't a shock, yet it still pained her. She'd never be in the Clarus kitchens again. She'd never see the sunset from the castle again. Never explore the royal forest again. Loss by a thousand little robberies.

"Solinsel berries are generally undesirable. Overripe and smashed from weeks of transport, I presume." The prince smirked, his voice haughty. "Fresh, they're exquisite. Worthy of a prince, even."

"Worthy of a fae," Snow said, thinking about Reinhold. Tarts were one of his favorite desserts.

"Yes, even a fae!" Leopold laughed and slammed a hand against the table. "Your servants must fill buckets with berries this time of year. Perhaps they can bring a fresh supply for us before we leave."

"I could pick them myself," Snow said, happy at the thought. "I know all the best places to find them."

"How droll," he said, laughing. "I love your little stories."

Leopold had been led to believe Snow was born a lower noble who'd been raised as a ward in Clarus. More alarmingly, Leopold's father, the king, believed he was building a kingdom alliance—as if Snow's ties to Queen Agnes would ingratiate him with the Solinsel crown. All lies.

Snow had tried to explain she was born a commoner, but Leopold laughed it off. She'd like to think it was magic dampening his ability to listen, but she suspected his pampered life made him soft and lazy. His manners were prim, from the way he sipped his soup to how he held his hands. But his eyes wandered to a serving girl as she leaned over to place a platter on the table. Snow jerked her attention away from her fiancé, avoiding his unpleasant emotions. Again.

"Prince Leopold," Snow said, "I hope I don't get seasick on our journey. How many days will it take to cross?"

Snow already knew the answer, but the distraction worked, and Leopold's eager emotions wavered.

As the prince droned on, Snow saw the pages of her life filling up with more of *this*. Over and over. Until she disappeared between the lines of her own story—behind a prince she didn't care for nor respect. But she would choose it again if it meant saving her friends. Saving Max.

Snow quickly shoved Max from her mind, attempting to avoid torturing herself with his memory. Too late. Always too late. Her thoughts were a never-ending cycle of loving, longing, and mourning Max.

She smiled at Leopold as he told of a swashbuckling adventure. But inside, she braced against his every wave of emotion.

"I was thrown overboard in the storm," Leopold continued his grandiose tale. "But the king of the water kingdom rescued me."

"You must be very important for the ruler of the underwater kingdom himself to know you even crossed his vast sea. And for him to come directly. Impressive." Elisabeth's hold on her fork grew choked. She strained to keep a pleasant expression, but her annoyance was so great Snow half-expected the entire room to feel its reverberations. And, strangely, Snow thought she sensed a bit of vindictiveness, too.

When Snow had been brought back to Clarus, she realized she had a decision to make. Swim or drown. She chose survival.

Like flexing long dormant muscles, Snow had begun to practice her gifting. When she'd pushed herself to her limit, Snow dropped her attention to her lap or above people's heads, letting their inner feelings pass by her unfelt. The work exhausted her beyond anything she'd ever experienced.

Part of Snow wanted to give up, but then she'd remembered her mother. When Rosalind knew the king would marry, she didn't wallow in self-pity. Snow's mother moved away and started anew, using all her skills and resources. Snow could do the same. She would use the fae gifting the way it was intended. Fully. And Snow would be prepared for a foreign land. She would never again allow her gift to atrophy to such a terrible degree.

Snow built her emotional stamina a little more every day. Though it was uncomfortable, Snow allowed herself to feel Elisabeth's disdain. Her dislike of the prince should've increased Snow's worry about marrying Leopold, but she felt oddly comforted that she wasn't the only one appalled by the prince's snobbery.

The queen abruptly stood, the chair scraping as it was shoved back. "The sun sets on one ruler. The king lies in repose. A raven's beak cracks glass. Another claws at the crown."

Elisabeth gave Snow a sideways glance, her body rigid. This wasn't the first irregular speech from the queen. The woman had gone from focused and cruel at the dwarves' cave to scattered and incoherent. The swings put everyone on edge, unsure of what she'd do next. The high judge patted the queen's hand, which calmed her, but the guards shifted uncomfortably as the visitors from the north stilled.

The queen stared at Snow with an unusual intensity as she continued, "I hide. Hidden."

The prince tugged his collar and cleared his throat. Perhaps he'd back out of the engagement. Would that be the worst thing?

It might be.

Snow had learned enough to know mad rulers created weak kingdoms. Weak kingdoms invited invasion and subjugation. Snow reached under the table and squeezed Elisabeth's hand, a silent plea to smooth things over. The princess subtly signaled to the guards, completely calm under pressure. Snow followed her example and smiled at Leopold. She rested a hand on his forearm, trying to distract the prince from the queen's spectacle, but he craned his neck to watch as guards ushered her from the room.

Elisabeth stood up, refocusing attention away from the queen's out-burst. "We are so delighted you came this morning to celebrate Snow White and Prince Leopold. Tomorrow at dawn, Snow will return with her prince. They'll wed this autumn—a bright joy for both kingdoms."

The visiting emissary relaxed, and the mood of the room lightened. Elisabeth emanated a sense of pride, which warmed Snow. The princess had faith in Snow's ability to wed a royal and integrate into a new culture. Yes, Elisabeth hired tutors and mentored Snow, but the princess's confidence bolstered her. Even so, regret plucked at Snow; she had studied and prepared to help her *own* people. She'd be leaving them with Queen Agnes whose policies were plowing the kingdom into despair. Snow knew enough to turn things around or perhaps enough to restore much of their idyllic lives.

But even if Snow stayed, she could do nothing while Agnes controlled the throne. And by leaving, she could protect the dwarves and the Hunts. Though, Max and his family would likely flee Solinsel. Staying far away from the queen was their best chance at survival. The thought of Max tore at her, and she found herself gripping her dress under the table, knotting it in her fists.

A servant approached, distracting Snow from her increasing discomfort.

"More wine, my lady?" a familiar voice asked.

Snow's attention jumped to the servant as he refilled Snow's goblet. She froze, recognizing Ludwig, her half-brother. The prince babbled on, Elisabeth still feigning interest, neither the wiser to his presence. Snow blinked at the sight of her brother, stunned. He wore an official palace uniform, blending in without notice. He gave Snow a quick wink, but she sensed his nervousness. Had he snuck in to say goodbye?

"Are your things packed?" Elisabeth asked Snow.

Snow wheeled her attention off of Ludwig. "Nearly so."

Ludwig hurried to the next table, refilling another glass without looking back.

"Our fashions are quite different," Leopold said. "You'll need new dresses when we arrive. Not to worry, Snow. I will make sure you sparkle on my arm."

So glad I can be your accessory.

Leopold launched into a discourse on the superiority of northern fashion, but Snow ignored him as she watched Ludwig from the corner of her eye. Suddenly, she realized that Max could be with him. Possibly. Would he?

She wanted to stand up for a better view, desperate to see him. Fortunately, Elisabeth stood, excusing herself, and Snow took the opportunity to do the same. Snow politely said goodbye to the prince, though her thoughts scattered as her attention flicked around the parlor. Scanning each face carefully, she searched for Max. •

As a guard escorted Snow from the parlor, she strained to look at everyone. She attempted to appear casual, but failed miserably. Even so, she was met with disappointment, unable to find her heart's desire.

Questions tumbled through Snow's mind as she strode back to her temporary rooms. Why was Ludwig at Clarus? Would he know where to find her? What did he hope to achieve?

Whatever he wanted to say to her, he needed to do it quickly. She would leave Solinsel on a ship at dawn. Entering her dim rooms, Snow ambled to the curtain that covered the mirror. Gripping the velvet, another question popped into her mind.

Could I sneak a private note to Ludwig for Max?

Snow hated the way they left things between them. She yanked back the curtain and discovered the mirror was missing. Perhaps Elisabeth relocated it to her room? Not that it mattered—a candle would do just fine. Snow rushed to Elisabeth's bedside, grabbing the tinderbox.

A young servant, only a child wearing a loose bonnet, emerged from the sitting room, her back to Snow as she dusted.

"Will you fetch me parchment and ink?" Snow requested.

"Fetch it yourself," she said, her voice distinctly not child-like, as she turned around, the corner of her lips curled in a smirk.

Snow gasped, the tinderbox clattering to the ground. "Runa!"

Runa hurried to Snow's side, grabbing her hand, her voice firm. "It's good to see you, too. We can celebrate my heroic appearance later. First, you must make an excuse to see your fiancé. Immediately. There's no time to waste."

Snow shook off her surprise and then threw open her door, only to find a stationed guard. The queen was taking no chances on Snow's possible escape. He didn't appear to be much older than herself and was lanky with bushy brows and a short beard.

"I need to speak with the prince. I'm leaving in the morning and have questions on what to pack," Snow said.

"Your servants should see to that, Lady Snow," the guard said, scowling at Runa though she kept her head down, hiding her features under the frill along the edge of her bonnet. Snow lifted her chin, refusing to be cowed. The guard huffed, relenting, and led them out of the royal wing. Because of Snow's noble rank—even though recently granted—the guards and servants thought long and hard before refusing her anything. Snow hadn't anticipated an official title, but Leopold expected to wed nobility, and Agnes wanted to keep the wedding contract intact.

Their hallway neared a wide art corridor where nobles often lingered with goblets of wine. It was hard to say how much gossip spread and how many trade deals were made here. They would need to cross the art corridor in order to reach the guest rooms, but just as they stepped onto the checkerboard marble floor, Runa pinched Snow's arm.

Snow bit back a yelp and glanced around the ornate corridor. Several paces away, among the busy servants and the social nobles, she noticed Prince Leopold talking to a man she didn't recognize. The northerners were easily marked by their gaudy northern fashion, especially Leopold. But the man he spoke with dressed like a Solinsel noble, though Snow had never seen him before. However, many people had traveled to Clarus in hopes of gaining an introduction to the royal visitor.

Spotting the prince, the guard pivoted and started toward him. Though the guard was lanky, he walked with a smooth, confident gait, indicating long hours of training. The queen had stationed a more capable guard than Snow had first assumed. This could be a problem as Snow had only wanted an excuse to leave the royal wing. She didn't know Runa's actual plan beyond that. Snow needed to discuss it with her, but not in this public place.

"On second th—"

Runa pinched her arm again.

"What was that?" The guard stopped and turned to face her, his thick brows furrowed in thinly veiled annoyance.

"On second thought," Snow scrambled for words. "This *will* be the perfect place to discuss my travel plans." *In this private corridor.* Snow kept her sarcasm to herself.

The guard raised a brow, but continued forward. Behind him, Runa whispered another instruction to Snow.

"Make an excuse to see Elisabeth. Bring the merchant."

"Who?"

"Snow," Prince Leopold called out to her, "my lovely bride-to-be."

The room seemed to shift, everyone's attention moving to Snow and her prince. The prince, who embodied a lucrative trade agreement to potentially save them from the queen's mismanagement of Solinsel. Snow glanced at the nobles and felt their expectations, their worry, relief, and more than a little mistrust.

She'd sensed them before, but this time, Snow *looked* at the people. Worn and drawn, their clothing the same fashion from two years earlier. Worry lined their foreheads, their false expressions of happiness thinner than late spring's ice on a mountain lake. Snow's footsteps grew heavy with pity for her kingdom.

They'd come to see if the rumors were true: An unknown girl from their kingdom might rescue them. Even the guard was curious, but he stepped back to give her and the prince a little privacy.

If Snow was going to be a pawn in the queen's game, she wouldn't let it stop her from attempting success in her new role. She couldn't control the throne, but she could choose to make the best of her situation right now, which would benefit her people.

Snow smiled at Leopold and snaked her arm through his, swallowing back her dislike.

He patted her hand and continued on with his conversation with the Solinsel stranger. "As I was saying, I will be sure to present your trade offer to my father."

Trade? This man is a wealthy merchant, perhaps?

He looked to be at least twenty years older than herself, and he sported a beard. Unlike the others, this man's clothing looked recently constructed and with beautiful stitching. But, disturbingly, intense jealousy rolled off him.

"I believe we can build a mutually beneficial partnership," the stranger responded, his words clipped. His gaze darted to Runa then back to the prince.

Who is this man?

Uncomfortable with his unfounded emotions, Snow dropped her gaze to his doublet and inspected the expert stitching. Next to her, the prince shifted closer, his side touching hers. Snow swallowed, reminding herself to stay the course.

"You want trade agreements," the merchant said, "and no matter who you marry or who rules our kingdoms, merchants are open to hearing all fair trading proposals."

Was it Snow's imagination, or was the man struggling to control his breathing? His arms tensed at his sides, and he pulled one hand into a fist. Snow looked closer at the stitching, noticing the fine detail of the white-petaled flowers. Delicate stems that sparked a memory. She recognized those flowers—anemones. The flowers bloomed in the late spring, around her birthday.

Snow's attention flew back to the stranger's face. He finally looked from the bracelet on her wrist up to her face, his green eyes locking with hers. Like a wave, she felt a rush of adoration wrapped in wistfulness that she'd only felt from one other man.

Snow glanced down at her friend in time to see Runa give her a little wink, then back up at the merchant in front of her.

Max?

CHAPTER 26: MAX

YEAR 10 OF THE MAIDEN COMET, SUMMER

Max flexed his fingers, willing himself not to punch the smug Prince-Third-Son in the face. He dearly wanted to, but launching him into the wall would draw too much attention. He knew Snow felt all the vehemence inside him, but he couldn't change his feelings.

He might have been able to console himself if Snow looked content, but her smile was fake and her motions stiff. He knew her too well to think she was the slightest bit happy.

Or had Runa changed the plan and told Snow about Max's glamour from Reinhold, and she was uncomfortable with Max's presence? The thought made his insides twist.

With Dottie's help, he'd drawn the fae to the kitchen—though this time, the fae hadn't been surprised. Reinhold had suggested the glamour as Max's presence would alert the queen. And, if Snow recognized

Max under some basic disguise, her reaction might tip off any number of people watching her. Max and the dwarves couldn't afford notice.

But when Snow's eyes locked on his and widened, he knew she'd figured out the masquerade—quicker than he'd planned.

"Leopold," Snow said. Max hated her familiar use of his name, though he knew he shouldn't. "I must speak with Princess Elisabeth. Tonight, before I finish packing."

"Fortuitous planning," Max said. "I have a gift for Princess Elisabeth from my travels. Would you deliver my little token to her?"

"You are a wise man," Leopold said. "A royal always appreciates favors from his people rather than being expected to dole them out all the time."

Runa rolled her eyes.

"With me as your escort, it wouldn't be inappropriate for you to deliver it yourself," Snow suggested.

Her escort guard raised a brow, but Snow pressed on. "As you two have been such *long-time friends*," Snow embellished, "she will welcome the visit."

"I appreciate the invitation," Max said, "and gratefully accept."

"Lead us to Princess Elisabeth's room," Snow commanded the guard.

The guard pressed his lips together into a stiff line. Inviting visitors into the royal wing pushed the boundaries of Snow's authority.

"I shall see you at lunch," Snow said to the prince, cleverly reminding the guard of her relationship with the visiting royal.

Leopold kissed her knuckles, which roiled Max's insides up into a knot. Then the prince stared expectantly at the guard. According to Dottie, the servants and guards had been instructed to keep the prince happy, so Snow played her part perfectly. The guard gave a curt nod and led them to the royal corridor.

Snow and Runa walked behind the guard, and Max took up the rear. As they entered the royal wing, Max's nerves increased. Once they involved Elisabeth, they would officially be discussing treason. Once the words were said, there was no taking them back.

As they neared Elisabeth's new rooms, he heard voices inside. They were muffled, but one sounded female and the other was deeper. A servant, perhaps? The guard knocked, announcing himself. Time seemed to stretch before Elisabeth answered the door. However, she quickly invited Snow, Runa, and Max into her rooms when she answered it, leaving the guard outside her door.

The large room had an unlit fireplace, leather couches facing each other, and a round table in the corner, stacked with books and maps. Based on the grand size, masculine style, and function, Max guessed these were once her father's rooms. The door to the bedroom was closed, as were the curtains, blocking the heat of the summer sun.

"Snow," Elisabeth said, looking from her to Runa and back again. "Why do I get the impression you're not here for a social call?"

"We've come to discuss the queen," Runa spoke first.

"I see," Elisabeth directed them to the couches, her face a mask. They all sat, except for Runa who leaned against the arm.

"The queen has magic, but it comes at a terrible cost," Max said, recounting what he'd noticed and Reinhold had confirmed. "She gained the throne but lost her mind."

"Even so, I don't underestimate her," Elisabeth said. "You shouldn't either."

"We don't," Runa said.

"What are we doing here?" Snow asked Runa and Max.

Elisabeth's brow rose. "You don't know?"

"I have my guesses," Snow said. "This is my friend, Runa." She gestured to the dwarf. "And you already know Max."

Elisabeth looked at Max again, her eyes widening. "You have a glamour? How?"

"Reinhold," Max said.

"But the fae cannot interfere with our affairs." Elisabeth's brows furrowed. "Fae law limits what they're allowed to do in our realm even with their Bonded's permission. The queen tried and failed to get them to help her."

Failed?

"What did she ask for?" Max said, his interest piqued.

"I tried to persuade her to tell me. But all she did was rant about my brother," Elisabeth said, worrying the edge of her sleeve. "The visiting fae requested to see Reinhold, but he refused to appear."

"What? Why?" Max asked, surprised.

"Coward," Runa muttered.

"Is he in hiding?" Snow asked.

Elisabeth shrugged. "He's humiliated perhaps? He should have saved the king, but the fae was outwitted. Or his opponent more powerful." Elisabeth's words sunk in, reminding Max that the queen had fooled an experienced fae. "Yet, Reinhold helped you, Max. With my brother's death, his fae is a spectator. Or should be."

"He said as much," Max confessed. "Reinhold said he cannot risk helping us directly. But he glamoured me and said he would stand before a judge and give witness to what the king signed in declaring Snow his rightful heir. That act would uphold his Bonded's wishes and the legal contract signed. But, only if Snow can find a second witness and proof: either the ring or the contract. Otherwise, he will not risk the fae council's judgment."

At this point, Reinhold wasn't risking banishment, not like the rest of them.

Elisabeth stood and paced the floor. "You know what you're asking of me."

Treason. The room fell silent.

"I can tell you're conflicted," Snow said. "And upset. That's understandable."

"But ask yourself if it's truly treason if the king wanted someone else on the throne," Max pressed. "Who should we support? The original choice or the usurper?"

Elisabeth closed her eyes, her voice quieting. "If you fail and the queen arrests me for treason, I'll be hanged."

"I understand why you're calculating your options," Snow said. "You're wise to weigh all possible consequences."

"It's more than just about me," Elisabeth said. "If I fail, who will remain to help our people?"

"How much help have you been so far, honestly?" Runa asked. "You're nice but impotent against the queen."

Max inwardly groaned.

"Elisabeth, you have softened the edges of the queen's moods," Snow said, "and everyone in Clarus appreciates your compassion. But even the nobles are wary of Agnes."

"And the guards only need a reason to change their loyalty," Max added. "A legal reason. You were there when your brother signed the contract. You can make a difference right now."

Elisabeth glanced over her shoulder at a closed curtain with a scowl and then resumed her pacing. Runa looked up at Max with a shrug, but Snow seemed to deliberately avoid his gaze, vacillating between watching the princess and staring at her lap.

"The contract disappeared with Helene. Which means it's lost to us." Elisabeth stopped pacing and squared her shoulders. "I will match Reinhold's risk. If you can find the ring, I will stand with the fae and attest to Snow's legitimate claim to the crown. But, you'll need to search Agnes's rooms soon. Snow is slated to sail away on a ship tomorrow. And Agnes is in quite a state. She won't be going anywhere for days. How will you check her rooms?"

"We planned for that possibility," Runa grinned.

Max had hoped it wouldn't come to this. But finding the ring was vital, worth any cost. He hoped Ludwig and Grim had done their part.

Their next steps would tip-off the queen that Max, the dwarves, and Snow were actively attempting to overthrow the throne. And nowhere in the Seven Kingdoms was there a rock they could hide under that Agnes wouldn't find them.

CHAPTER 27: SNOW

YEAR 10 OF THE MAIDEN COMET, SUMMER

"The queen asked to see me," Snow said to her escort-guard with the bushy brows.

The guard almost recoiled at the request.

"I'm leaving tomorrow," Snow said, adding to the urgency.

As Snow was supposedly in the queen's good graces and the favorite of the court, thanks to her 'fortunate' engagement, the guard didn't question her demand. He marched to the queen's rooms farther down the hallway, with Snow, Max, and Runa behind him. At the queen's door, two of her personal guards stood sentry, and a lone servant greeted them.

"The queen is not to be disturbed," the servant said nervously. The polite language didn't cover the queen's ranting in the next room.

"As the queen's ward," Snow said, "it's improper for me not to meet with her before I depart."

Max piped up, acting oblivious to the impropriety of him standing outside the queen's rooms. "Queen Agnes did forge an advantageous match for the kingdom. And the bride will never return to Solinsel. She must give the queen her due appreciation in person."

The people, even the castle guards and servants, hungered for a different ruler. But they needed—no *deserved*—legitimate proof that it was Snow, or they risked a traitor's death. She sucked in a breath, remembering every bit of training to act the confident queen she was meant to become. Then she lifted her chin and pushed into the queen's room without official permission, Runa on her heels.

They strode through Agnes's sitting room, the destruction glaringly clear. Torn window curtains hung by mere threads, and what little furniture remained was broken. Behind them, Snow's bushy-browed escort exchanged sharp words with the queen's guards at the door, but she didn't stop to hear the argument. Marching ahead, into the sparse bedchambers, splinters of wood lay strewn on the floor—bits from the chair collapsed in the corner. The queen's massive mirror had been shattered, leaving jagged, sharp pieces behind. Only one cabinet stood untouched as if defying the mania of the resident.

Agnes thrashed on her bed, her hair a knotted mess with braids partially pulled apart. A servant, healer, and the high judge were all attempting to calm her. But the servant and healer weren't the queen's usual aids. One was Ludwig, dressed as a healer with a pile of medicines stacked next to him. The other was Dottie, wearing servant's clothing instead of her kitchen apron, which meant Grim had fetched her as planned when he saw Max leave with Snow into the royal wing. Red welts marred Dottie's arms, likely from the queen's nails, and Snow sensed her friend's distress.

"What is the meaning of this?" The judge shot to his feet and approached Snow, stunned at the intrusion.

Runa circled the periphery, her hand sliding behind her, unnoticed . . . until she neared the cabinet. The queen hissed, lashing out with her claw-like fingers at the dwarf.

"I'm here to address the queen's obvious insanity," Snow said defiantly.

The high judge's attention snapped to Snow as he marched toward her. With the judge's back to the queen, Ludwig had the opening he needed. He pressed a rag to the queen's nostrils. Her eyes rolled back, and she collapsed on the bed, her chest still rising and falling.

Snow rushed back to the door, addressing the guards. "Send for a lower judge. Something is amiss with the queen, and we can't rule out the high judge as the culprit. We need someone impartial."

One of the queen's personal guards sprinted away despite the high judge's protests.

"How dare you accuse me," he shouted. "I've been nothing but loyal to Queen Agnes."

"That *may* be true," Snow said. "But we must act prudently."

The queen's other guard started to remove Max, but Snow stopped them. "An impartial witness is exactly what this situation calls for."

"I think not," the high judge argued, his emotions a swirl of frustration, disgust, and swelling panic.

"According to the Law of Solinsel set in year one of the Crone Comet, Age of Reflection, a noble can request a judge's investigation," Snow said, relieved that she'd spent all those moons studying at the dwarven caves.

"B-but . . ." the judge stuttered. He fumed as he stormed from the queen's quarters, the queen's guard following. "This isn't over."

"Thank the Abundants he left. Fortunate." Runa hissed to Snow under her breath. "For him." She lifted the hem of her skirt enough to reveal the small but sturdy pickaxe she'd concealed.

"Do you want to have the queen removed to the healer's quarters?" Max asked overly sweetly. Behind him, her guard watched them from the bedroom door. Snow realized the room would be easier to search without the queen and her constant, bushy-browed shadow.

Snow glanced from Ludwig to Agnes and then commanded her guard-shadow, "Please take the queen to the healer's quarters. This healer will stay with her, but keep a close watch on our queen. We want to keep her safe."

Snow gave Ludwig a meaningful look. Could she trust her half-brother with the queen that he hated? As bushy-brows and the queen's servant carried Agnes away, Snow stopped her brother.

"She deserves proper justice," Snow whispered. "Not vengeance."

"She won't die on my watch," Ludwig whispered back. She sensed the conflict in him fade. "I will do no harm to her today, I swear it. Tomorrow, I make no promise."

When they left, Max shut the door behind them, leaving her, Runa, Max, and Dottie alone.

"What next?" Runa asked.

"The judge has gone to gather support for himself," Snow said, combing through the queen's vanity, each drawer more cracked and dysfunctional than the last. "And the guards will grow suspicious of us in here. So, we don't have much time."

"What be we looking for?" Dottie asked.

"The queen took something from me. And I need it back."

CHAPTER 28: MAX

YEAR 10 OF THE MAIDEN COMET, SUMMER

"Most of everythin' be cleared out from the rooms 'cause of the queen's tantrums," Dottie said, scurrying to the entryway to listen for returning guards. "Even her garb be gone. Servants fetch her a single attire each day."

Max and Snow dug through the messy drawers of her vanity. No jewelry boxes remained, nor wine decanters on the countertop. Runa's attention was on the stone walls, trying to discern if dwarven metal or magic was hidden in the stones. Max checked the top of the mattress and the bed, finding nothing. Before he made to crawl under it, Runa stopped him.

"Hold on." Runa stretched her arm. Then in one quick motion, she flipped the bed over, the crashing sound reverberating as the frame cracked.

"Was that necessary?" Max raised a brow.

"Are we pretending the mad queen hasn't broken a dozen beds in the last moon?" Runa scoffed

"She's not far off the mark," Dottie called out from the next room.

Runa returned to checking the wall, and Max dropped to his knees, continuing his inspection of the wooden frame for hidden compartments or holes in the mattress.

"The cabinet is pristine, which is odd," Snow said, moving toward it.

"No one dared lay a finger on that furniture," Dottie shout-hissed information from the sitting room.

"Wait," Runa said. "Did you see Agnes's violent reaction when I neared her? I was also next to the cabinet."

Max turned around just as Runa threw open the cabinet doors. Inside, they found two dresses in the northern fashion. Agnes had kept them all these years. Max didn't realize she was so sentimental.

"Ohhh . . . what's this?" Runa pulled out a puzzle box from the back of the cabinet.

"All of this was one big game to Agnes," Snow said, shaking her head. "She's clever, one step ahead of me the entire time. Or she was until now."

Max felt along the walls of the cabinet, looking for any abnormality. On the bottom, the nails were bent. Like they'd been yanked out and then hastily reset by an amateur.

Dottie rushed into the bedchambers. "Guards are coming."

"I think the bottom of this cabinet was pried open at one point," Max said. "I need to do it again."

"We'll stall," Snow said, hurrying to the doors with Dottie.

Without asking, Runa tossed him a dagger from under her skirt.

Max reflexively caught it by the hilt. "A little warning?"

"You're welcome." Runa bolted to the door separating the bedchamber and the sitting room, silently closing it and staying with Max.

If the guards breached the bedchamber doorway, they'd easily spot Max. He jammed the dagger between where the bottom plank met the frame, aiming for the area between the nails. The cabinet creaked just as the queen's main door thundered open.

"Judge, I appreciate you coming so quickly," Snow said, speaking loudly. The gap under the door between them was wide enough that the conversation carried. "Solinsel law states that if the crown isn't fit for duty, a regent will be placed until the next heir is selected. We need to review the statute. Where can it be found?"

"Lady Snow," a judge responded, her voice stern. "I'm not comfortable with any of this questioning. I am here because you have accused the high judge of acting against the queen. A bold accusation indeed. Yet for the question you ask, it is only appropriate for the high judge to task the scribes to search the archives."

An awkward silence followed, and Max paused, staying quiet. But, Snow didn't have long to argue until she'd risk arrest herself. Giving up on discretion, Max used a broken bedpost piece as a hammer, slamming it against the handle of the dagger and sliding it between the nails. Trusting the sturdy dwarven craftsmanship, Max used his weight to leverage the plank, ripping up the nails.

Boots marched closer. Runa shoved the vanity in front of the door just as someone careened into it with a thud. A guard yelled, but Max ignored him. He shoved his arm into the enlarged crack in the cabinet. He didn't have time to see if anything dangerous was hidden inside. A finger-breaking rat trap? Poison? Worse?

Runa rushed toward the bed, but before she could shove it in front of the door, the vanity was thrown back, and two guards rushed in. Runa caught the first guard from behind, kicking behind her knees and sending her sprawling.

Max frantically felt around the bottom of the cabinet. There was no box. No ring.

Another guard, older with a mustache, stepped in farther, pulling Snow with him. The guard's hand was wrapped around Snow's arm, his fingers white from the tight grip. Max's instinct was to use the dagger against the guard, but the king's written words were stronger than any blade.

"Snow?" Elisabeth's voice sounded near the entrance, feigning surprise.

Max's fingers brushed up against an object. There *was* something at the bottom of the hidden space. Rolled parchment. Grabbing it, he slid it out, glancing at the seal before cradling the parchment to his chest.

Elisabeth stormed in with Dottie, demanding answers. "What is the meaning of this?"

"These are legal papers for the judge," Max waved the parchment, wanting to be sure that both Elisabeth and the lower judge saw them.

The first guard was already on her feet, and she grabbed Max's document, handing it to the judge. The king's seal and the hiding place signaled that this was the very contract that King Friedrich had signed over two years ago. And the smile on Snow's face confirmed it. The queen must've found them after dismissing Helene. She'd had them hidden all this time. In her delusional state, she'd hoarded rather than destroyed the evidence.

Elisabeth's eyes widened, seeing the parchment. She knew what it was. Good. The princess read over the lower judge's shoulder, their eyes darting frantically across the words. Fortunately, the princess could validate the contract, which would end this mess quickly.

"The ring can't be far. We'll find it, too." Max said to Snow as the lower judge read the parchment.

"Take this merchant out of the royal wing," the older guard instructed his counterpart, still keeping a tight hold on Snow's arm while glaring at Max. "You'll be lucky if you don't find residence in the dungeon."

Max folded his arms. "I'm not leaving this room unless this judge demands it."

The first guard pressed the tip of her sword to Max's side. In his periphery, Runa shifted, her hands sliding to retrieve her pickaxe. And Snow mouthed, 'no,' to them both, her brow scrunched.

The judge gasped, obviously getting to the good part of the contract. "Wait!"

Everyone froze in place as she read the text slowly, her lips moving. Then she read it again, seemingly oblivious to the drawn weapons and iron-hot tempers rising. "Bring me the high judge."

"Can he be trusted?" Snow asked the lower judge. "The queen appointed him."

"Let's find out," the judge said.

The first guard huffed off to find the high judge, and the older guard released Snow. Max couldn't take his attention off her. He was desperate to hold her, comfort her, but she held herself back, refusing to look at him. She was engaged, and it wouldn't be proper. And, Snow was the heir to the throne, far beyond his station.

This was the scenario they'd dreamed of. Worked for. And he knew success meant Snow would officially be on a pedestal, too high for him to touch. His heart twisted as she seemed to soar out of reach.

While they waited for the high judge, the guard stood outside the door, acting more like a warden than a protector, and Elisabeth stayed, seemingly lost in her own thoughts, worrying the edge of her long sleeve. By the time the high judge arrived, the princess had calmed, her head high.

The high judge read the document, his eyes darting to Snow. "Can this be true?"

"She had a ring to prove her legitimacy to the throne, but I suspect the queen confiscated it, too," Elisabeth said, stepping forward.

The high judge looked from Snow to the princess and then back again. Then he dropped to his knee.

"My queen."

Grim ran into the room, a pickaxe in hand, and slid to a stop. Quickly evaluating the broken furniture and mirror, Snow's smile, and everyone else bowing, he frowned. "Dang, I missed all the fun."

The initial adrenaline from the morning gave way to exhaustion after Max oversaw his father's release from the dungeon. Heinrich's hanging had been stayed, but holding his father's thin frame in his arms and half-carrying him to the healers was the real beginning of unchaining his father from the queen's atrocities. After the healers assured Max that Heinrich was in good hands, he hurried to give his full report to the captain of the guard and a council of lower judges.

After his report, Max was told that the lower judges of Caston and Clarus had questioned the queen's appointed high judge, and they believed he had no knowledge of the queen's dark magic nor her depraved actions against King Friedrich's children. However, the high judge resigned due to his blindness to the queen's evil dealings. By the time Max was finished with the judges, the sun was well past its zenith. With the queen in the dungeon, Max found Ludwig, Runa, and Grim in the kitchens with Dottie. The cook pressed hazelnuts and walnuts into a pot and sprinkled nutmeg on top while smiling from ear to ear.

"I didn't expect to see you baking at this hour," Max said.

"Well, can ye blame me? I was busy gnawin' me nails and waitin' for Grim to send me to watch the mad queen," Dottie said. "But now, I reckon a bit of honeyed nuts are the least we can do to celebrate."

"Here-here!" Grim shouted. "Who doesn't like snacks?"

Max turned to Snow's half-brother. "Ludwig, I hate to ask for a favor, but—"

"Anything you need," Ludwig looked more relaxed than Max had ever seen him.

"Will you let my mother know that the danger has passed?" Max asked. "In an hour, tell her she can come see her husband." The healers would need time to get Heinrich cleaned up before his wife rushed to his side.

Ludwig quirked a grin, though with a bit of sadness behind his eyes. Even with the heavy weight lifted, his scars would take longer to heal.

"I am truly happy that you're getting your family back," Ludwig said, putting a hand on his shoulder. Then he turned to Dottie and asked her to save him a piece of the dessert.

"No promises," Runa shouted after him.

"I'll fend her off of the treats!" Grim shouted right after her.

When the nuts were in the oven, Dottie turned to Max. "Speakin' of kin, have you spoken with Snow?"

"She went out for fresh air," Runa said. "Answering all the judges' questions took a toll."

"I'll go find her," Max said. He knew exactly where to look.

In the empty courtyard, Snow sat under the apple tree on a bench that had been fashioned by her father for the woman who'd betrayed them all. Her face was downcast, one hand fiddling with the bracelet he'd given her.

"I thought I'd find you here," Max said, adjusting his bow at his back. "Would you like company, or do you want to be alone?"

"Elisabeth sent everyone away, giving me some peace," Snow said, looking up at him. "But I'd love your company."

He glanced up at the balcony and the open corridor between the castle wings, finding them both blissfully empty. The guards kept watch outside the wall but well out of sight. Most of the others were on high alert, watching all the entrances to the dungeon until the fae arrived to do their own investigation. Agnes must have received her dark magic many years ago, but no one dared risk that she might have an accomplice. The fae would assuredly offer advice and their services to confine the queen going forward. Even Runa and Grim respected—feared—the fae's creative punishments.

Max stepped closer to Snow. Something in her expression looked particularly vulnerable. As if she had finally allowed herself to uncoil after years of tense plans and 'what-ifs'. The unvarnished difficulty was apparent in the way her shoulders hung. She looked up at him, a declaration and a plea in her voice. "I can finally breathe."

"Without Agnes watching your every move with her fae magic," Max said, softly agreeing. "How do you think she did it?"

"She could've used anything, even a silver goblet."

Max nodded, but the queen's room was in shambles. "Perhaps a shard of what was left of her mirror? Or something I missed in her alchemy lab."

The cluttered lab had a semblance of order, unlike the madness they'd seen in her rooms. He couldn't understand Agnes, and he probably never would. Shaking off the last few hours of interrogation and explanation, he sat next to Snow, leaving a wide space between them.

"When will you become the queen?" Max asked, getting right to the point. No reason to deny what came next.

"Soon," Snow said. "When the fae council arrives, I imagine Reinhold will appear and give his witness. Between his word and Elisabeth's, the coronation will officially roll into motion. Moreover, the captain testified that he saw my father's ring on my finger and that the queen took it. His word backs up the contract. So even without Reinhold, I'll be crowned."

Max hoped the fae would find the ring in the alchemy lab. No one but their council was allowed to enter.

"I never worried about a guard or an assassin's blade," Snow said, running her fingers over the amulet bracelet. "I can never thank you enough. But now that the trouble is over, you should take your amulet back." She unclasped it and pressed it into his hand, her fingers sending a warmth through him.

"Keep it, my queen," he said, wrapping his fingers around her hand and the bracelet.

She flushed, and he flipped his wrist upside down, letting gravity drop the bracelet back into her palm.

Snow looked up at him through her dark lashes, and he couldn't help but notice the red of her lips. She leaned forward, her voice a whisper, "Max..."

"You know..." Max said, taking on the burden of what needed to be said. He released her hand and gently re-clasped the bracelet around her wrist as he spoke. "I hear the prince is more in love with you than ever. You agreed to marry him under duress, but you're in charge of your destiny now."

His fingers lingered on the clasp, a growing tension between them. He wanted to add that she should pick a strong kingdom partner or a skilled noble to help her right the crumbling kingdom. But he didn't. He almost hated that he didn't. How selfish was he for wanting to keep her to himself?

Snow leaned closer, closing the distance between them, one hand gripping his forearm. Max's heart thrummed against his ribs, a vain hope expanding in his chest. Was she choosing him? Her attention dropped from his eyes to his lips, her chin lifting.

Max moved to grab her hip when their peace was broken by footsteps on the gravel.

"Snow," Princess Elisabeth called out, striding closer to them, her hands tucked behind her. "It's almost time for dinner, and the guards are restless to have you in their sights."

Snow stood, greeting Elisabeth. "Very thoughtful of you to arrange a quiet moment for me. Thank you."

Elisabeth grinned and produced an apple from behind her back. "These apples are yours now. They're from the last year's stores. Did you know the queen had them waxed and *labeled*? She was absolutely fastidious."

From her body language, Max anticipated Elisabeth's throw before the fruit left her fingertips. He caught the apple mid-air as it sailed gently toward Snow, flashing a smile at the future queen.

"Max!" Snow said, exasperated.

He jogged back away from them both, clutching the apple in his hand, and Elisabeth frowned.

"Catch," he said, laughing. He feigned as if he was going to throw it, hard. But instead, he strode back to Snow, pulled by an invisible string, and put it gently into her palm, but didn't release it. They stood for a moment, balancing the apple between them. Max should've spoken of strategy, of alliances, of her other options for marriage. But all he could envision was him by her side; he wanted to be in her life as more than a friend. More than her royal huntsman.

"So, the prince and his envoy were planning to leave tomorrow," Elisabeth said. "Should I tell them to leave without you?"

"I've already told Prince Leopold that my place is here," Snow said. "The engagement is done; we ended it on good terms."

Max released the apple—dropped it—but Snow gripped it with a grin. Relief washed over him, and her grin turned mischievous. His heart thumped, and he very much looked forward to getting Snow alone again.

"How does the apple taste, now that you're queen?" Elisabeth asked.

Snow grinned at Max and lifted the apple to her lips. Then she bit down, juice dribbling unceremoniously down her chin. Max should've laughed. Should've kissed her. But his attention was drawn to the tingling sensation in his hand. He flexed his fingers, perplexed. Had he strained his hand at some point? Maybe when leveraging the bottom of the queen's cabinet open?

Snow turned and continued her conversation with the princess. While they spoke, Max flexed his hand, trying to shake off the discomfort. Beyond Snow and Elisabeth, in the dark tunnel that led to the training yard, something stirred. Was his paranoia from the last few years playing tricks on his mind?

In the tunnel, Max saw the movement again, animalistic, and crouched near the ground. The shadow stalked toward them. Before he saw the black fur, he heard the low growl.

CHAPTER 29: SNOW

YEAR 10 OF THE MAIDEN COMET, SUMMER

The apple's scent was strong and sweet. Familiar. It reminded Snow of something, but before she could place it, a growl sent a chill down her spine.

Impossible.

"Elisabeth?" Snow could barely whisper the word, her throat tight. Her aunt slowly pivoted, both their attention drawn to the apparition moving in the darkened tunnel.

The Shadow Beast stalked out and into the light, its black hair a sharp contrast to the white fleshy scar slashed across its nose. Snow's insides turned to water, and the apple slipped from her fingers. No guards were stationed close enough to see the beast, let alone fight.

The beast leaned back on its haunches, letting out a low growl which quickly grew higher, louder. An unnatural wind whipped through the courtyard. The leaves of the apple tree violently shuddered, several unripe fruits crashing to the ground in an uneven pattern.

The tone of the growl shifted into a slight keening waver. Snow dragged her leaden feet and put herself between her aunt and the beast, searching the area for someone controlling the creature. Someone with fae magic.

The beast dared Snow to look into its crimson eyes. But she ignored the pull; she wouldn't make herself easy prey. She couldn't afford to fall into its trap—she could barely function to begin with. As the beast's patterned keening began to climax, her heart raced, a warning blaring somewhere in the back of her mind. The beast would attack—they had just moments before certain death.

But what could they do? In the Rosewood attack, they'd had four armed individuals, and now they only had Max's bow and arrow and a couple of short blades between them. It wouldn't be enough.

Snow used her greatest weapon, opening herself up without reservation. She'd been so focused on Max earlier that she hadn't noticed anyone else. Whoever controlled the beast, they wouldn't be far. She quickly scanned the area, including the balcony, but sensed no one other than her aunt and Max. Snow glanced back at him, finding his stance wide as he readied his bow and arrow. Fear pressed on him, but he was pushing it back by sheer will, determined to fight.

Just behind her, Princess Elisabeth emanated surprising calm. Focus. Her usual bitterness was overshadowed by another emotion: vindication.

Snow's stomach cramped, and she wrapped her arm around her middle. Elisabeth stepped to Snow's side with a glint in her eye and an expression that Snow had seen once before—one of unrestrained delight. But when Snow had seen that quirk of the lips and the lift of the chin before, it was on the face of the queen—when she'd cornered

Snow in the dwarves' cave. Snow tilted her head, trying to understand the sneer on her aunt's face and the feeling of triumph rolling off her.

"Finally, you begin to understand," Elisabeth said quietly. Coldly.

Stunned, Snow could barely think as her stomach clenched like a vice, and she doubled over, wishing she'd vomit. In her periphery, Max trained his arrow on the beast. Even in her condition, she noticed that his grip was slightly off, but she couldn't figure out why.

Her head swam.

It doesn't matter. A single arrow cannot take down that beast.

Snow's knees weakened, threatening to give way. The princess grabbed Snow's arm, holding firm. Then Snow collapsed, but her knees didn't hit the ground—her shoulder screamed as the tissue strained under the full force of her own weight.

"Magic is affecting Snow," Elisabeth, feigning assistance, cried out the lie to Max over the beast's keening. "Probably connected to the Wild creature."

"Poison?" Snow rasped as a burn ripped lower through her gut.

"There's no stopping it now, Snow," Elisabeth cooed, sarcasm cutting at the edges. "Your dosage is infinitely higher than your father's."

Snow gasped, stunned at Elisabeth's machinations.

"I thought I could ensnare the north in a trade deal," Elisabeth whispered, pivoting so Max couldn't see her lips moving. "But we can't have everything, can we? And the real prize is the crown. It was rather comical watching you fumble, thinking *you* could ever rule Solinsel. You were born nothing and will die with less. I must admit you caused me a few headaches, but your latest attempt to thwart me worked in my favor. With the queen dethroned, I can step in and fill the void even sooner than I'd planned. In the meantime, I can't have an illegitimate orphan running around fixing things I've intentionally broken. I've set the stage to become a beloved queen. Which means I need the people's gratitude for my improvements. As *small* as they might be."

Greed flared, practically choking Snow. From the corner of her eyes, she saw Max trained on the beast, sweat beading along his brow. The creature shifted onto its haunches, waiting. Poised to pounce. Max would never defeat the creature, no matter how long Elisabeth waited, toying with them.

"The queen? You poisoned her, too," Snow guessed.

"Just her mind. I needed her body whole, at least until the people revolted. With her imprisoned and you dead, the people will be desperate. They'll beg me to take the throne. And I'll give the nobles who judged me *exactly* what they deserve. Once I get rid of that dolt high judge Agnes selected, no one will dare challenge me. Can you believe Agnes tried to outsmart me? She confiscated Friedrich's legal succession declaration before I could steal it. I should thank you for confiding in me today about your little ploy. Though, I never expected you to actually find the papers—just to be caught by the witless guard that I alerted. But even after that little miracle, I again outmaneuvered my brother's bastard child."

Max's stance shifted just slightly. Was he aiming at Elisabeth? Trusting he was following his instincts, Snow drew the princess's attention before she noticed.

"You killed your own brother?" Snow wriggled, testing the princess's grip, and the dull ache in her shoulder roared with the movement.

Elisabeth's emotions flared with jealousy, and Snow half expected the Shadow Beast to lunge and feast. However, the princess reigned in her runaway hatred and ignored Snow's pathetic attempts to free herself. "Honestly, I calculated a more prolonged death, just like your sister's."

The princess's self-cathartic words inwardly calmed, finally releasing all the secrets she'd held so close. Pride oozed from her, wildly discordant with the repulsive horror Snow felt at Elisabeth's every syllable. Snow couldn't speak. Not because of the searing pain but because of the roiling disgust in her stomach.

Snow couldn't hide her reaction. Every abject thought running through her mind shone on her face. Between the poison of the apple and the princess's confession, Snow didn't have the capacity to don a mask for her thoughts. And Elisabeth seemed pleased. Behind the princess, Max's blurry form stepped closer.

"I poisoned you moons ago, but the comb didn't carry a lethal dose. Even so, you didn't get as sick as I'd anticipated." Elizabeth eyed her, curiosity rising.

"You were the vendor in Isolzing?" The cramps in Snow's gut threatened to shred her insides. "Why not kill me then?"

"Careful where you point that arrow, huntsman." Elisabeth glared at Max. "I control the real weapon. If I die, the beast will be loosed. Remember that. For now, I'm holding my pet at bay. What do you think will happen to the woman you love if I'm not here to stop the beast? Besides, we wouldn't want it to find its way through the castle or race down the mountain and meet your mother along the way, would we?"

Max lowered his arrow to point at the ground, his jaw clenched. Elisabeth's attention slid back to Snow. "Why would I kill you, Snow, when I could weaken you instead and use you in my negotiations with Leopold?"

Every time Snow wore the comb, it poisoned her a little more. She'd embraced sentimental memories and not trusted her instincts. She groaned, her stomach clenching. "How?"

"My fae found you before you even arrived at the trading post last year," Elisabeth said.

"You don't have a Bonded," Max shot. "Not anymore."

Elisabeth leveled a withering glare at the huntsman. "Know your place, huntsman." The princess turned to Snow, her features twisting into a sickening triumph. "It wasn't a stretch to figure out you would show up in Isolzing. So predictable. Though, I'd nearly given up when my paid informants alerted me to your arrival. The rest was easy. The posters were a contingency in case I couldn't find you, but of course, I did. And I couldn't have the guards snatch you up when a better plan—a more lucrative plan—was possible with Prince Leopold. So I glamoured you. A simple bit of magic."

"The bee sting," Snow forced her words, despite the pain. "How often did you glamour to look like Agnes?"

"*You* sent Heinrich Hunt to kill Snow and bring back her heart and liver," Max spat.

"You took my ring in the cave," Snow added.

Snow was a pig Elisabeth had fattened for slaughter. How had she been so blind? From this angle, Snow caught movement on the balcony, above Elisabeth's gaze—Runa, pickaxes in both hands, slipped closer. Her narrowed eyes were on the princess—good. Still, Runa was too far to aim decently; she might hit Snow. But could she maim the beast?

Snow retched onto the gravel, feeling a momentary reprieve before a wave of nausea hit again followed by an instinct even more frightening—the urge to sleep.

"You weakened the kingdom so the suffering people would gladly put a scorned princess on the throne," Max spat.

Elisabeth's emotions shifted along with her torso, a feral anger released as she looked upon the beast. Without her walls, Snow felt as if she were doused in blistering water. She cried out but didn't attempt to block Elisabeth's emotions. Instead, Snow dove deeper. Something slithered below the princess's anger. Almost as if a thread of crystalized intent swam like a sea snake away from the princess. A command.

The princess's grip on Snow's arm loosened, and she felt herself drop to the ground.

She waited to be ripped to shreds. Snow looked up at her aunt, not shrinking from the unavoidable pain. But Elisabeth wasn't looking at her dying niece.

She stared at the huntsman.

"No!" Snow screamed as if she could stop the inevitable as her heart shattered. But the words echoed only in her own head.

A roar sounded from the creature as it raced toward Max. He cried out, and Snow was sure he'd gotten off one arrow, but she couldn't see much past the mass of fur in her direct line of sight. Runa called, a flash of metal flying from her hands followed by a clatter on the cobblestones. The pickaxe landed steps behind the princess.

Elisabeth's attention was focused on her beast-puppet, her mind still consumed with oily indignation. With every drop of strength, Snow dug her fingers against the stones, willing away the pain and the sleepiness. Could she jolt Elisabeth's connection with the Shadow Beast?

With strength beyond her, Snow surged up. Using her uninjured arm, she punched her aunt in the diaphragm. Without waiting to see if her plan worked, Snow crawled, uncoordinated, toward the axe.

Was Max injured? Had the beast claimed Max as it had her mother?

Finding herself on one knee, Snow wrapped her fingers around the smooth wooden handle. From the castle tunnel, Ludwig raced into the courtyard, catching her attention. He yelled as he raised his sword. Determination filled him . . . but Snow was closer.

Snow spun, weapon raised.

The creature had paused, distracted by Elisabeth's momentary lapse in magical control and Ludwig's cry of vengeance. Snow didn't waste her chance. Using every technique she'd learned and every fiber of her being, Snow hurled the iron axe. As it left her fingers, the tear in her shoulder ripped deeper. But her aim—for the Shadow Beast's neck—was true.

CHAPTER 30: MAX

YEAR 10 OF THE MAIDEN COMET, SUMMER

Pinned under the beast's paw, Max's heart pounded. At Ludwig's cries, the creature leaned back, decreasing the pressure from Max's chest. Desperate to escape, he attempted to roll away, but the beast's foreleg was too heavy. Snow cried out a sob, and it pierced him more painfully than a Shadow Beast's claw. The creature's body shuddered, and the earth trembled. Max spotted the handle of the pickaxe; the blade sunk deep, above the front shoulder.

Elisabeth's screech was drown by the beast's own guttural cry. The creature reared, and Ludwig's blade sliced along its side. The beast countered, but this time its injured limb was slower—though its extended claws were just as deadly. Snow's brother had learned his lesson from the last battle, and he dodged in time.

Ludwig's gambit gave Max the chance to scramble away. Unable to put weight on the injured foreleg, the creature shifted onto its back legs.

Ludwig lunged and slid his sword into the beast's soft underbelly; with the expertise of a butcher, he stabbed through the space between the ribs.

"No!" Elisabeth shouted.

The creature didn't seem to quite realize its injuries as it stumbled. Ludwig jumped and rolled away from its open maw, unable to retrieve his sword. Max pushed up to his knees, wiping sweat from his eyes, taking in his surroundings in a blink. Snow crouched on the ground, and Elisabeth loomed too close, her hands curled like claws. But the princess's attention was on her dying beast. For now.

Overhead, Runa watched covertly from the balcony—Max had to give the dwarves time to alert the guards.

"You never really broke your Bond with your fae, did you," Max shouted at Elisabeth.

That's who you were talking to in your rooms earlier.

"Oh, but I did," Elisabeth said, spittle punctuating her angry words as her attention flitted between her beast and its attackers. "When my parents suspected I was behind the mysterious 'abominable deeds' in the palace, I had to do something drastic. I'd been sloppy. And too soft. But, I was young. Foolishly, I broke my Bond. I begged my parents for forgiveness and blamed my mistakes on the bad influence of my fae."

A keening sounded from the beast. Not the feigned mourning from the beast Max had heard before—this sound was no trick. The beast faltered, disjointedly falling on the ground under the apple tree, his breath a ragged gurgle.

"Your fae was wrongly imprisoned?" Snow gasped.

"You assume he is innocent? Like calls to like, child. That's why our Bond was so strong—he said that is why we were matched." Elisabeth took a step toward her beast, her nostrils flaring. "The fae council had no idea the depths of himself that he'd kept hidden. We helped each other. But after the Bond broke, I spent *years* gathering enough magic from the Wildwood to contact him. I can never touch my fae again with him trapped between realms, but he still mentored me through my mirror."

"You idiot," Runa spat from the balcony, shouting loud enough for the valley to hear. "The fae was building your abilities so you could break him out. And then he would have ruled us all. Including *you!*"

Max grit his teeth, willing Runa to run for help.

"He would never do that to me," Elisabeth's voice rose while she took another step toward her Shadow Beast, the hilt of Ludwig's blade marking the killing blow.

"You betrayed him. What loyalty would he really have to you?" Max said. Poison had touched his skin—his hand. The tingling in his palm had progressed deeper into his muscles and well past his wrist, leaving his fingertips numb.

Snow heaved, crouched on the ground, the apple near her feet. Her skin was grey and waxy. She winced but dragged herself to the apple, kneeling over the fruit so it was hidden under her skirt.

Now that the princess had stepped away from Snow, Max slid his hand to his quiver. Then, in a quick motion, he yanked out an arrow and had it nocked and aimed. His string wasn't properly taut, his aim slightly off-kilter. But he kept his expression the same, not indicating that the poison had compromised him. Instead, he calculated how he'd need to adjust his aim.

The beast stilled, and the courtyard seemed suspended in time. Then, breaking the silence, a feral scream ripped from Elisabeth's body—a culmination of anger, desperation, and frustration combined into evil unleashed. Max half expected the clouds to darken and lightening to strike.

Elisabeth spun away from the Shadow Beast, facing Max. "You have no idea how much I suffered after the Bond was broken. But you will."

"I might be poisoned, *dear* aunt," Snow interjected, her voice weak but unfaltering. "But I am your biggest threat."

From Elisabeth's sleeve slid a long, slender dagger with an onyx blade. Her eyes narrowed in deadly hatred, her attention on the huntsman.

Max let the arrow fly. However, instead of coming straight at him, she spun to the side—and the arrow flew impotently past. Then Elisabeth leapt next to Snow, crouching next to her, the dark blade at the ready. So close to Snow that Max didn't trust his shot. Not now.

Ludwig began to charge.

"Stop!" Max screamed and signaled for Ludwig to back up. Elisabeth would kill Snow—it wouldn't take much. Snow teetered on the edge of consciousness.

Elisabeth grabbed Snow's arm upward, revealing the gold amulet on her wrist. Not taking her attention off Max, Elisabeth unclasped it, a sickening grin forming on her face.

"Snow, let us see how smart your friends are," Elisabeth sneered, pressing the edge of her blade to Snow's neck. In her other hand, the gold bracelet swung like a tiny rope, glinting in the afternoon sun. "Your huntsman knows his life is forfeit, but his parents are negotiable. Depending on his choices right now. And he knows I'm resourceful."

There was no decision to make. Though he didn't reveal it, Max would not sacrifice Snow.

"I have nothing left to lose," Ludwig shouted.

"You have three *relatively* good reasons to rethink that comment," Elisabeth said coolly. Ludwig froze in place, his chest heaving. The princess glanced down at the amulet in her hand, then at Max. "My fae ally is quite resourceful. He knows about many fae relics. Even ones that have been in certain human families for generations."

Elisabeth quickly clicked the clasp into place, signaling her protection against any arrow tip or dagger blade. For a moment, her brow scrunched as she inspected the dwarven chain. She frowned, her lips moving slightly as she seemed to be trying to interpret the dwarven markings. She shook her head, seemingly shrugging off the symbols. Then she slowly looked up at Max, the edge of her lip curling in a cocksure smile.

The princess stood tall, defiant. She'd won, and she knew it.

"Shoot her," Ludwig hissed under his breath at Max.

"It won't work," Max muttered back, growing desperate.

Snow was dying right in front of him, and if he stepped any closer, Elisabeth would mercilessly end Snow. Runa had disappeared, but if a guard showed up after Snow died, it would be the princess's word against Snow's unknown half-brother and the huntsman Snow had jilted in favor of a prince.

"I'll never forget how you eat fruit like a child who's been given an arrow," Snow's voice was a hoarse whisper, but Max made out the words. "Dangerous. Illogical."

He remembered the game.

"And I love you for it," Snow said.

"Ahh, a touching goodbye," Elisabeth said. "But you'll see him in Fairen'la soon enough."

Snow shifted her hand in front of her, moving her skirt just enough to draw Max's attention to the apple half-hidden beneath her, one bite missing.

"Don't think, Max. Trust." Snow mouthed more than whispered. "Instinct."

She lifted the apple and tapped it to her own heart. Did she want him to shoot Elisabeth? His arrow tip would pass right through the princess. The wooden shaft might do some damage, but would it be enough?

The princess smiled and held her chin high, sure of her victory. But then Snow pulled her legs under herself and squared herself into a crouch, sitting directly in front of the princess. Max could only imagine how difficult that was for her, fighting for that specific position.

Snow tapped the fruit's red flesh with her finger.

The poisoned apple—it all made sense.

Snow tossed the apple straight up in the air. And time seemed to slow.

Her plan—a desperate attempt to stop the princess—became clear.

For a moment, the apple hung, suspended in midflight, before descending. Max aimed on instinct, compensating for his weakened arm. He only had one chance. He released the arrow. The string snapped. The shaft flew. A familiar *thwack* sounded as the metal tip pierced the apple then a reverberating *thunk* as the wood shot into its target.

Elisabeth gasped, the apple pinned to her chest, directly over her heart, secured in place with the arrow. Her smile vanished as she looked down and gripped the shaft. She huffed, more irritated than concerned.

"A bit of wooden shaft isn't going to stop me," she spat.

"The wood won't kill you," Snow said.

"The poison carried through from the apple will," Max said.

Elisabeth's eyes widened, her nostrils flaring. She muttered an incantation in a language Max had never heard. She shook her head, panicked, muttering the words again, louder.

"No, no, no!" The princess bolted for the castle's main doors, but she only got a few steps before she stumbled. Swaying on her feet, she yanked the arrow from her chest.

In the shadow of the tallest Clarus spire, Elisabeth collapsed onto her knees. She shifted, revealing the blood staining the front of her dress. Elisabeth pressed her hands to her chest as if willing the poison to *not* stop her heart. Or for her blood to reverse polarity from sickly to clean. Either option was an impossibility.

"We were so close. After all these years," Elisabeth muttered, her voice strained, gazing at her Shadow Beast.

If she said anything else, the words were swallowed by the pounding of guards' boots through the castle tunnel. Max dropped his bow and ran to Snow's side, pulling her into his lap. She blinked up at him, her skin cold, as he brushed her hair away from her face with numb fingers. Runa was leading the contingency of guards quickly through the corridor. But they couldn't help Snow now. Whatever the poison had done to her, no sword could undo it.

As if hearing Max's silent cry of despair, Reinhold fluttered down from the balcony, landing next to the skewered apple.

Ignoring the tingling numbness in his own hand, Max blurted, "Snow, she's been poisoned."

Reinhold nodded, his face drawn. "Hurry. We have work to do."

CHAPTER 31: SNOW

YEAR 10 OF THE MAIDEN COMET, SUMMER

S now blinked awake, finding herself in a room . . . she didn't recognize. She lay in an enormous bed situated in the center of a
spacious chamber. The walls came into focus, painted in hues of soft
blue and silver, which shimmered in the glow of the crystal chandeliers
suspended from the ceiling. Blooming lavender wafted from the win-
dowsill and mingled with the sweet aroma of beeswax candles.

Snow propped herself up on goose-down pillows amid the soft,
plush periwinkle linens.

Where am I?

Morning light drifted in through embroidered, gossamer curtains,
framing the tall windows. A gleaming vanity stood against one wall,
holding an assortment of silver brushes and delicate bottles. A cozy
sitting area with a cushioned bench sat under the window, and the
nearby table held an ornate goblet and a petite vase filled with flowers.

The fresh air beckoned Snow to the window. Moving to the edge of the bed, Snow felt only the slightest wave of nausea before swinging her legs over the side.

Her toes brushed against soft, pliant fabric—something decidedly *not* floor.

"Hello?" Max mumbled, his voice rough from sleep as he sat up from his position on the floor. His eyes met hers then widened as he shot to his feet. "Snow! Thank the Abundants!"

"What happened?" Snow asked, her memories of the Shadow Beast jumbling in her mind.

She pushed herself off the bed before realizing she was only wearing a thin nightgown. In a blink, Max held a sunny robe of butterscotch velvet and draped it over her shoulders, his fingers grazing her neck. Snow warmed at his touch and happily took his offered arm as he guided her to the window seat.

Out the window, her gaze wasn't drawn to the king's forest in the distance but instead, to Clarus's courtyard and the apple tree below. Memories flashed: the triumph before she bit into the crisp apple. The way acid burned at the back of her throat—the bitterness of betrayal. Her stomach cramped, and she tightened her grip on Max's arm.

"Princess Elisabeth?" Snow pushed the words out past the tightness in her chest.

"Gone," Max said with a sharp finality at odds with how tenderly he situated Snow on the cushioned bench, putting a pillow behind her back. "The fae council planned to remove her mirror to the fae realm to destroy it."

Snow shuddered; the dark fae had spied on her using the mirror in Elisabeth's rooms. At least it was in the sitting area, not watching her while she slept. Elisabeth had taken the mirror back, which explained the frantic conversation they'd overheard right before Runa, Max, and herself had entered her room.

"Wait, you said the fae *planned* to destroy it? What happened?" Snow asked. Why was Max just standing there? He had to be exhausted, too. It would be far better, for his sake, to sit next to her. And maybe for hers, too.

Max leaned over and brushed his thumb over the furrows of her forehead. "Don't worry. Runa and Grim took pickaxes to the mirror and then handed over the shards."

Snow's frustration momentarily cleared. "I'll bet the fae council appreciated their help. So . . . proactive."

The moment stretched as Max held her gaze, and Snow's heart began to pound.

Then Max shook his head and straightened, keeping his attention averted from her face. "Well, there were some choice words said, but our friends didn't get cursed, so I figure that's a win."

It *was* a win. So, why did Snow feel sad?

Max cleared his throat and stepped back. "I'll fetch Reinhold now. He insisted I send for him as soon as you awoke."

Panic seized her, and she snatched his sleeve. "No."

Her breaths grew shallow. If he left, would she see him again? It was irrational, but she was afraid nonetheless. "Don't go."

Max hesitated. Then his hand enveloped hers, and Snow's heart nearly shattered as he peeled her hand from his sleeve. But then, instead of letting go, his fingers slid between hers. Her heart, so heavy only a beat before, took flight.

Max.

He'd nearly been lost to her so many times. Yet, he was here. At least for now.

"I'll have a servant fetch Reinhold, then," Max said, his voice rough. She sensed his hope but also a sadness she didn't quite understand. He squeezed her hand and then released her. "I won't go anywhere until you wish it."

There was something more to his words, yet every nerve in her body tingled as if awakening from a long slumber. In that tender moment, Snow's thoughts spun like gossamer threads, weaving a tapestry of affection . . . and she let them go unchecked, blaming it on her exhaustion.

The morning light warmed Snow's back, but her attention remained fixed on Max as he strode to the door. She soaked up the assurance of his presence as he spoke with the old steward and a guard outside. As the door clicked shut, he strode back, and her gaze followed his every move. Her eyes traced the lines of his form, lingering on his broad shoulders before skimming lower to his narrow waist. He moved with the deadly grace of a hunter—or more accurately, the queen's huntsman.

"How long was I asleep?" she asked as Max neared. "Have you spoken to Heinrich and Addy? Ludwig? How was I cured?"

"Slow down." Max chuckled, but she noticed things she'd missed before. Like the fatigue rimming his eyes and the stiff set of his shoulders. "Two days. Yes. And my parents and Ludwig are hale. Everyone is just worried about you."

But Snow was awake now. She felt better. Yet, he was still worried about something.

"Reinhold cured you. He can explain more when he gets here." Max's attention shot to the side table. "I nearly forgot; he left this for you."

He picked up the delicate crystal goblet brimming with elixir and extended it to her. But Snow's attention remained on the table, or more specifically, on the anemones in the vase there. They must have been the last ones of the season. Who else would have bothered to gather them for her . . . except Max? Her heart melted, and questions burned her tongue, but when she turned to Max, his posture was stiff as he held out the goblet.

Maybe she'd read too much into the gesture. Maybe it wasn't even him. Maybe . . .

She turned her attention to the goblet and the liquid within. When the morning light touched the elixir, it shimmered. Snow sipped, and the liquid cascaded over her tongue in a symphony of flavors including citrus, lavender, and . . . elderberry. The mixture left a lingering sweetness on her tongue and quieted the vestiges of her nervous stomach.

A servant knocked and entered, bearing a tray of assorted fruits and a small dish of honey to drizzle on top. Strawberries, raspberries, and slices of perfectly ripened melon glistened invitingly. She set it on the table and maneuvered it closer, taking Snow's empty goblet when she departed.

"Dottie is upset with herself for letting you out of her sight that night," Max said, frowning at the table now between them. "I expect she'll spoil you rotten during your reign."

"She's sweet, but what could she have done?" Snow replied. "Truthfully, I'm grateful Dottie wasn't in the middle of that fight. If she had been . . ." She couldn't finish the sentence.

Max stepped past the tray and slid onto the bench.

"Dottie is safe," he said softly, reminding her the danger had passed.

His hand rested in the gap between them. The space felt like a rushing river, making her skin prickle. His gaze dropped to his hand between them. Clearing his throat, again, he shifted his sleeve, revealing the amulet bracelet.

"Reinhold put a drop of some elixir on my tongue and then commanded that I wear the amulet until you awoke." Max fiddled with the clasp. "But apparently, I'll need some help getting this off."

Snow swallowed. But her fingers deftly worked to release the clasp. Max stared at her with widened eyes, not moving as the metal dropped from his wrist.

He was affected by *her* touch. Max snapped his mouth closed and took the bracelet in hand.

Snow chastised herself. Just because she could sense people didn't mean she should. So, she pulled back. And found that she could. Naturally.

Relief flooded her. She'd never needed the witch's help forever. Snow simply needed maturity. And a safe emotional space to practice.

She wanted to assure Max that she hadn't sensed anything from him. But that wouldn't be strictly true, so she kept silent and held out her arm. Max's fingers slid under her wrist, rough and calloused. He wrapped the bracelet around her and fastened the clasp before brushing his fingers over the soft skin inside her wrist.

"There," he said. But his hands lingered, suspended in that space, and Snow couldn't move.

She *hoped* he would pull her to him, to promise to stay with her. Always. She searched him, seeing the longing etched in his face. But there was something else, too. Something fragile.

Max released her, pulling back. The gap between them became a chasm, and the rushing river widened.

"The dwarven runes that Wielbran and Gertrild added to the chain," Max continued, "I heard the fae talking about them. Somehow, the dwarven magic layered on top of the fae amulet, altering it."

"I didn't know that was possible. What does that even mean?"

"After I showed the fae Elisabeth's alchemy lab, they discussed the amulet with Reinhold. When the fae remembered I was in the room—mind you I had been there the whole time—they stopped talking. But shortly thereafter, Reinhold instructed me to wear the bracelet."

"You were poisoned, too," Snow said, worried at the realization.

"I'm fine." Max shrugged, reassuring her before continuing. "The fae had me put the bracelet on you, too, for three hours each day. But from their expressions, I don't think you really needed it. Not in the way they expected."

"Elisabeth disguised herself as a vendor and sold me a wooden comb. I was wearing it the day you showed up with Nora," Snow said, clutching the amulet to her chest. "I was sick the day you gave me the amulet, but never after. And Elisabeth said that I didn't get as sick as she'd expected. Not as sick as everyone else, anyway, including Agnes."

"You should know—Agnes will heal, but she's still nonsensical," Max said slowly. "Even so, from what we have gathered, Agnes knew someone was manipulating her. We found Helene very much alive. In the dungeon."

"What?" Snow wasn't sure if it was the shocking conversation or the elixir, but her mind was clear.

"According to Helene, the queen dismissed her while Elisabeth was away. Probably in Isolzing, waiting for you. We think the princess's spells ebbed after a time, which is why she returned at regular intervals to Clarus. Agnes began to realize what was happening, but she couldn't clearly communicate. She did manage to instate a new high judge, though. We can only assume that Agnes sent Helene to the one place where she would be protected by guards day and night: the dungeon. I think that, once Elisabeth realized that Helene no longer had the papers, the judge no longer mattered to the princess. Agnes took a calculated risk, which probably saved Helene's life. And Elisabeth's fae was so focused on finding you during that time that he didn't realize Agnes had taken the papers."

"So, I have two high judges?" Snow mulled, absently spearing a piece of melon with her fork. "This will be interesting."

"Helene is an expert in the law, a loyal servant of the people *and* you—yet dismissed without cause," Max said. "But the new judge did admirable work. I think Agnes picked him because she knew his family and that he wasn't part of the established upper crust of Solinsel. She didn't know who else to trust. Anyway, I don't envy your decision, whatever you do."

It was one thing to imagine being the queen but quite another to actually be responsible for real people's lives. Was Snow ready?

Max reached out and took Snow's hand, and she gripped it like a lifeline. But she didn't look at him, not wanting him to pull away. Did he want to put all the trauma behind him, including Snow? Did he want to still be her royal huntsman? Or something more?

But was he giving her what she needed at his own expense? Max was the kind of man who would do just that. Even if he wanted to stay in her life, could she give him the love and attention he deserved? The answer was a sinking stone. No, not when her kingdom was falling apart. She couldn't make any promises to anyone until she did everything she could to buoy up her sinking kingdom.

And Max knew it. It explained his reticence. He relished the ever-changing woods and she was destined for an unyielding crown.

Even so, Max deserved an honest discussion. Snow racked her brain searching for the right words, but before she could speak, Reinhold burst in.

"Lady Snow," he said. "*Princess* Snow," he corrected, rushing to greet her with a quick bow. "I'm glad you are finally awake."

The fae looked harried with his hair mussed and his expression drawn. Reinhold wasn't one to panic, and Elisabeth was gone, so why was he swirling with internal turbulence?

"Reinhold," Snow said. "What's wrong?"

"Come with me," he said to them both. "To the king's tomb."

Max shook his head. "Wait, I almost thought you said 'tomb'."

"Help the princess," Reinhold snapped at Max. "She's still weak. But she'll survive."

"You may be a fae, but you're bound to laws while you reside here," Max said. "You cannot force a human ruler to do anything."

"She's not the queen," Reinhold shot back. "Not yet."

"I'll be fine," Snow assured Max, her curiosity outweighing any danger she sensed. She took Max's arm and turned to Reinhold. "Lead the way."

Snow and Max followed Reinhold, all three of them glamoured to look like merchants, as they hurried through the courtyard. Apparently, real fae glamours were painless, nothing like Elisabeth's bee-sting-slap. An unknown fae stood near the apple tree, inspecting the leaves. The vitality of the tree had been restored, likely thanks to fae magic, though the fruit that had prematurely dropped would never be harvested.

Snow couldn't help but search the ground and notice there was no evidence of Elisabeth's gory demise. Her mind reeled back, envisioning when the Shadow Beast took its last breath. The creature who had killed her mother was no longer a threat. Max grabbed her hand, comforting her. Or perhaps he needed a little comfort, too.

Before they exited the courtyard and started down the hill, Max whispered to Snow. "Reinhold helped us, but we're leaving without alerting anyone. Is this wise?"

"I trust him. And I owe him." Reinhold wouldn't risk getting cast out, but her reasoning was more than that. Snow sensed nothing malicious. And she trusted herself.

If she'd honed her gifting earlier and learned to listen to her instincts, she would've seen through Elisabeth much sooner. She might've been able to save her father. Max moved his arm to wrap around her waist, pulling her closer as they walked in tandem down the hillside.

"Reinhold," Snow said, trying to keep up with his long strides. "Your glamour on Max is flawless, even the shadows. Could a witch ever master the art?"

"Humans don't live long enough to perfect most magic spells," Reinhold said. "Elisabeth was unable to master refraction. I would have easily spotted whenever Elisabeth posed as Agnes, but I wasn't residing at the castle."

"Just in the kitchens?" Max objected.

"A fae must eat," he huffed. "Anyway, now that you've seen a witch's work, you won't be fooled so easily."

"If you haven't been at Clarus," Max asked. "Where have you been?"

"I never left the Clarus property," the fae said. "I just wasn't in the castle."

Reinhold turned onto another path, which was only a few paces until it ended at a rocky cliff face. The fae snapped his fingers and pointed for Snow to stand in front of it. Snow took a tentative step forward, wondering if this was the famed tomb of past rulers. She hadn't been able to see the entrance from the castle window. Without warning, Reinhold grabbed her wrist and slapped her hand on the rock face.

"You may have time to waste, but not everyone is so fortunate," Reinhold said flatly.

The entrance lit up, just like the dwarven entrance. A doorway cracked open, widened, and then thudded into place. Inside, plain grey rock surrounded the open space, and a soft light shone down from a single shaft overhead. In the center lay a single glass coffin. Snow stood frozen in place.

"Quickly, now," Reinhold said as he transformed into his smaller form and flew toward the coffin.

The perimeter of the space was lined with doorways—resting places for past rulers and their spouses. Why wasn't her father in one of those side rooms? Snow stepped inside, Max right behind her.

"Your cure," Reinhold began as he alighted on the top of the glass, "another fae might have called 'pure luck,' but I think the Abundant, the Maiden herself, held you in her palm. Righting the wrongs of Solinsel, she brought together an unusual confluence of magic to counter the darkness. That's the only possible explanation, and it makes me hopeful that . . ." Reinhold choked up, which was almost as shocking as seeing her father in repose. The fae continued, his words getting faster and faster. "Elisabeth used tainted magic, impossible for light fae magic to fully undo. But, the dwarves gave me the poisoned comb you'd purchased and worn. I extracted the comb's poison in the very lab the princess used to create it. I added my own magic to the reduction to reverse its effects. But *still*, it wasn't enough to save you. I hate to admit it, but the dwarven magic made the full antidote possible."

"What?" Max asked. "That doesn't make any sense."

Reinhold sighed, slowing his words like Max and Snow were children. "When the poison from the comb entered Snow's body, the magic of the fae-created amulet and the dwarven runes layered and worked together. They are both types of *protection* magic."

"The magic mixed?" Snow asked.

"Layered." Reinhold looked affronted at the thought. "The amulet's power imbued your blood with strength to fight the small amount of poison leeching through your scalp. The princess created a signature poison, only known to herself. Your body's ability to fight Princess Elisabeth's *particular* poison saved you in the courtyard. After you bit into the apple, your amulet recognized the poison from the comb and staved off the toxins long enough for me to create reinforcing antidotes."

"The cure wasn't in the goblet I drank from this morning?" Snow asked.

"That was a basic clarity and healing potion." Reinhold waved off the idea. "The reduction I created from the comb was merely two drops. I gave one drop to you, Snow." Reinhold looked down at the coffin. "And the other to the huntsman."

Did he want to give it to someone else? Snow took another step forward.

"I still cannot believe it was Elisabeth. I was such a fool," Reinhold said.

Reinhold's self-loathing shocked her. She'd never heard of a fae admitting to a mistake, let alone one of this proportion.

"Your father," Reinhold continued, "he's alive, but just barely."

Snow blinked, wavering on her feet. Max's hand was at her back in an instant, steadying her. Reinhold's sincerity signaled the unguarded truth of the statement. It explained why the fae hadn't returned to his own realm. And why he lingered at Clarus, but not in the kitchens.

He'd held vigil. Isolated and alone.

Snow gently pushed away from Max, approaching the coffin. As she walked forward, Reinhold tapped the glass once, and the top portion vanished, revealing her father. He was breathing, but his skin was waxy and pale. Snow fell to her knees, realizing the queen had hidden Friedrich away, hoping to save him. And Reinhold had barely left his side, believing Agnes had betrayed them all.

"The fae council said that Queen Agnes invited them to Clarus," Reinhold explained. "Based on what I'd said about the queen's behavior, the fae refused her. Though they likely would have anyway as

Agnes had raved about cracking glass, poison, dark magic, and witches. Now we know that Elisabeth had destroyed Agnes's ability to string thoughts together. She was never able to explain the king's situation. However, I doubt that, even if they'd known, the fae council could've countered the poison. Elisabeth's fae conspirator was clever, having her create a new, unknown spell. It's unlikely that even he knew the weakness—dwarven magic."

Snow's heart clenched with sorrow as she stood before her father's glass coffin. Reinhold had given the precious cure to Snow and Max, knowing they had a greater chance of survival. Or because he knew it was what Friedrich would wish. But now her father had no hope of reviving—the comb was gone along with Elisabeth's poison.

All of Snow's frustration, her haunted memories of the Shadow Beast, the worries about her friends, the kingdom, and even Max spilled out of her. Tears burned hot trails down her face. The weight of missed opportunities with her father and unspoken words pressed upon her, filling the air with an overwhelming sense of sorrow. Her father, the king, was needed. He had become a pillar of wisdom and strength for the entire kingdom; Solinsel blossomed during his reign. But now Friedrich lay before her, dying, beyond the help of fae magic.

Trembling, Snow leaned over his frail form, her tears falling. In her mind, Snow painted vivid scenes of a different life, a life where she could have shared countless moments with her father—laughter over meals, heartfelt conversations by a crackling fire, and his comforting presence during times of uncertainty. She yearned for his guidance, his stories, and the warmth of his love that she'd barely begun to experience. Snow wept for the loss of what could have been, for the moments cruelly denied them. The weight of her emotions engulfed her, pouring out as a torrent of grief that echoed through the chamber as if the very mountain mourned alongside her.

But then, amidst the depths of her sorrow, Snow felt a subtle shift in the air. Her father's breathing, once faint and feeble, seemed to deepen and steady. It was a small change but a miraculous one. Reinhold gasped in astonishment, confirming that she wasn't imagining improvement.

Snow pulled away and turned toward her father's face, her eyes widening in disbelief. A weak cough broke the silence, shattering the veil of despair that had settled over the room. With bated breath, Snow's heart pounded with anticipation. And then, in the hushed stillness, Snow White witnessed her father's eyes flutter open.

CHAPTER 32: MAX

YEAR 10 OF THE MAIDEN COMET, SUMMER

"This is no place for a human," Reinhold said as Max entered Elisabeth's alchemy lab.

No one had been allowed to touch any of her things. And only members of the fae council had been allowed inside her lab, other than Reinhold . . . and Max. A note-taking fae council member nodded in agreement, and two other councilors stood nearby as witnesses to the elimination of the lab.

Max hated the darkness that permeated the air and was happy to leave and report to the king and queen. He spun on his heel but didn't get far.

"We appreciate the king and queen's discretion," the female fae said, stopping him before he left. "And yours."

"You were quite brave, considering you were so very outmatched," the male fae said. "Humans are known for such rashness. Foolish, but brave nonetheless."

Your flattery needs some finessing.

The female fae quickly spoke, "What we mean to say is that we hope this incident doesn't reflect poorly on bonding. This could have a ripple effect across the Seven Kingdoms."

Max kept his voice calm, not wanting to irritate the powerful fae. "If you care about the reputation of the fae, start by clearing away the taint of the fallen one from the castle."

The female fae cleared her throat, and both fae gave Max a nod, a sign of respect.

Leaving their conversation on a positive note, Max hurried away. He was done with the fae, witches, and the lab. He was halfway up the stairs when he felt a tremendous force pulling at him, threatening to suck him back into the depths of the castle. Using all his strength, Max struggled to his feet and bolted back up to the main floor where the magical pull was barely noticeable. A moment later, he felt a pulse of energy. Then the invisible force vanished.

Runa and Grim hurried over to greet him, and Grim spoke first. "I felt it, too. It's done then."

Max nodded, and Runa let out a sigh of relief.

"We're off to the Darkstone Mountains," Runa said. "Our family will be irritated we've waited this long to return."

"Visit us soon, when you have things figured out," Grim said.

Runa grinned. "Several families get together for The Battle of the Axes and a feast. We will have the *best* story this year!"

"But we're taking the King's Road back, right?" Grim asked.

"Of course," Runa said. "We don't need more drama. But, next year, maybe we'll need a fresh adventure?"

"Definitely," Grim said. "But it'll be hard to top taking down a fallen fae and his once-Bonded mad princess."

"You weren't even *there*." Runa smacked his arm. "You could fight off a squirrel on the road and it would be more than what you did at Clarus."

The two of them wandered off, teasing each other. Max had thanked them several times, and they'd brushed him off, only telling him to visit. He couldn't be more fortunate in such good friendships.

If only he could choose the woman he loved, his life would be perfect.

Max made his way to the royal wing where the guards saluted him and let him pass without question. He could get used to this treatment. The thought made him smile. Just as quickly as it had appeared, the smile fell. He would be returning to his regular duties soon. The king had been awake for a few days, and he'd been devoted to assisting with his wife's recovery. Max had *tried* to speak with Snow, but the steward had sent him away. She was busy.

Too busy for him.

A well of hurt opened inside him, and he shook his head. As much as Max hated to admit it, Snow was pushing him away.

Perhaps it is for the best.

Heinrich would soon return to being the royal huntsman, and Max wasn't sure he could go back to being an apprentice. Nor could he ignore how he felt.

Lord von Hohenberg had sent word of a wealthy noble in Rosewood who would like Max to be his huntsman. A tempting offer, considering the extensive surrounding forests. As much as he loved the woods he grew up in, if Snow didn't want him near, he couldn't stay and keep his sanity.

'What was best' tasted of bitter heartache, and Max was loathe to swallow the pill. But what else could he do?

Max entered the sitting room that adjoined the king and queen's chambers, their place of respite, but also where they occasionally received visitors. Sunlight streamed through the tall, arched windows, and tapestries of family exploits lined the walls. Vibrant flowers in every corner and comfortable chairs and plush cushions invited him inside their sanctuary. The queen relaxed on a chaise lounge, and the king perched on a chair next to her, leaning close.

"Maximilian," the king said brightly, inviting him closer.

Max approached, and the queen smiled and sat up, offering him a box nearly the height and depth of her hand.

"A gift," she smiled. "And don't be alarmed. It's not poisoned."

Max chuckled as he opened the gift but froze when he saw the ruby red apple inside. The fae had explained that the tree in the courtyard was healthy. Elisabeth had stolen an apple, taken a seed, and fed it poison in her lab, creating one of her own. They found traces of the poison in the king's goblet; Elisabeth had poisoned her brother's favorite wine, little by little.

"I appreciate the kind gesture," Max said, hiding his discomfort.

The queen smiled, unaware of how little Max wanted an apple, especially after watching what the last one had done to Snow.

"I hope you are both feeling much improved," Max said, changing the subject.

"All meaningful healing takes time." Agnes took her husband's hand, a look passing between them. The royals had always stood by each other, but something had changed. Softened. Agnes continued. "Please, sit, Maximilian."

The queen explained that she had figured out that the king's children were being hunted after Snow arrived at Clarus. A year before she faked Friedrich's death, when he was very ill, she sent notes to Heinrich, pretending they were from the king. *She* was the one having the king's children moved around. Max could tell from her tight expression that she had mixed feelings over her husband's previous affairs. Even so, she'd done what she could to protect his unclaimed children.

She had kept her actions a secret from everyone, desperate to try and save the innocent children. She had even begun to suspect Elisabeth, but she knew the king would never believe her, so she worked in secret, telling no one of her plans.

"You may wonder why I sentenced your father to death," Agnes said quietly. "After all, he was the only person I'd trusted with the children's locations."

Max stilled, realizing he hadn't processed that betrayal yet. Then he paused, realizing what had happened. "Elisabeth manipulated you?"

"She tried to force me to have him hanged immediately," she said. "But I was able to push back her enchantment long enough to add 'after a year'."

"Saving his life," Max added.

"Yes, well, after that, Elisabeth started glamouring, appearing as *me* whenever she needed to do something particularly ugly. She couldn't risk me pushing back in any way. But she also buried my mind deeper, not ever really needing me to do anything except be her puppet on display."

The king pulled on a long silk cord, calling a servant. While they waited, Agnes continued, "Ludwig is traveling to contact his remaining siblings, letting them know they are safe. The king and I decided to move them here if they wish."

Max grinned, knowing Nora would love living at Clarus. Maybe she'd spend time learning about the magic of the Wildwoods like Snow did, down in the cottage with his mother. Addy would probably like the wintertime distraction.

Instead of a servant, Reinhold strolled through the door, accompanied by Snow.

Snow!

Max's breath caught in his chest. Her skin appeared healthy, warm, and soft. He loved how her eyes danced as she spoke to the fae. He longed to tuck her body close to his and kiss the top of her head. Time seemed to stand still, and the world around him faded into the background. His heart swelled as her mere presence illuminated the room.

Engrossed in her conversation, she didn't immediately notice Max. But seeming to sense his presence, her words trailed off, and their eyes met, the crash of the connection consuming him. She was brilliance and thoughtfulness and laughter. She challenged him and leaned on him in equal measure.

But she didn't feel the same.

The warmth inside turned to ice.

She hadn't sent for him. Hadn't asked for him. Not once.

"Max!" Snow rushed to him, but her footsteps slowed. When she reached him, she didn't grab his hand. She jerked to a halt as if remembering something, stopping just outside his personal space. Yet, tantalizingly within his reach. He ached, wanting to pull her closer.

Something within him broke.

He definitely could not stay in Clarus.

This, whatever *this* was, would drive him mad.

"Huntsman," the king said, getting his attention. "I am the ruler of Solinsel, but Snow will be announced as my official heir on the morrow. Announcements will go throughout the kingdom. And beyond."

Prince-Third-Son will definitely increase his offer. But, Snow would never accept. Would she?

"Lady Snow will soon be Princess Snow Albrecht," Agnes said. The king patted his wife's hand, and she wrapped her fingers tighter around his. Agnes turned to Snow. "Elisabeth purposefully undermined your education, selecting ill-fitting tutors to your learning style. I'll do much better, I promise."

"Eventually, I wish to spend time with my wife in her northern kingdom," the king said, surprising them all. "So I will transition the crown to Snow in a decade. She'll have plenty of time to get used to the weight. And I think I'll make a fantastic ambassador, don't you think?"

"Y-yes, father," Snow said. "Of course."

Reinhold frowned. "Are you sure?"

While Reinhold discussed the plans with the king, Snow asked to be excused. Max watched her go silently, despite the sense of falling from a cliff. Why was she so desperate to get away from him?

The door shut behind her, and Max blurted, "May I be excused?"

"Yes, of course," Agnes said, incredulous. "Go and catch up to her. Run!" She mumbled something about them being adorable and ridiculous as he rushed out of the room.

Max raced down the hall, his heart pounding as he gave chase. He had to catch Snow before she disappeared in the maze of corridors. He had to know...

Seeing him coming, guards backed out of his way. One of them pointed to which direction Snow had gone, a grin on her face. Max would have to thank the woman later.

"Snow!" Max called, rounding the corner.

She immediately stilled but didn't turn.

Why?

Max checked over his shoulder, but the corridor was vacant.

"Can we talk?" he asked.

She nodded, short and curt, still not deigning to look at him.

"Maybe somewhere private?"

She nodded again, and that was all the permission he needed. He put his hand on Snow's lower back and led her into an alcove near the balcony entrance. The area was smaller, darker, and far more intimate. Her scent—lavender and jasmine—enveloped him, and he wondered if that was a mistake. This close to her, he could barely think straight.

"Why are you avoiding me?" Max asked, getting right to the point.

Snow lifted her gaze, staring up at him through her dark lashes. The flicker of knowing in the depths of her eyes far surpassed the realm of mere acquaintance or even good friends. He saw the reflection of shared experiences and unspoken understanding, a lifelong connection that defied logic. So, it defied all possible explanations that she could just walk away from him, leaving him behind. Her lips parted, but *still,* she uttered no assurance.

"Did you decide to marry Prince Leopold?" Max's voice cracked, hating the thought of her being with anyone else, despite the rumors of the prince's very sizeable offer for Snow's hand.

"Who?" Snow asked, her brow scrunched. He could tell the moment she understood his question and her expression cleared. "Um, *no.*"

Max growled. "It's really unfair that you know everything on my mind, but I know nothing of yours."

Snow put a hand on his chest, not pushing him away but seeming to draw him closer. "I wanted you to have time to think about what *you* wanted. We've been through so much, it was . . . selfish of me to drown you in the depths of royal life without giving you a chance to decide."

Wait . . . what?

"If . . . if we're together, you'd be giving up your role as the huntsman one day, becoming the prince consort."

"There are worse things than becoming a royal," Max said with a huff of disbelief. He didn't need time or space to think; he had thought through their future together. A thousand times. A thousand scenarios. All of them worth any sacrifice. She was worth it.

"I know you, Max. You'd much rather be in the woods than at festivals and chatting with visiting dignitaries," her voice cracked, her fingers trembling.

His shock melted into concern.

"Snow," he said, pressing his hand to hers and then entwining their fingers.

Warmth spread from their hands, igniting a spark that transcended the boundaries of the physical world. This was the dance of souls, whispering of possibilities yet to unfold. Their connection was not only rooted in the past but held the promise of an interwoven future. His future. With Snow.

"I'd suffer through the mind-numbing chatter of a million nobles if it meant I'd get to be with you," Max said, grinning.

In the secluded alcove, the world faded into insignificance. Slowly, Max's hand cupped Snow's cheek, his touch tender and filled with reverence.

"If you'll have me, I'd love for you to become Prince Maximilian," Snow said, her eyes alight.

Max leaned in, his heart pounding in sync with hers, feeling the soft brush of her breath against his lips. Time became suspended in the delicate space between them.

Their lips finally met, a soft caress that spoke volumes. The world seemed to cease its chaotic whirl, and all that mattered was the connection between them. Max finally pushed away the precarious uncertainty of the last two years. He and Snow had taken on malevolent forces and had won.

And the fact that Snow was with him now, confessing her heart's desire . . . it was almost as unbelievable.

Snow clutched his tunic and leaned back. "The guards will continue their rotation at any moment."

Max smiled, gazing down at the woman he loved. The kiss was everything Max needed to know—a testament of their shared feelings. And, it whispered of a future filled with love, adventure, and unbreakable strength.

"Want to go for a ride in the forest?" Max asked. "I know a spot where fireflies might already appear this time of year."

"I thought you'd never ask." Snow got on her tiptoes and kissed him again. "I'll prepare a lunch with Dottie while you get the horses ready."

EPILOGUE

YEAR 11 OF THE MAIDEN COMET, SPRING

Hundreds of guests watched as a little-known Attuned from the poorest part of Caston officiated the wedding of the most beloved prince and princess in generations. For Snow, the audience faded to a blur as she focused on the man in front of her: Max.

The grand hall, unused for many years, was filled with joy once again. Warm light streamed in from the stained-glass windows as if the setting sun celebrated along with all of Solinsel. After nearly a year of official courtship, Snow's best friend was finally her husband, Prince Maximilian.

Max slipped a simple gold band on Snow's finger, and he kissed her hand, which wasn't strictly traditional, but who would complain? Certainly not Snow. She grinned as he straightened, squeezing his hand. He pulled her into an embrace, her lips meeting his on instinct, the most natural thing in the seven kingdoms. Scents of pine and leather encircled her, which perhaps was not very prince-like, but she preferred it. She could hardly believe her good fortune—a far better outcome than she ever dreamed.

The Attuned smiled as she finished the ceremony, and the crowd roared in celebration. That wasn't strictly traditional either, but Grim and Runa led the cacophony, and everyone else quickly joined. As soon as Max guided Snow off the elevated platform, the room slowly . . . magically . . . shifted, courtesy of Reinhold. The wedding platform recessed into the ground, and another one lifted the somewhat startled musicians, though they began playing without hesitation.

Heady scents of roses, hydrangeas, and lilies floated across the ballroom as nobles from the nearest kingdoms and emissaries from much farther danced in celebration. Lifting her gown slightly so it wouldn't drag—the very one that the dwarves had so kindly procured—Max led her in a dance. Wearing a jeweled headband that matched her exquisite dress, Runa gave them a wink while Grim sighed with a contented smile.

"So, why is Runa grinning like she'd just loosened the legs on the dining chairs?" Max asked.

Snow snorted a laugh then quickly composed herself, attempting dignity. She was the next ruler of Solinsel after all.

King Friedrich and Queen Agnes greeted guests as did Max's parents. Heinrich had never been one for small talk, but with all his practice in currying favors while he was shuffling the king's children, he'd gotten good at it. Even better, he'd actually made a few friends, including Lord and Lady von Hohenberg, who had privately introduced Snow to her little brother moons earlier.

The king had reinstated High Judge Helene, who was mentoring Agnes's appointee; he'd held the courts with integrity during Helene's absence. And unless things went awry, Helene planned to retire soon. Both of the judges stood along the periphery, chatting—likely in another deep discussion on ethics. Not far from Snow, Nora danced with a few friends, looking quite grown-up and comfortable in her finery. She'd taken well to castle life, unlike Ludwig, who had opted to leave. Snow didn't blame him, and she hoped he would find what his soul needed.

Max's hand pressed against her hip and lower back, drawing her attention.

"Are you sure we can't leave for our honeymoon tonight?" he teased. "I know a captain who has a boat waiting. I've always wanted to see the north."

"It's waiting because the king commissioned it." Snow laughed. "And we'll leave in the morning after breakfast, or the King will not be pleased."

He pulled her closer, his breath on her neck sending a warm shiver down her spine. His lips brushed her ear as he whispered, "Let him be displeased."

Snow grinned, running her fingers through the hair at the nape of his neck.

"Before you say 'no,' look at who just arrived." He spun her effortlessly so she'd spot several fae flying through the open window into the room, silhouetted against the vibrant sunset.

"Just as Father warned," Snow said to Max under her breath.

As the fae transformed into their larger forms, the crowd stirred with delighted surprise. Two of the fae flicked their hands, and suddenly the ceiling sparkled with ethereal blue motes of light, followed by impressed *ohs* from the crowd. Max escorted Snow to the dais to take her proper place next to King Friedrich where Reinhold introduced her to several fae, including the head of the fae school. Snow was polite, though she knew what the fae were really after. She didn't need to use her inner gift to know they wanted access to her future children.

Though there would be no Bonds in her household until she fully understood them. She would no longer leave decisions solely to the fae, as had been done with Elisabeth.

A bell rang, signaling the first course of dinner. With a swish of Reinhold's wand, the far wall disappeared, revealing an extension of the grand hall with a mouth-watering, sumptuous feast. Snow's friend, Dottie, had outdone herself, creating all the best dishes, most of them desserts.

As the group meandered toward the perfectly appointed tables, the main doors flew open. Everyone stopped in their tracks, looking toward the disturbance. Even the musicians' notes hiccupped as five dwarves marched into the room, dressed in their finery. Nora's exuberant giggle as she ran to embrace Lielinda broke the momentary tension.

The scent of the forest clung to them, and Snow imagined they entered through the same old entrance Max had told her about. Grim and Runa joined their family, mischievous grins on their faces. The matriarch, Ingrihild, carried a beautifully wrapped gift, and she presented it to Snow. Nestled inside the box, Snow found a stunning necklace adorned with seven massive emeralds nestled inside the box. Emotion welled, her heart full as the necklace was more than jewels: it represented their acceptance and celebration of Snow. Not just because she would become a powerful ally, but because they cherished *her*.

Looking around the room, Snow felt overwhelmed with the love and support of her family, friends, and the people of Solinsel. She thanked the Abundants for bringing her Max, who was both her best friend and the love of her life.

Max helped her put on the necklace, his hands brushing the back of her neck filling her with warmth. When he looked down at her, she longed to unravel the layers within, to uncover the depths of his thoughts and dreams. She yearned to be part of his world, to stand by his side and weave their stories together.

Hours later, as everyone sat to enjoy the final round of dinner, a servant handed a note to Snow from her stepmother. Quickly glancing at it, she read:

Your ship awaits.

Snow jerked her attention to Agnes, who raised a teasing brow.

Snow leaned over and whispered to Max, "Did you still want to leave for our honeymoon tonight?"

Max immediately grabbed Snow's hand and led her out of the hall, slipping away while everyone laughed and ate. In the quieter corridor, he pinned her to the wall, his voice a growl, "How soon can you be ready to leave?"

"Apparently, our things have already been sent and the horses readied."

Max kissed her neck, which had Snow's stomach warming with a different kind of hunger. Snow grabbed the front of his gold-threaded tunic, suddenly breathless. "I'll race you to the stables."

"Will guards be escorting us to the bay?" Max asked, checking over his shoulder.

"Don't worry, my prince," Snow said, gingerly running her thumb over his lips. "If we can handle a Shadow Beast, a vengeful witch, and a creepy magic forest, we can handle an evening ride."

"True," Max said, his lips brushing her collarbone.

Snow cupped Max's cheek and kissed him then quickly dipped under his arm and bolted for the stables, very much looking forward to their next adventure.

More "Once Upon A Prince" books:
The Unlucky Prince by Deborah Grace White
The Beggar Prince by Kate Stradling
The Golden Prince by Alice Ivinya
The Wicked Prince by Celeste Baxendell
The Midnight Prince by Angie Grigaliunas
The Poisoned Prince by Kristin J. Dawson
The Silver Prince by Lyndsey Hall
The Shoeless Prince by Jacque Stevens
The Silent Prince by C. J. Brightley
The Crownless Prince by Selina R. Gonzalez
The Awakened Prince Alora Carter
The Winter Prince by Constance Lopez

Afterword

Thank you to every reader who took a chance on a new spin on Snow White, a long-time beloved fairytale.

I always loved a prince love interest, but do you know what is even more swoony? A huntsman. And another thing I changed from the original tale was the prince's insta-love *after* Snow had already died. Weird. Walt Disney reworked the story so the prince and Snow met before her demise, but I took their relationship a step further and made them best friends.

More importantly, I always—even as a child—thought Disney's prince angle didn't work because Snow was the daughter of the king. Snow was born a princess! So, who the heck is this random prince at *her* castle? Snow didn't really need a prince to save her. She just needed to get rid of the queen and take back the throne that was hers by birthright!

So, because Snow is a potential heir, why not match her with the strong and capable huntsman?

For the magic system, I created this world a year ago when I was doing "story starts." I sent two different story openings to my readers, and they loved the one about a princess and her sassy, Bonded fae. (A future fairytale story.) I absolutely loved the world, so I set my Snow White within that same magical realm, too.

So, here's the story I wanted as a child . . . a princess, heir to the throne, taking back her kingdom and getting the super-hot-huntsman (who is her BFF and totally loyal) to join her on her quest. And she finds half-siblings and makes new dwarven friends along the way!

More Books by Kristin J. Dawson

The Unchosen Series

-epic fantasy
-female protagonist with a massive character arc
-cunning female mentor character
-kingdom's survival at stake
-unique magical system and language
-romantic thread: friends to fall-in-love (sweet romance)
unravel the mysteries, secure the smartest alliance, win the crown

Elven House of Ivy, coming 2024

-romantic fantasy

-enemies-to-allies-to-more (sweet romance)

-elusive elves & dangerous fae

-pet dragons and comical warrior orc friends

gather allies, end the Seekers before they end you, and stop a war before it

begins . . . again

More fairytales in the Seven Kingdom world are coming in the future!
Be sure to follow Kristin J. Dawson on Amazon or subscribe to her
newsletter to receive updates.

Acknowledgments

Writing a novel is always a collaboration of minds, and I was fortunate to have so many great people in my corner for this project!

Thank you to Alora and Constance for reading the very rough early version of this story and for coordinating the Once Upon a Prince series! Herding ten other authors is not for the faint of heart. My awesome Eugene Writers Anonymous friends helped me in early brainstorming and again later to elevate the opening chapters (Paul, Polly, M. K., and Sarah). Special thank you to Raye Wagner, who waved her magic wand over key romantic elements. And to my childhood BFF, Amy, who shared insights that helped create Snow's fae gifting ability.

Big thank you to Jeanna Mason Stay, who gave me a phenomenal line edit on the story. We worked together at Deep Magic E-zine, and the stories we edited together were all recognized as "must reads" by Tangent Reviews (a huge feat!), so I knew we made a good team. (I highly recommend Jeanna for anyone writing fantasy!)

And as always, thank you to my copy editor, Kathleen, who has been red-lining my work since my childhood. And to my lovely proofreader (and cheerleader), Dawn, who has proofread all my published books!

Beta readers are critical to making sure the final reader experience is wonderful, so thank you to: Jessica, Sandy, Jacque, Kimber, Mandie, and Hanna. Thank you to the ARC readers who combed through the details to find pesky errors that seem to slip through all the previous edits. (Seriously, some of those errors should get an award for tenacity!)

And thank you, dear reader, for taking a risk and trying out a new story world!

About the Author

Kristin loves chocolate (*quality* chocolate, because ... life is short!), research (I know, I know, who loves research ... *raises hand*), English movies (especially with my mom or my sisters), and reading science fiction and fantasy novels (like Raye Wagner, Jeff Wheeler, Melissa Caruso, J.K. Rowling, Suzanne Collins, and ... a thousand other great stories with fun characters and lots of tension!).

I was born in L.A., grew up in Utah, spent a short stint in Bristol, England, then ended up in the Pacific Northwest. I've been here ever since!

Note: When Oregonians say, "I live in the country," they're not talking about living near cornfields or cows. They're talking about the woods. The woods! (I know, it's not like the farmer stories I grew up with, either.)